"Ridge, I —"

"Enough. We got off on the wrong foot, Dr. Roarke. Let me buy you a hat as a peace offering."

His face was so earnest that Alexsana faltered. Suddenly, he was like a little boy on a mission. She set her lips grimly as she entered the store behind him, steeling herself for the inevitable. She had five 'Indiana Jones' hats at home, gifts from past suitors. Why had men always wanted to put her under a masculine cap? She was an archaeologist, but still a woman.

But as Alexsana looked around the hat shop, past the leather and felt fedoras, she discovered that Ridge had headed straight to a more feminine section of the store. He held a beautifully crafted, tightly woven linen hat with a white taffeta ribbon around its crown. He looked at her, then back to the hat again. "I saw one like it in the window," he said proudly.

A shiver ran down her spine. Had he picked it for her?

"It's perfect, don't you think?" he asked, placing it on her head before she could say a word. "I looked around, and it was as if it had your name on it."

Palisades.
Pure Romance.

Fiction that features credible characters and entertaining plot lines, while continuing to uphold strong Christian values. From high adventure to tender stories of the heart, each Palisades Romance is an undiluted story of love, from beginning to end!

A PALISADES CONTEMPORARY ROMANCE

CHOSEN

LISA TAWN BERGREN

PALISADES

CHOSEN
published by Palisades
a part of the Questar publishing family

© 1996 by Lisa Tawn Bergren
International Standard Book Number: 0-88070-768-2

Cover illustration by George Angelini
Cover designed by David Carlson and
Mona Weir-Daly
Edited by Shari MacDonald

Printed in the United States of America

For information:
QUESTAR PUBLISHERS, INC.
POST OFFICE BOX 1720
SISTERS, OREGON 97759

Library of Congress Cataloging–in–Publication Data
Bergren, Lisa Tawn.
Chosen/Lisa Tawn Bergren.
p.cm.
"A Palisades contemporary romance." ISBN 0-88070-768-2 (alk. paper)
1. Man-woman relationships--Middle East--Fiction. 2. Women-archae-
ologists--Middle East--Fiction. 3. Terrorism--Middle East--Fiction I. Title.
PS3552.E71938C48   1996   96-5324
813'.54--dc20   CIP

96 97 98 99 00 01 02 03 — 10 9 8 7 6 5 4 3 2

To Bob and Pam:
Friends, family, hosts to house guests who never go home.
Thanks for your hospitality,
going through this book to make sure I "got it right,"
making me meet Tim, and all your love and support.
You guys are the best!

*"But you are a chosen people, a royal priesthood,
a holy nation, a people belonging to God,
that you may declare the praises of
him who called you out of darkness
into his wonderful light."*

1 PETER 2:9

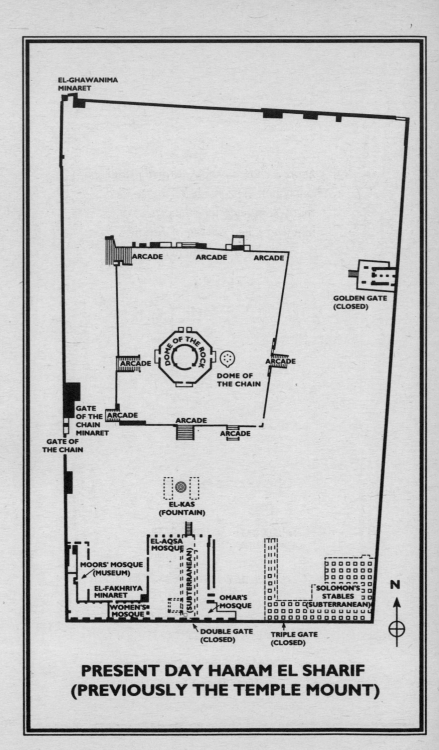

PRESENT DAY HARAM EL SHARIF
(PREVIOUSLY THE TEMPLE MOUNT)

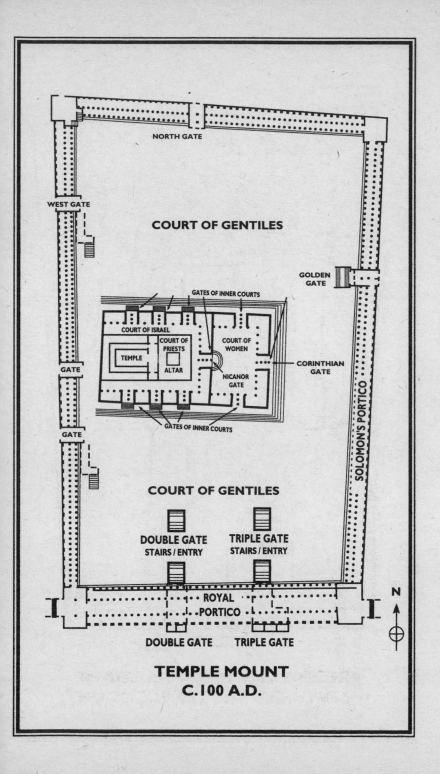

TEMPLE MOUNT
C. 100 A.D.

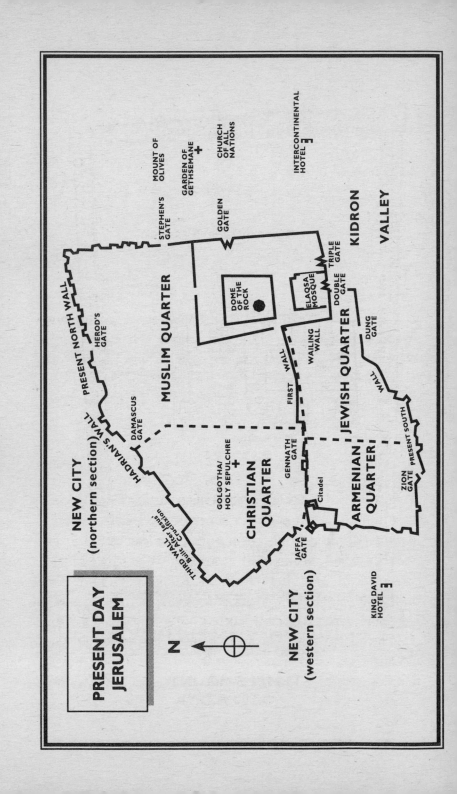

Prologue

❧

The Coast of Israel
late January

S amuel Roarke Jr. gazed out at the Mediterranean, thinking about the incredibly preserved, sunken ship he had seen an hour ago. In his mind's eye, he could just begin to see what the ancient harbor must have looked like in its glory. He wished for the thousandth time that he could travel through time to stand beside Herod, observing his ways, his work, his wonders. *One hundred years before Christ was born.*

Sam glanced back at his partner, forcing his mind back to the subject of the ship. "It's gotta be Greek," he said.

Robert Hoekstra, head of the Center for Maritime Studies back in the States and current supervisor to Israel's Caesarea Maritima dig, nodded in agreement. "It's at least as old as the one they found off the coast of Athens. We need to fly in a consultant to advise us on how to pursue this part of the project. It's a thousand years older than anything I've had hands-on experience with."

"Christina Alvarez?" Sam suggested. He and Robert had recently discussed the innovative dive site protection system that Christina had developed while excavating the American

Civil War wrecks, then perfected during work on nautical archaeological sites in the Caribbean.

Robert stood before him, rubbing his forehead, which was bronzed from weeks in the mild winter sun. "If she'll agree to it. That lady's got her fingers on more projects of economic importance than anyone else I know."

"It's that treasure hunter husband she hooked up with."

"I need to find myself a treasure hunter wife," Robert said, grinning down at his frayed, sun-bleached shorts.

"That you do," Sam said with a laugh. Then he grew more serious. "I think we can get her to come see this. If I know Christina, just the chance to check out a ship like this will bring her, at least on a consultant basis."

"Very good," Robert said, stroking his gray beard. "Give her a call right away. We haven't a day to lose."

Jerusalem, late January

Alexsana Roarke walked up the wide, grand stairs and handed her briefcase to the Waksf guard. No matter how often she went through the procedure of passing the guards at the gate of the Temple Mount — referred to by Muslims as the Haram el Sharif — she was irritated by the amount of time they took. The guard smiled in recognition and quickly searched the case, waving off his companion who moved to body-search her.

"Yes. She is too pretty to be carrying a bomb," the second guard said in Arabic, misunderstanding the first guard's wave. He smiled at Alexsana in appreciation, noting her stylish clothes — signature white chinos and blouse under a khaki blazer — and the slim figure beneath.

14

Her smile in return was perfunctory at best. Yes, she hated this process more each time she endured it. *Weaselly guards who think they wield so much power....*

"But sometimes they send their prettiest to do the dirty work," the second guard muttered as he scrutinized her, continuing his monologue as though he thought someone was listening. Warming to the power of his position, he pushed onward. "As I look at her more closely, I think she is not so pretty. Just blond. You always like the blonds."

"Be quiet, fool." The first guard switched to English. "This is Dr. Alexsana Roarke. She has been summoned to meet with Abdallah al Azeh."

His cohort's eyebrows lifted in surprise.

She nodded at the first guard as he gave her permission to pass, then turned to the second. "I will be sure to inform Abdallah al Azeh that you do not like blondes," she said in perfect Arabic. She did not stay to watch his response.

Moving quickly, with purpose, she passed the El Aksa Mosque and the ornate, golden Dome of the Rock without looking twice; she had no time for sightseeing. Besides, the dramatic structures of Jerusalem had been part of her life for as long as she could remember; they blended into the background of her days like towering mountains to an Alps hermit.

A group of tourists passed her, straining to hear their guide who led them from one location to another. She felt sorry for the people who buzzed through Jerusalem this way, passing in a mad frenzy from one holy site to another. How could one truly come to experience this wonderful, crazy, complicated city in one week? The Temple Mount, or the Haram, had been breathtaking to her the first thirty times she saw it as an educated adult. Covering an area equivalent to five football fields in size, the monstrous structure could be explored for weeks on end.

But that was her archaeological head speaking. Still, there was so much to this place…the city Jesus had lived in and loved. The city *she* lived in and loved. Alexsana drew in a deep breath of air, fresh from a light rain. It smelled like clean stones to her. She approached the offices on the northeastern corner of the Haram where al Azeh conducted business.

She racked her brain as she had done since yesterday for the reason Abdallah al Azeh — head of the Waksf and Islamic Affairs — had summoned her to meet with him, then shrugged her questions away, drew a breath, and knocked on the official's door.

A male guard opened it and nodded her forward.

Alexsana stopped in shock at the inner office door. Standing to her left and right were two Mossad agents, easily identified by their trademark secret service aviator glasses. Sitting across the desk from Abdallah al Azeh was Abba Eban, head of the Israeli Antiquities Authority.

Eban was seldom seen in or around the Haram. Convinced that the Jews only wanted to destroy the Haram to rebuild their biblical temple, many Muslims would consider Eban's presence an act of treason by al Azeh. *The mystery deepens,* she thought.

"Come in, come in," Abdallah said, motioning to a plush, green chair beside Abba Eban. Both men politely stood. Abdallah watched Alexsana sit and inquisitively study them.

"You wonder why we both wish to meet with you."

A tiny smile edged her lips upward. "To say the least."

"Alexsana," Abba Eban said, smiling broadly. "Under the new peace accord, Abdallah has paved the way for an unprecedented dig." He paused dramatically, letting the information sink in. "We are to have unlimited access to Solomon's Stables."

Alexsana drew in her breath sharply, struggling to maintain her composure.

"Due to your long-standing reputation, the work done by you and your family in the region, and the ability to remain neutral between Palestinian and Jew alike," Abdallah said, "we have chosen you to be dig supervisor."

One

࿐

January 25

The desert was hot for a late winter day. Ridge McIntyre wiped his brow as he pulled the Jeep off the highway and onto a subtly marked road that led deeper into the Negev Desert south of Jerusalem. The newest correspondent for CNN, Ridge had managed to land the prime news region of the Middle East in which to prove himself, and he was intent upon setting up his contacts. He had already established three key sources of inside information; if he could nail this fourth, he'd have a strong network set up to funnel him politically hot stories.

He drove the Jeep up a steep hill, hoping that he was going in the right direction. Just over the crest he spied two men standing in the road with their arms crossed in front of them. As Ridge neared, they pulled their black and white Bedouin robes aside, displaying Uzis at the ready.

Ridge sighed, wondering how many more times he would have to risk his life for a story in this region.

The smaller man motioned with his head for Ridge to get out of the vehicle. Ridge started talking before his foot was out the door, a customary defense mechanism for dealing with stressful situations.

"Ridge McIntyre. I'm here to see Khalil al Aitam."

"Shut up," the taller man said. He turned Ridge toward the car, forced his arms to the sun-scorched roof, and frisked him for weapons. The other man searched the Jeep for the same.

Ridge submitted to the search without moving, ignoring his painful palms. "I'm a United States citizen," he began in protest. "And a correspondent for CNN."

"Shut up," the man repeated and stood away from Ridge.

"Your American citizenry buys no love here," the smaller guard said in practiced English. "Your connection to CNN is all that allows you to breathe your next breath."

Alexsana Roarke smiled back at her handsome Palestinian host, lounging in his Bedouin robes amongst the traditional pile of brightly colored cushions. The tent around them was surprisingly cool and smelled of sweat, broiled lamb, and very strong tea and coffee. Beside her, a woman served the hot, sweet tea customary to the Middle East.

"Thank you, Sarah," Alexsana said. The dark-eyed beauty smiled shyly with her eyes — her nose and mouth hidden by a light veil — then ducked out of the tent. Alexsana turned toward Khalil. "When are you going to marry that girl?" she asked him calmly.

"When I get tired of you saying no," he said. A row of even, white teeth gleamed at her.

Alexsana snorted and shook her head. "I said no in third grade and in seventh *and* when we graduated and left Ramallah." She reached out and took his hand.

The man continued to smile, but hurt showed in his eyes.

Alexsana studied him carefully. Tall and muscular, at ease and relaxed in his robes, Khalil was a man who would be admired by women of any nationality.

Spotting his serious expression, Alexsana's own smile faded. "Oh Khalil, come on. We have definitely taken different paths. A marriage between us would be disastrous."

"A good marriage can conquer any obstacles."

"If you begin from the same foundation. Our lifetime of friendship doesn't count." Alexsana ignored the stubborn set of his chin. "We've covered this before. You've become a militant Muslim. A political fundamentalist leader — of Hamas, no less. I am and will always remain a devout Christian. Your life has become unavoidably entrenched in the ways of Middle Eastern men — how would it look for you to have a professional Westerner as a wife?"

She lowered her voice, conscious that Sarah probably was listening outside. "I will not be parked in some tent, serving tea. I would be desperately unhappy and you would be very dissatisfied."

Khalil rose and walked toward the curtains. His actions reminded Alexsana of those exhibited by a king, and she struggled not to openly admire this childhood friend who had become very much a man. He pulled aside the animal skin that hung over the window and watched a Jeep approach along the sandy road leading to the tent. "So, my *friend*, what is it that you seek from me today?"

Alexsana closed her eyes and wished away the tension that had risen between them. "I'll cut to the chase," she said, phrasing her words carefully. "Word has it that Abdallah al Azeh and Islamic Affairs are going to let me lead a team under the Haram and excavate Solomon's Stables."

"I have heard. The Hamas will not allow it. Decline the invitation when it comes."

Alexsana laughed aloud. "You've got to be kidding! This is the chance of a lifetime! Of my career!" Forcing herself to lower her voice, she rose and went to him, touching his shoulder. Khalil let the curtain fall as the vehicle pulled up outside the tent.

Alexsana's eyes widened as understanding dawned. "This is the reason that you agreed to see me today? The reason for another marriage proposal? Because I am in danger?"

Khalil turned to her and cradled her jaw in his strong hand. He looked lovingly into her eyes. "You would be safe as my wife."

Her brow furrowed, but she did not look away. "Even if I agree to lead the team under the Haram?"

He dropped his hand and moved back to the curtain. "No. There are many who consider you a menace already. I've intervened to keep you off the hit lists as even a *potential* leader to the project."

"I cannot accept that!" She grimaced, unwilling to accept his words. "The Hamas knows me, my family. I've grown up here! Never have I proven myself untrustworthy! I am considered a friend to Muslim and Jew alike."

"That is no longer possible."

"We will make the Haram's foundation *stronger*. We will not harm the El Aksa Mosque."

"You don't understand the ramifications!" Khalil said, uncharacteristically letting his voice rise. He dropped the curtain again and stared angrily back at the slim blonde in front of him.

"*I* don't understand?"

A voice from outside the tent interrupted the intensity of the moment. "Hello? Ridge McIntyre, CNN. Anyone home?" The animal skin fell to one side as a tall, handsome man stepped into the tent. Squinting in the darkness after being in the bright desert light, he shifted his gaze from Alexsana to her regal companion, then back again as she moved to collect her bag.

"I — I'm sorry," Ridge stammered, noting the tension in the room. "Didn't mean to interrupt. I was invited by Khalil al Aitam."

"You didn't interrupt." Alexsana studied him intently for a moment, then brushed past. She quickly shoved away a moment of admiration for a journalist who could actually ferret out Khalil. "I was just leaving." The last thing she needed was to deal with Khalil *and* another hotshot American reporter.

Khalil reached out and grabbed her arm. "We are not finished here, Alexsana."

She looked defiantly up at him. "Oh, yes we are." She shook off his hand and ducked out of the tent.

Ridge stood back, watching the interchange and wondering what the story was. *I bet it's a good one*, he mused silently. He admired women with gumption, like the one who had just left. "*Women*," Ridge said amicably, shrugging, as Khalil scowled back at him.

"Your visit was ill-timed, Mr. McIntyre," Khalil said.

"So it seems. If you'd rather I return later...."

"No, no," his host said, waving off his dark thoughts. "I will see her later. You are here. What is it that *you* seek?"

Alexsana sped past the two guards in her old BMW, feeling exasperated and suddenly tired. Was it wise to accept the position without Khalil's protection? She pushed away all thoughts of doubt. Archaeology was in her blood; her great-grandfather had studied Israeli biblical sites in 1905; her grandmother was on one of the first teams to excavate the Temple Mount in 1928; her father had excavated the site where the Dead Sea Scrolls were found in the '40s. Alexsana saw no other path, felt no other passion.

Still, she had hoped to secure Khalil's nod of approval, which would have guaranteed noninterference from the Hamas and assured her own personal safety. Samuel Roarke would not like the danger surrounding this assignment, and Sam Jr., her brother, would be impossible. Alexsana sighed. "Dear God, I just know there's something fantastic down there beneath the Temple Mount," she prayed aloud. "Please clear the path. Help me show the world the places where you walked."

She checked herself. One-sided conversations with God had become habit long ago. "Do I only want to please you?" she asked. "Okay, okay, I admit it. There *is* glory in it for me. Help me to keep my priorities straight and give me wisdom in choosing my path, Father." Oh, how she wanted this! How could God not give it to her?

"I want it for you. I do. *And* for me. Help me to do the right thing, not just act on my own greed. Use me if you choose to do so."

The miles sped by and Alexsana sighed repeatedly as her car climbed the streets of Beit Jala, a Palestinian village on the road to Jerusalem. Reaching behind her seat, she grabbed a bright, red-and-white-checked *kefiyah* and threw it over her dashboard in a half-hearted attempt to appease potential rock-throwers on the walls and rooftops that lined the road. In years past, she had replaced many windshields damaged by the guerrilla tactics of protesters who assumed she was a Jew; today she passed the rows of simple limestone houses without incident. Either the *kefiyah* protected her, or the Palestinian boys did not bother to lob a stone.

The next neighborhood, a Jewish settlement, consisted of more limestone houses, surrounded by hundreds of hastily constructed modular units. Alexsana shook her head. The "town" had been placed on land allegedly purchased from an elderly Palestinian. Before the PLO or Hamas could act, hundreds of Israeli settlers had moved in. Over three hundred acres had been usurped by vigilant Israelites, dedicated to taking back their homeland by pushing out the other natives, the Palestinians. It was a never-ending, circular battle.

As she neared the Old City, Alexsana decided she needed some fresh air and her brother's company. After parking outside Damascus Gate, she made her way toward the western, Christian quarter of the city, walking the quarter-mile to her apartment. There was no direct access to her home other than by foot.

Suddenly, she could not wait to see her brother. Sam would certainly have a new joke to tell her, and working alongside him at Caesarea Maritima would feel more like play than work. It would be like a vacation compared to the heavy days she had been through recently.

Alexsana smiled and nodded her way through the quiet afternoon streets, brightening at the prospect. She purposefully looked away from Temple Mount as she passed it, pushing away thoughts about the caverns underneath, unexplored.

Turning her thoughts instead to the afternoon ahead of her, Alexsana smiled. It would be good to return to Caesarea, good to get in the water again.

Twenty feet under the Mediterranean is just where I want to be.

Two

February 1

R idge exited a second highway and headed toward the
ancient harbor of Caesarea Maritima. The week had continued to run in the eighties, unseasonably hot. He rolled
down his window as the road crested and the brilliant blue
of the Mediterranean opened up before him.

The sea was bluer than the Pacific and greener than the
Atlantic, a beautiful combination. If there had been palm
trees swaying along the coast it would have resembled an
island paradise; instead, the harbor created its own mystique
marked by grassy, sandy banks and quietly lapping water.
The smell of saltwater filled Ridge's nostrils. *Yes. I like this
assignment.*

He neared the ancient site of Caesarea Maritima and
pulled to a stop in the parking lot. A quarter-mile off were
the crumbling remains — surprisingly intact in places — of
a Herodian aqueduct that had once carried fresh water from
the mountains and valleys to the coastal residence of the
Roman governor. Inside the city walls were the remains of an
amphitheater and numerous buildings. Above, a restored

Crusader castle was now used as a restaurant for tourists.

Ridge briefly looked over the sites before heading toward the harbor. He had done his homework. Through America Online, he had seen drawings of what Caesarea once looked like: Herod had accomplished an amazing feat by constructing the first artificial harbor on the coast of what was then Judea. Built of massive blocks and constructed through the use of slave labor, it had become one of the most prosperous harbors of its time. Entire buildings had stood on the artificial walls, welcoming seafarers from all over the known world.

Most of what remained of the harbor two thousand years later was under water, leading to this excavation led by Goldfried and Hoekstra, and reportedly cosupervised by the man he sought, Dr. Roarke. Ridge spotted people alongshore: some were working under several white tents that flapped in the breeze; others were walking between them and beached rafts. The group was a flurry of activity as he neared. One group carried artifacts from the rafts to giant sieves, then to a large work tent. The other group appeared to be heading back out to what Ridge supposed was a dive site in rafts powered by small motors.

Shielding his eyes against the sun, Ridge looked out toward the dive boat, where he could barely make out several figures climbing aboard, scuba tanks on their backs. Another motorized raft came toward shore as Ridge reached the tents. He checked his watch. "Good," he muttered. "Lunch time. The gang should all be here."

"Good afternoon," he called cheerfully to a college-aged girl entering the nearest tent. *Catching some extra credit from the university,* he surmised.

Her eyes widened and she self-consciously touched her tousled hair as she looked the handsome man over: three days' beard-growth over a deeply tanned, strong jawbone. Eyes with a mischievous spark to them. There was no mistaking it: Ridge McIntyre stood right in front of her. The girl's expression communicated her thoughts as clearly as words could have done. *He's even more attractive than he is on television.*

Ridge's eyes crinkled with impish delight as he smiled back at her. His dark hair was neatly slicked back, but a section on top was out of place. It fell across his eyes, giving him a practiced casual look as he brushed it back into place.

In the international news pool he had made a stir with his roguish looks and unconventional style, but he was an undisputed female viewer favorite. It was this fact that had helped him land this plum assignment. Ridge knew it. He could not argue with what God had given him and, in truth, did not hesitate to play up his assets to get what he wanted.

"Ridge McIntyre," he said, introducing himself despite the fact that the girl had clearly recognized him.

"Jill Jensen," she said, smiling shyly. "Ridge McIntyre of CNN?"

"That's happening more frequently now," he said, raising one eyebrow. "I'm still not used to losing my anonymity," he said conspiratorially, leaning closer to her. A visible shiver of excitement shot through her body.

A large man came out of one of the tents and rang a triangle bell. Ridge smiled at the young woman again, letting his silver-blue eyes meet hers. "We're a long way from the Ponderosa, but I guess whatever works to call in the troops there should work here, too."

She giggled and glanced at the ground self-consciously. His deep voice brought her head back up.

"Jill, I'm looking for Dr. Roarke. Can you point me in the right direction?"

"Which one?"

Ridge frowned. "Alex Roarke, I think it is."

"Over there," she said with a small smile, nodding toward the raft that had just reached shore. "Come join us for lunch after you're through," she invited.

"Why, thank you," he said graciously, but his attention had shifted to the woman and man who had climbed out of the raft and were walking up the beach to the tents. *Where have I seen her before?* He racked his brain, but nothing came to him. *Better just go introduce yourself to the man you came to see, McIntyre,* he chastised himself. *Work, not women. Work.*

"Excuse me," he called. Halfway up the beach, the man and woman turned toward him and in a moment met Ridge outside the main tent. Ridge looked into the man's eyes. "Dr. Alex Roarke?"

The man laughed and glanced at the woman beside him. "Bad first move. There's nothing my sister hates more than being overlooked."

Alexsana nudged her brother and smiled at the handsome reporter, enjoying his discomfort. He obviously was rarely caught in such a gaffe and was hemming and hawing, trying to figure a way out of the *faux pas.*

She decided to show some mercy. "This is my brother, Dr. Samuel Roarke," she said cheerfully. "I'm Dr. *Alexsana* Roarke."

"Oh, I'm very sorry," Ridge said smoothly, drawing on charm to try and save himself. "I obviously needed to do a bit more research on the Roarke family. I'm —"

"Ridge McIntyre, CNN."

"Have we met? I'm sorry, I thought you looked familiar, but...."

Alexsana watched him squirm without apology. She enjoyed putting playboys, particularly journalists, in their places. During their years in the business, the Roarkes had encountered their share of world-renowned correspondents and had been treated unfairly at times. Besides that, she remembered clearly where she had met the man. And right now, the last thing she needed was for Ridge McIntyre to make up a story about Dr. Alexsana Roarke and Hamas leader Khalil al Aitam.

Alexsana ignored his question, inwardly acknowledging that it would keep him up all night. All journalists shared one thing: the need to know. "What can I do for you?"

"The news office says that you're my best contact for archaeological news in the region," he said distractedly, obviously still trying to place her.

"Might be. But I'm sorry — I don't have time to babysit an American journalist." She walked into the tent and collected a plate full of fruit, cheese, and crackers. The two men followed closely on her heels. Sam tried to suppress a grin as he gestured for Ridge to try again.

"Please, help yourself if you're hungry," Sam said inside, waving to the platters in front of them.

"Thank you," Ridge said, grateful for the excuse to stick around. Alexsana walked away from the serving table and sat on a bench among several raucous university assistants. Her brother joined her, smiling into her frowning face as he left an empty seat beside her for the newsman. Ridge quickly gathered his own lunch and sat down, ignoring Sam's apparent enjoyment of the scene unfolding before him.

Alexsana scowled at Sam, feeling like she was three years older than he, rather than the other way around. She did not appreciate the fact that he was egging Ridge on. Sam loved to see her put journalists in their place, and Alexsana knew that he would love doing it himself even more. *I've had my fun. Now I just want him out of here,* she decided, growing more uncomfortable by the minute. It was only a matter of time before the ace reporter placed her.

"Look," Ridge said, after taking a bite of watermelon. "The network would pay you good money to help me out. We're talking ten, maybe twenty hours a month."

The group had quieted, eager to hear what this man wanted from the Roarkes. They broke up laughing at his statement.

"Big mistake," Sam said with a grin. "The Roarkes have never been motivated by money. Witness our lavish working conditions."

"Well, I don't know, Sam," Alexsana said, returning his smile. "I've been wanting a new BMW...."

"I can smell a trap," Ridge backpedaled, holding his hands up in a gesture of submission. "What can I say to convince you? I need a reputable source in the scholarly and field communities of biblical archaeology. According to the central office, you're the one I need."

"And since I'm not interested in money, what do I get out of the deal?" she asked forthrightly, taking tortoise-shell glasses off to polish them with a napkin.

Ridge studied the unkempt woman, her hair a damp mass of tangles after her dive. And suddenly his eyes sparkled as he made the connection. Carefully, he chose his next words, spoken so that only she and her brother could hear.

"Help me, and I won't dig into the story about the current personal relationship between you — the prominent choice to lead the Solomon's Stable dig — and international terrorist Khalil al Aitam."

Sam's blue eyes darkened and he rose slowly, physically menacing in his anger.

"Come on, Sam," Alexsana said quietly, placing a firm hand on his arm as she stood. She replaced her glasses and looked at Ridge, her lips set in a grim line. "Perhaps the three of us should take a walk down the beach."

"Wait here," Sam said to Ridge firmly, pulling his sister further away from him and the spellbound group inside the tent. Sam and Alexsana walked about twenty feet, then stood face-to-face, quietly arguing. To not hear their conversation was excruciatingly painful for Ridge. Still, he took comfort in the fact that he had found something that could make the seemingly impenetrable Alexsana Roarke — and her brother — squirm.

Seldom had Ridge met a woman who did not cater to his needs and desires in one way or another. It both infuriated and intrigued him. He stared unabashedly at the twosome across the sand.

"Sana, tell me you haven't seen him…" Sam said, shaking his head as if he dared her to tell him otherwise.

"Look, Sam, I *needed* to — just for a moment. It was purely professional." Her tone was firm, not wheedling.

"Khalil's intentions have never been professional toward you," Sam sputtered. "It's no longer safe to 'drop in for a visit' with him, even if he is an old school chum. And you let someone like Ridge McIntyre see you? What were you thinking?"

"Sam, you and I both know that I've practically been handed the Solomon's Stable assignment. I thought I'd try to establish some security for the team, and Khalil was the best man to see about it."

Sam snorted. "Right. What'd he say?"

Alexsana turned away. "He asked me to marry him again," she said, avoiding the real issue.

Her brother laughed. "And you said?"

"What do you think I said? 'Yes, take me away'? Obviously, my mission was futile. Just forget about it. I got out — safe, unharmed." Her tone brooked no argument as she took command of the situation. If Sam knew that Khalil had told her that even he could not protect her from a Hamas reprisal, her brother would try to stop her from accepting the assignment. She turned back to the reporter.

"McIntyre," she beckoned curtly, furious that she had to deal with this at all. *If he hadn't been meddling, Sam would've never found out....*

As Ridge approached the Roarkes, Sam looked out to sea, seemingly ignoring what his sister was about to say.

"Khalil would never hurt me," Alexsana began carefully. "Nor is he some Bedouin lover of mine. We've been like family since we were this high," she said, indicating the height of her denim cut-offs. Alexsana frowned when Ridge's eyes lingered on her tan legs and waited until his eyes met her own clear blue ones. She pursed her lips and then shook her head. "You can't be serious about making up some story about Khalil and me. We're just two old friends on two very different paths."

"If you're on such different paths, why look him up?" Ridge questioned suspiciously.

"No comment. You obviously know nothing, so your 'story' can't go anywhere. Idle threats don't work any better with me than promises of money," she said haughtily.

"I've made some good connections in the three weeks since I've arrived in Jerusalem," Ridge said. "You of all people should know that, since you saw me track Khalil down — something few have been able to do." He stopped to take a breath and regain some control, running his hand through his hair.

He began again, his voice much calmer. "Look. I'm not going to make up some *Current Affair* story of intrigue and love in a Bedouin tent…although it's tempting. I know that in the past, archaeological digs have been stopped or handicapped by Jewish or Palestinian subgroups who protest. People have been injured. What I offer you is this: the inside scoop on anything I hear that impacts archaeological excavations in the region — including your own — and financial remuneration, simply for being neighborly and giving me a few of your hours."

Alexsana stood back and thought. She hadn't the time to keep up with all the politics that might impact her work or those she loved. Besides, if he had connections with men like Khalil, perhaps he would actually obtain some useful information. And who knew if the man would actually develop the story on her and Khalil, if pushed to it? It could be aired in a juicy fashion that might endanger her position as supervisor for the Solomon's Stables excavation.

She studied him intently before speaking again. "I usually manage to keep up on anything that might impact my dig, but I'm going to be very busy in the next few months," she admitted casually. "I suppose I can consider your offer, give you a couple of days." Her face remained impassive. "But after this month, I cannot promise you any particular amount of time. I can only give you what little I can spare."

"Great," Ridge said, taking her admission for agreement. "An in-depth analysis of the people and politics of the Old City is what I need the most. I'm leaving town for a few days. Can we meet at the end of the week?"

Alexsana turned away, walking back toward the tent. "I live in the Old City. You can look up my number," she said over her shoulder, dismissing him.

"I'll just do that," he muttered, averting his eyes before Sam caught him staring at Alexsana's legs again. He turned to walk back to his car. Her voice stopped him. She stood, twenty feet away, blond hair flying in the ocean breeze.

"One more thing, McIntyre. As I said, I don't have time to babysit a journalist. You step on any of my friends' toes, and we're done."

"I don't need a babysitter, Alexsana. I need a competent source."

Three

February 11

The ancient black telephone rang for the eighth time. Alexsana sleepily reached for it with one hand, while holding a pillow over her head with the other. Blindly locating first the huge dial holes, then the cradle, she lifted the receiver and slowly brought it to her ear. "Roarke here."

"I've been trying to reach you for days. I thought we were to meet at the end of last week."

Alexsana recognized the famous voice which she had heard on her brother's television. She supposed many women would be thrilled to be on the phone with the man who had been labeled "News Junkie Hunk of the Year" by *People* Magazine, but she did not consider herself a part of the man's fan club. "I just got in. I was away doing research," she said idly, determined not to explain herself further.

Alexsana smiled as she listened to the static on the other end. *That put him in his place.* The reporter, for once, was silent. It probably shocked him that she didn't jump to be at his beck and call. Perhaps he had expected her to call *him* for breakfast as soon as he got back from wherever he had been.

Alexsana could just picture the playboy with a girl in every port: a shapely model from Madrid, a flight attendant in Paris....

Ridge cleared his throat. "Yes, well, I was wondering if you'd be available to meet me for lunch today. I've cased the streets — gotten to know the city pretty well. But I need more. I need to know it like the locals know it."

Alexsana yawned and looked at her calendar. After leaving him hanging for a moment, she finally responded. "Tomorrow, not today. I'll meet you at St. Stephen's Gate at noon." She hung up without another word.

A half-mile away in his hotel room, Ridge stared at his own telephone receiver. Alexsana's brusque manner irritated him. Yet his interest was piqued by a woman who could so easily turn him away.

February 12

The next afternoon was glorious, and the sun grew hot as Alexsana and Ridge met up at the Old City's northeastern gate. Alexsana was dressed in a loose khaki skirt and a crisp white blouse that was buttoned to the neck and tucked in, showing off her slim figure. A brown leather belt was wrapped around her waist, and stylish sandals covered her feet. Ridge smiled appreciatively, yet refrained from commenting.

"Dr. Roarke," he said with a nod, still smiling as she came near.

"Mr. McIntyre," she said, noting that his eyes were the same pale blue as the Jerusalem sky. She motioned to a Palestinian vendor who carried an elaborate dispenser made of silver on his back. After she had handed him a half-shekel, the man poured something that looked like fruit juice into a battered tin cup. Alexsana drank deeply and considered Ridge over the tin lip. "So you want to know the city as the locals know it, huh?"

"That's my intent, yes."

"*Tamarindy?*" she offered in a casual challenge. "All the locals drink it. I'll buy."

Ridge stared back at her, obviously weighing his options.

"You've gotta be tough if you're going to be a correspondent in the Middle East." She turned and paid the vendor for another serving. He poured it and handed it to her. She, in turn, handed it to Ridge.

Ridge met her gaze, then took the cup and quickly drank it. "Can we get going now?"

Alexsana smiled, taking the cup and handing it to the skinny tamarindy vendor. He gave her a wide grin that showed many missing teeth. She turned back to Ridge and nodded. "Come with me."

"Where are we going?"

"A fine local restaurant called The Green Door. You're hungry?" Her blue eyes again held a spark of mischief, and she cocked an eyebrow innocently.

"I could eat," he allowed doubtfully, looking as if he wondered just how bad the restaurant was. "But I thought you were going to show me the town, not take me to lunch."

Alexsana stopped and looked up at him, her face uncomfortably close to his own. "Look. You're going to have to trust me or forget this whole thing. If you want to know Jerusalem, stick with me. If you want the thirty-buck tour, sign up at the King David Hotel."

He bit his tongue and followed her silently through the labyrinth of alleyways and streets that made up the Muslim quarter. "Men who have known persecution," Alexsana pointed out, "tend to build their cities upward. Note the narrow, winding streets and high walls — the Old City is made up of walls within more walls." She gestured up and around them. "You've noticed it, too, I'm sure, in every quarter: the locked gates, bolted doors, first stories without windows."

She said little else until they arrived at last in front of a stone building with a moss-colored door.

"Let me guess," he quipped.

"Oh, you're fast, Mr. McIntyre. Welcome to The Green Door."

As they entered a dark, large room, several men looked up at them, then away as if uninterested. The blonde spoke to a young woman who then hurried to another room. Then Alexsana turned back to Ridge. All around them, old mattresses were strewn about in piles and cats freely roamed the room. To his credit, and Alexsana's surprise, Ridge did not let any feelings of distaste show in his expression.

"Where shall we sit?" he asked calmly as a tabby cat rubbed against his legs, purring.

Alexsana looked about and chose a meeting place closest to the ancient, open oven, where a man was cooking something that looked like pizzas. She smiled as Ridge watched him. "Not what you're used to in America, and not quite what they do in Italy either. It's somewhere in between."

"We came here for the food?" he asked with an arched brow.

"No," she smiled, "for the ambiance. And to see an old friend."

After the young girl had taken their order — which Ridge trusted Alexsana to place — they sat, silently observing the cook and, more discretely, others in the room. Soon, a large Palestinian man, slightly stooped with age, walked over to greet Ridge's guide.

"Alexsana, *marahaba*," he said.

She rose to kiss him on the cheek. "Ghasan, *salaam al eikum*." The Arabic words, meaning "God's peace to you," was Alexsana's favorite greeting, although she also used Ghasan's word for hello on occasion. "Please, let me introduce you to my guest, Ridge McIntyre. He is an American correspondent for CNN. Ridge, this is Ghasan Khatib, proprietor of The Green Door."

Ridge reached out to shake Ghasan's hand, smiling warmly. There was instant dislike in Ghasan's eyes, but Ridge held his gaze without flinching.

"Please, Ghasan. If we could just have a moment...." Alexsana motioned toward their "couches," inviting him to join them.

With a sigh, the elderly man moved forward. Ridge sat down again after dropping his ignored, proffered hand and wiping it on his jeans as if he had never raised it in the first place. He gave Ghasan a polite smile as if he weren't offended, and Alexsana turned before he could see her admiring grin. It took guts to look into Ghasan's eyes and not cower.

Alexsana left the men to size one another up and went to an old white Frigidaire in the corner. She helped herself to three bottled Cokes, ignoring the filthy handle and black fingerprints all over the relic's thick door.

She returned, impishly smiling first at one man, then the

other. The young girl joined them again to open the bottles.

Ghasan spoke first. "You were never one to keep company with journalists, Alexsana," he said, keeping his eyes on Ridge.

"It wasn't my first choice."

"Oh, no? Is this man blackmailing you?"

"In a way," she said calmly, holding Ridge's gaze. "But don't worry about me. I don't plan on keeping company with him for long."

Ridge looked momentarily irritated, then his face was expressionless once again.

Alexsana drank deeply from her bottle. "I'm showing him the real Jerusalem, Ghasan, and I'd like for you to tell him what you think of the Peace process."

"The Israelis are dogs, but we are tired," Ghasan said without preamble, warming to his old, well-rehearsed diatribe. "We are tired of burying our women and children, so we agree to 'peace,' to certain borders, certain rights. Now, after the so-called 'peace' we still bury our children and the Israelis still eat at our borders, 'settling' more villages while being protected by the government, for which our own soldiers are mere puppets."

Ridge frowned as he listened to Ghasan lament the murder of friends and family members. The old Palestinian had many stories that no news correspondent had ever covered.

Ghasan excused himself twenty minutes later, rising to greet other guests.

"How reliable is he?" Ridge asked Alexsana when the man was out of earshot.

"Very."

"He did not appreciate you bringing me here."

41

"Journalists have been notorious for telling slanted stories," Alexsana said, digging into her "pizza" made of a thin crust, olive oil, cracked eggs, and vegetables. "They denounced their pledge to report the news without bias long ago."

Ridge raised his eyebrow. "Why do you think that?"

"I've seen it over and over. American dollars help fund the Israeli military, and many of those dollars belong to wealthy businessmen who have powerful friends among politicians and the media."

"Fabulous," Ridge said, a trace of bitterness entering his tone. "The old 'you can't trust the media anymore' story."

"Well, can you?"

"Are you suggesting that the American media has been deliberately biased in their reporting?"

"I'm saying that it is human nature to choose a side, no matter how hard you try to be impartial. And American money and emotion tend to flow toward the Israelis, not the Palestinians."

"You speak as if you were burned yourself."

"I've seen friends I considered family get crucified in the media."

"Friends like Khalil al Aitam?"

Alexsana's practiced look of nonchalance broke. Her eyebrows settled into a frown. "I don't approve of the path Khalil has chosen, but I do understand his reasons."

"I see." Ridge seemed pleased to have finally pushed her off-center.

Alexsana's mask of control was quickly reestablished. "Maybe you do, maybe you don't."

From his minaret — a tall, thin, tower high above the lime-stone streets — a *muezzin* called the Muslims to prayer, as he did five times a day. His haunting wail echoed around them as Ridge and Alexsana exited The Green Door and blinked in the bright sunlight.

"I keep thinking I need to shop for a hat, but I never have time," Alexsana said.

Ridge looked at her, appreciating her first real conversational comment. "I know just the place," he announced, an idea taking root.

"What?" she turned toward him.

"Come on," he said, motioning left with a nod, "we can take care of your hat needs. I passed a shop on the way to meet you."

"No, Ridge, I was just commenting...I wasn't asking...Ridge!" The man was leaving without her. Sighing, she followed, stretching her long legs to catch up with him. Just outside the Old City walls was a line of high-end shops that catered to Jerusalem's wealthy.

She reached out to grab his arm as they passed a furrier shop. "Ridge, I really don't want a hat."

"What? Are you kidding? You'd look great in a hat. Come on. I'm buying. You bought the drinks this morning. I'm buying you a hat."

"Ridge, I —"

"Enough. We got off on the wrong foot, Dr. Roarke. Let me buy you a hat as a peace offering."

His face was so earnest that Alexsana faltered. Suddenly, he was like a little boy on a mission. She set her lips grimly as she entered the store behind him, steeling herself for the inevitable. She had five 'Indiana Jones' hats at home, gifts from past suitors. Why had men always wanted to put her under a masculine cap? She was an archaeologist, but still a woman.

But as Alexsana looked around the hat shop, past the leather and felt fedoras, she discovered that Ridge had headed straight to a more feminine section of the store. He held a beautifully crafted, tightly woven linen hat with a white taffeta ribbon around its crown. He looked at her, then back to the hat again. "I saw one like it in the window," he said proudly.

A shiver ran down her spine. Had he picked it for her?

"It's perfect, don't you think?" he asked, placing it on her head before she could say a word. "I looked around, and it was as if it had your name on it."

She glanced at him quickly to make sure he wasn't making her the target of some joke, then blushed as he looked at her in open admiration. Alexsana searched for words as she looked from him to a mirror, becoming even more tongue-tied as she realized that she did not know what to say. The brim of the hat rolled up in front and was slightly oval, making it longer in back, reminiscent of styles popular in the 1920s.

"It's beautiful, Ridge…but I…I know it must be expensive…."

"Nonsense. I'm buying it for you. Not as an expense that I'll submit at the office. As a gift from me to you." He warmed to the idea as he recognized just how much she wanted the hat. "No arguments. If you don't accept it, I'm just going to buy it anyway and toss it on my bureau at home to remember the day by."

"You'd spend this much on a memento?"

"I'd rather see the memento on a certain tour guide."

Alexsana looked back in the mirror and felt her heart soften toward the man. He might be a cocky, overly self-assured womanizer, but no man had ever made her feel so feminine by such a simple gesture. She ventured a shy look of gratitude as he paid for the hat and they left the store.

"Ridge, that was very generous. I want to reciprocate in some way...."

"No need, Doctor. I like the fact that you owe me."

Her heart pounded at the thought. Alexsana Roarke rarely let herself be indebted to anyone. "Listen, I could pay for the hat myself...."

Ridge grinned at her smugly. "But it wouldn't be the same, would it?"

She wanted to deny it, but it was true. The simple beauty of the moment was that Ridge, a near stranger, had picked the one hat, out of a sea of options, that she would have chosen for herself. Yet it was a hat that she would not have purchased on her own. It was too expensive, too frivolous, but so wonderful!

"Yes, well, I...I could at least buy you dinner tonight at the Seven Arches."

"You're asking me out to dinner? Dr. Roarke, I think we had better take this slow," Ridge said, reaching out to stroke her arm.

Alexsana moved away, aware that he was trying to bait her. "I am merely proposing that we continue your crash course education on the real Jerusalem," she protested.

"At the Seven Arches restaurant? Pretty swanky and romantic for a Jerusalem 101 class." He was giving her a run for her money and enjoying every moment of it.

"It will balance out The Green Door," Alexsana said, allowing a tiny smile to reach the corners of her mouth.

"A smile! Your whole face lights up," Ridge said appreciatively with a wide grin of his own. As she looked back at his handsome face, Alexsana frowned at the sudden hammering of her heart. *The guy buys you the right hat and he's got you all aflutter. Get ahold of yourself, Sana.*

"Shall I pick you up at seven?" he asked, noting the change in her expression, but letting it pass without comment.

"No," she said firmly. "I'll pick you up in front of your hotel at six. And Ridge...."

"Yes?"

"This is not a date," Alexsana said firmly. She turned and walked away, casually putting the hat on as she did so. She did not notice Ridge catch her admiring her reflection in a shop window down the street.

"Not a date, huh?" Ridge muttered under his breath, still unable to stop himself from grinning. "Whatever you say, Doctor. Whatever you say." When she had turned the corner and was out of his line of vision, Ridge turned on his heel and whistled all the way back to his hotel.

Four

❧

February 12

Alexsana waited for Ridge in the back of a black BMW cab, smoothing the fabric of her stunning ivory silk jumpsuit. With its dramatically sleeveless, fitted bodice and stylishly flared pants, the outfit emphasized both her narrow hips and gentle curves, and Alexsana felt terrific in it.

Completing the ensemble was an oversized silk shawl of rust, royal blue, and gold, which she had knotted around her shoulders to guard against the chill of the evening.

Briefly she wondered why she had gone all out for Ridge, then quickly decided it was all an act to show him that he couldn't peg her, as he seemed to do with everyone else. *I'll surprise him left and right,* she thought coolly. She toyed nervously with her hair, which had been smoothed into a French twist, revealing the tiny dropped pearls at her ears. Glancing out the window, she inhaled sharply in spite of herself as Ridge appeared at the door of his hotel, dressed in a black, tapered tuxedo jacket that flattered both his broad shoulders and lean waist.

Alexsana took a deep breath as Ridge approached the car. She could not allow herself to consider it a date, even if he was drop-dead gorgeous and they were going to the most romantic place in town.

Ridge opened the door and leaned in with a broad grin. He looked her up and down, then whistled.

Alexsana scowled at him. "Get in, McIntyre," she said with the humorless tone of a schoolmarm to an errant boy.

"Sorr-ry. Just thought I'd give you a compliment," he said, getting in. His face did not ask for forgiveness. Alexsana knew that he felt he had bought some latitude with the hat. *I have to nip this in the bud....*

"Are we in grade school?" she asked curtly.

"No-o," he said, sobering quickly. "I..." his voice trailed away as he looked out the window, searching for words.

"What?"

"Forget it. I'm not very hungry. That pizza didn't agree with my stomach."

"What?" she laughed, backpeddling from her harsh tone. The mood lightened again. "Ridge McIntyre, unable to handle street food?"

A gentle smile eased back into Ridge's face as the taxi sped off. "Yeah, yeah, laugh it up," he pretended to grumble. "I'll start our dinner with some tonic water and be fine."

At a quarter after six, Ridge and Alexsana entered Intercontinental's elegant, five-star, Seven Arches hotel. Along each wall, huge arrangements of flowers adorned antique tables that had been oiled to a deep shine. Neither Alexsana nor Ridge spoke to the other, and Alexsana's heels seemed inordinately loud as they clicked down the marble hallway toward the restaurant.

The maitre d' greeted Alexsana by name. "This way, Dr. Roarke. We're so pleased you and your guest could join us tonight." His eyes held thinly veiled curiosity as he looked Ridge over, obviously trying to place the familiar face. Never before had Alexsana eaten in his restaurant with someone other than her father and brother.

"Thank you, David. We are pleased to be here."

He pulled a chair out for her at a window table. "I trust the other Doctors Roarke are well?" he asked as she sat down.

"Very well, thank you for asking," she answered, taking the offered menu from him.

"Good, good. May I suggest the *osso buco* tonight? It looks outstanding. Your waiter will be along shortly to tell you about it in detail."

"Thank you, David."

Alexsana looked over at Ridge, allowing the tiny smile to return. For some reason she enjoyed surprising the man, and he seemed genuinely awed by the incredible, panoramic, sunset view of the Old City. She squinted as the sunlight hit the golden roof of the Dome of the Rock, its reflection momentarily shining directly into their window.

As she shielded her eyes against the glare, Alexsana gave in to the feeling that had nagged at her all afternoon. "Ridge, I have a confession to make."

"You?" he asked sarcastically, leaning forward.

"Don't make this tougher than it already is," Alexsana protested, shooting him a warning look. She gazed at him earnestly, the effect heightened by the absence of her glasses.

"Look, I've had bad experiences with journalists in the past. Poor, inaccurate reports. Misuse of contacts. Misrepresentation." She sighed. "But I know you have a good reputation, and it hit me this afternoon that I really haven't given you a break. It's not fair, and it is very unchristian of me."

Ridge had studied her as she spoke. After her confession, he shifted in his chair nervously, then shrugged. "We all have to protect ourselves. I'm used to it."

Alexsana leaned back, wondering. "Do you do that?"

"What?" Ridge asked, pretending to not understand her question.

"Protect yourself."

Ridge weighed his answer carefully. "To a certain extent."

"Ahh." Alexsana buried her face in her menu. After several moments of silence, she looked up again. "Tell me, McIntyre. Do you have any weak spots in your protective walls?" she asked.

He blinked slowly and raised one eyebrow. "Isn't this getting a bit personal?"

"Yes," she said with a tiny shrug. "Are you as brave as you make yourself out to be?"

He frowned at her, trying to think of a way to change their course of conversation. "Are you challenging me?"

"In a way," she said calmly, and closed her menu. "Are you the typical reporter, incapable of relating on a personal level?"

Ridge sat back, regarding the woman before him. "I can get personal." He sounded slightly defensive.

"Good. I don't care to spend time with people who can't get beyond a superficial level. Life's too short."

"Boy, you lay it on the line, lady, don't you?"

Alexsana smiled with her eyes and nodded.

"You want to know where I am weakest? Did you ever consider being a reporter?"

Her smile grew slightly wider, yet Alexsana merely took a sip from her crystal water glass, giving him time to formulate an answer.

Ridge looked out on the Old City. "Weaknesses...weaknesses. Let me tell you my strengths first. It'll make me feel a bit more secure when we get to that more distasteful subject."

"If you must."

Ridge leaned back, appearing calm. But Alexsana noticed that he was unconsciously twisting his napkin into a corkscrew as he spoke. His words should have sounded cocky, but Ridge managed to make it sound like he was just reporting the facts.

"I did well as a reporter from the get-go, going farther, faster than most of my cohorts. I started at a local station after college, back in Coeur d'Alene, Idaho. I was 'discovered' and sent to the Boise station. From there I went to CNN as a junior correspondent, where I happened upon a few hot stories and was promoted to international news. Two years later, *voilá*, here I am in Jerusalem."

"Professionally, a star. I know that. I want to know what most people don't know about Ridge McIntyre."

"Right, my weaknesses. You're tough, aren't you?"

A waiter came to take their order, and both absently opted for the special, osso bucco, wanting to get back to their conversation. Their salads arrived shortly thereafter.

"Ah, where were we? Weren't we talking about my strengths? Did I tell you I had a full-ride football scholarship at Idaho State?"

Alexsana smiled, enjoying the banter and Ridge's unease. "No, I did not know that," she said idly.

Ridge regarded her determined, calm expression. "I can see that you're not going to let me charm my way out of this one. Okay. I'll be frank. Women. Women are a weakness for me."

"I know that," Alexsana sighed. "That's too easy, too obvious. Tell me something that no one else knows about Ridge McIntyre."

He looked out to the City, his eyes running over the length of the Temple Mount and the grand mosque on top of it. A thought seemed to come to him. "All right, then. My faith," he said simply. "Here I am in the holiest city in the world and I don't know where I stand with God."

Alexsana stopped eating, flabbergasted at his frank confession. She never anticipated that he would actually share something so real, so deep. "Thank you," she said, setting down her fork. "That took a lot of guts to tell me." She stared at him in genuine admiration. "So where does that leave you? Are you seeking him?"

"Seeking him? What does that mean, anyway?" Ridge asked, lost in thought. "We're talking about God here. Someone or something so huge, it overwhelms me. I look out at this city," he said, waving toward Jerusalem, "and I think, men have been looking for God here for years. But being in a place where so many have found him is almost off-putting. What if I don't find him? Does that mean I'm lacking in some way?"

"So you fear the process itself? Or what you'll find?" she asked gently, no judgment in her voice.

"Both."

Alexsana nodded, swallowing a bite of salad nonchalantly while her heart pounded. There was nothing more exciting for her than watching someone near understanding of his Creator. It was better than anything she'd ever find on an excavation.

This was the priceless life goal that had dominated peoples' lives in the past. The present. The future. All wrapped up into one. It made her skin tingle with an awareness that the Spirit was with them.

She reached across the table to lightly take his hand. He looked from the Old City to her. "Ridge, it's worth the effort. It's so vital, there's nothing more important for you. No story will rival the feeling of what you'll find in Christ. I know it's scary. I know it takes work. But I can't emphasize enough how important this is."

Ridge stared at her, obviously warming to the fact that the subject was bringing him closer to the beautiful archaeologist who had rebuffed him in several ways already.

Alexsana sensed this and quietly withdrew her hand. "Don't confuse this with me," she said. "This is a relationship between you and God. I'm not part of the bargain. As a Christian, I hope and pray that you'll find him. For you."

Ridge sobered, raised one eyebrow, then nodded. "Okay. So how would you suggest I check out this relationship with the Almighty, Dr. Roarke?"

"I have someone you should talk to. We can meet with him tomorrow."

They filled the rest of their evening with conversation about the Middle East — politics, people, passions. But Alexsana could not stop her eyes from holding his own intense gaze, could not ignore the fluttering inside her stomach. The man — usually, so strong, so irritatingly sure of himself — had swiftly cut down her defenses simply by admitting that there was something missing in his life. It unnerved her. Was it all a ruse just to get close to her?

Five

❧

February 13

Alexsana and Ridge exited the city and walked along a paved road toward the Mount of Olives, ignoring the vendors selling olive wood figureheads of Jesus and the camel drivers who called to them in the hopes of giving the two "tourists" a ride.

"Special deal for you!"

"I take your picture, lady! Special deal today!"

"*Shou kran, la,*" Alexsana repeated over and over, dismissing them with a polite but firm "no thanks" as she led Ridge away.

"I thought you were introducing me to someone," he said, looking back over his shoulder at Jerusalem as they walked.

"I am."

He shrugged and followed her lead, stretching his long legs to catch up with her, then shortening his stride to match her own.

It was a cooler day. Alexsana and Ridge both wore sweaters: his, a thick, silver-blue, Norwegian knit that set off his eyes; hers, a long, Irish knit worn over thick, ivory leggings.

Alexsana gave him a bright smile. "Tell me what you know, so I don't bore you with basic information. Give me your foundation and I'll expand on it."

"All right. I've done my research: Jerusalem has been run by the Jews since 1967. It's a land of conflicting religious and political parties that keep it in constant turmoil...."

"How much have you learned about those religious parties?"

"Enough to know that there is religion atop religion — Muslim, Christian, and Jew, among others — and various subgroups within each religion, from the ultra-orthodox to the more liberal.

"Then you have the Arabs, who refer to themselves most often as Palestinians," he continued, "They include both Christians and Muslims, who have been trampled by Jews. After the war of '67, the Jews suddenly had a homeland. For a people who have never seemed to fit in anywhere and who have been widely persecuted, 'coming home to the Promised Land' must have seemed like a calling from God. In the face of their immigration, the Palestinians have scattered and dispersed, but they remain an angry force here. The Jews, for the most part, have better financial resources and wield more political power. I see a lot of similarities between the Palestinians and our own American Indians."

Alexsana nodded in admiration. "That's a good start. You won't be entirely slanted as a journalist to the Zionist cause. As much as my own sympathies lie with the Jews and their desire to see their Promised Land reestablished, I don't always agree with their methods. It pains me to see what happens to the Palestinians every day."

"Well, I try not to be biased. That is the goal of the profession, regardless of a reporter's personal opinions. But my knowledge comes from research, the internet, and personal interviews. What I still lack is more difficult to describe. I want to know, to see, some of these people firsthand so I can feel what they feel. Like Ghasan. *That* will give me the vision so I can accurately report to the world what transpires here."

Alexsana nodded again, understanding his passion and smiling at the realization that he had caught what many called "Jerusalem fever." A few minutes later, they reached the Mount of Olives, where she led Ridge down a path and into an ancient olive grove. They hiked up a steep, stony path that ended on a flat rock, shaded by a olive tree. An older man awaited them there, sitting on a small, portable stool with a cane in hand.

"Professor O'Malley," Alexsana introduced, "This is Ridge McIntyre." She smiled from one man to the other, enjoying the look of surprise on Ridge's face before it was quickly buried. She was pleased to see that Ridge had heard of the famous biblical scholar.

"Ridge," she explained as the men shook hands, "I invited Jerome up here because last night you said you didn't know how to start your search for God." She ignored his subtle scowl. "All my life, Professor O'Malley has been there for me when I wrestled with details of my excavations and even my own beliefs. As you probably know, he is the preeminent scholar at the École Biblique. If anyone can field your questions, he can."

Ridge nodded and sat down, his face expressionless. Alexsana tried to read his feelings. No doubt he would not appreciate her meddling into his affairs. He might have discussed it with her alone, but to bring in an expert? But she hadn't a choice. She felt as if God had directed her to do so. Fortunately, Ridge appeared unperturbed, caught up in the spectacular view of the city before them, which was entirely visible from north to south. He whistled in appreciation. "It's almost as good a view as from the Intercontinental," he said, shooting Alexsana a look.

Alexsana smiled and sat down, pulling off her backpack as she did so. "Have you guys eaten?"

Professor O'Malley nodded, but Ridge shook his head. She unzipped the bag and pulled out fresh *challah*, a Jewish braided egg bread, and several huge, ripe oranges. Then she dipped her hand into the bag and lifted out three bottles of water. "Hope you don't mind simple fare — I don't have time to pack elaborate picnics."

"Looks great. It was quite a hike up here," Ridge said as she sat down beside him. "I didn't even think about food after breakfast this morning." He looked out to the city, then back toward her. "I do appreciate all this," he said, raising his eyes to hers.

Alexsana met his gaze, never faltering. "I'm happy to do it." As she peeled an orange, she first studied the ripe fruit, then her companion.

The elderly professor interrupted their semiprivate moment. "So, Mr. McIntyre, your body is here…in the city of religion. Where do you find your soul?"

Ridge raised his eyebrows in surprise. "Forgive me, but you're about as subtle as my guide here." He leveled a stony gaze at the man, who appeared to be in his late seventies.

Jerome was unflappable. He peered unflinchingly at

Ridge from beneath heavy folds of skin. Age spots and wrinkles covered his balding head. "I need to know more about your own foundation. Were you raised as a Christian?"

"On Christmas and Easter," Ridge said simply. He watched the professor for a reaction.

"Ah," O'Malley said knowingly. "So you know about biblical teachings? The importance of this place for Christians worldwide?"

"I reread the gospels on the plane over…" Ridge began.

"You don't understand your own spiritual beliefs, yet you're trying to understand the religious fervor and passion of an entire nation?"

"Hey, now, don't go slapping some judgment on me," Ridge said angrily.

Jerome sighed. He looked at Alexsana, who was gazing at the city as if she were only half-listening, then back to Ridge. "I'm not judging, Mr. McIntyre. I am simply trying to determine where you are beginning so I can help you understand others — like you requested of Alexsana."

Alexsana halved the orange and handed Ridge a juicy section.

"This wasn't exactly what I requested…what I wanted to know…. Oh, okay," Ridge accepted haltingly. He chewed a bite of orange and swallowed. "Treat me like a rookie," he said, carefully looking at the city and not at his companions.

Alexsana smiled. Like herself, Ridge apparently did not enjoy admitting that he did not have everything under control.

Jerome said, "Let me begin with what we know best — Christianity. If you can understand, feel the passion Christians feel, you can transfer that knowledge to other religions. It will give you a start." He measured his words carefully.

"We are sitting on the Mount of Olives. Below us is the Garden of Gethsemane. This is the place where Jesus Christ spent his final days as a free man. It is here that the enormity of the task before him truly hit him and his companions. Looking out at that city," he said, gesturing forward, "Jesus knew what God had called him to do. It was here that in a moment of fear and anger, he said to his father, 'Take this cup from me.' Before coming here to pray, he had distributed the bread and the wine, telling his friends that they should practice communion in remembrance of him. He had prepared them, you see, to go on without him.

"The soldiers came and took him from this mountain. Jesus went peacefully. They led him into the city, to the house of Caiaphas, then to the palace of Herod, where Pilate was staying. Pilate believed Jesus was innocent, despite the fact that the Jewish leaders themselves proclaimed him guilty." He paused. "It must have been awful for Pilate. Can you imagine looking into the eyes of God, Mr. McIntyre, and knowing that what you were about to do would condemn you? Even if he did not recognize him as the Messiah, he certainly knew Jesus was innocent."

During the moment of silence that followed, neither Ridge nor Alexsana chewed or spoke as they contemplated such an idea. Jerome began again: "When Jesus would not speak in his own defense, Pilate 'washed his hands' of him and sentenced him. They took him to 'skull hill' — Golgotha, a rocky outcropping that resembled a human skull — and crucified him.

"After he died, his followers took him down and laid him in a tomb. Tradition holds that the tomb lies under those domes over there," he said, gesturing to the west, "beneath what is now the Church of the Holy Sepulchre. There he was laid to rest; three days later, his body was gone. He had risen. In his passage, he began the Great Hope for us: because of his ultimate sacrifice, we are forgiven of our sins and promised eternal life. Through ourselves, we die; through him, we live."

Ridge nodded, trying to absorb the information. His brow was furrowed, as if he were concentrating very hard. "Go on," he urged.

"You have heard Jesus referred to as 'the Lamb of God'?"

"I believe so."

"It builds upon the biblical imagery and Jewish tradition from which he emerged. The Jews traditionally offered a lamb in the temple each year as a sacrifice. Ideally, it was a perfect lamb — unblemished, in good health, of a good demeanor. To give up such an animal was truly a sacrifice — in the modern sense of the word. One lamb could provide food or money for a family. It could even be bred to produce *more* food and money. But they wanted to atone for their sins, and so they sacrificed the animals as God had dictated.

"When Christ — the Lamb — was sacrificed, Jesus gave the ultimate gift, and the need for animal sacrifice was eliminated forever. For how could one compare the death of an animal to that of a man, let alone the man we consider to be the Son of God? It was the end of salvation based on observance of religious law and the beginning of grace. Some believed Jesus was the Savior; others condemned him, seeing not the Messiah, but a weak, beaten man. They wanted a political king, the new David. By turning away, they missed the King of kings. They missed salvation."

Ridge looked at the professor, then at Alexsana, appearing a little irked at their obvious religious enthusiasm. "So you're saying that all of the Jews and Muslims and any other religion in the world are condemned?" His voice was tense.

Alexsana spoke up for the first time. "The Bible and Christ were very clear. Jesus said, 'No one comes to the Father except through me.' I know," she said, placing her hand emphatically on her chest, "that I am saved. I know the Messiah in a very personal way. That brings me great hope for my life, now and in the future.

"Will everyone else be condemned?" She echoed his question. "I don't know. My God is a gracious, loving and fair God. I trust him to make those decisions; I'm not capable of saying who will 'get in' and who will not. But as for me, I know. I *know*." She stared into Ridge's eyes, willing him to understand, to grasp the passion, until he looked away.

"I hear you," he said, "But I must admit, I don't understand."

O'Malley turned back toward Jerusalem and the others followed his gaze. "The City of David," the professor mused. "The Golden City. To understand Jerusalem is to understand a piece of God. Passion for their Lord drives Palestinians to despair in their displacement, Christians to panic at the thought of losing access to their holy sites, and Jews to distraction at their tenuous hold on things. They all want to hold her. But you cannot 'hold' the Golden City any more than you can hold God."

He gained momentum as he spoke, becoming more impassioned with each word, and Alexsana suddenly saw him as a young man: strong, stalwart, intense. "It is like a volcano, ready to erupt. It is foolish to think that anyone could hold a natural phenomena like a volcano." O'Malley smiled benevolently.

"Yet despite its potential for destruction, a volcano warms the earth's crust and spews forth minerals that enrich her soil, bringing new life. God is like a volcano — capable of destroying in a moment's notice, yet seeming to slumber peacefully for centuries. Can you grasp it?" He turned toward Ridge. "It is a primal, basic need, to know God." He looked at Ridge curiously. "You know him, Mr. McIntyre. You've just forgotten him."

Jerome sat down again. Ridge waited patiently for him to finish. "Ask yourself if you've gone so far here," Jerome said, pointing to his head, "that you cannot know the light here," he said, pointing to his heart. "Sometimes we try to *think* out something that is better *felt*."

Ridge looked from Jerome to Alexsana, seeming unsure of what to say.

"Search, my friend," Jerome entreated softly. "It will be here in Jerusalem, if anywhere, that you will understand the Christ or walk away from him. He knocks; open the door, or your future will be darker than the Solomon's Stables that Alexsana will soon explore."

His tone was sure and confident, and Ridge did not ask another question. The three finished their oranges and bread in silence, each lost in his or her own thoughts.

Later that afternoon, Ridge and Alexsana approached the West Jerusalem neighborhood of Mea Shearim. Before them, a sign proclaimed in poor English: MODEST DRESS, SKIRTS REACHING UNTIL BELOW THE KNEE. Ridge scanned the rest of the oddly translated sign, which asked visitors to respect the Jews' code of righteous clothing, while Alexsana removed her backpack and pulled out a paper *yarmulke.*

"Here," she said, handing it to him. "I'm dressed to walk through, but you need to cover your head."

Ridge unfolded the small disc and awkwardly placed the cap on his head, but his heavily moussed hair made it difficult for the yarmulke to stay in place. Alexsana grinned at him, despite herself. As they were passed by several men in long, black coats and shaved heads with one long curl at each temple, she struggled to control her laughter. "You fit right in," she managed to say, smiling behind her hand.

"Yeah, right," Ridge said looking down at her. "Lead on, my new friend," he said grandly.

She passed in front of him, through the limestone brick gates of the *haredi,* or "God-fearing community." "As you might have been able to tell from the entrance, this is an ultra-Orthodox section of Jerusalem. They maintain the old traditions and religious lifestyle of the Eastern European Jews." They turned a corner and walked several blocks, then Alexsana pointed toward the window of a classroom.

Ridge looked in at sixteen sleepy-looking boys. "How old are they? They're just tots!"

"Four," Alexsana said. Catching the eye of the teacher, she waved and smiled and kept on talking. "That is Rabbi Josef Shek, a friend of my father's. This *yeshiva* preschool is the heart of the community, where boys study and discuss the Torah and Talmud."

She pointed past Ridge at three neatly bundled little girls walking down the street, following their mother like goslings after a goose. "For one of those haredi girls to marry one of the little scholars you see inside is the highest hope of any haredi father. They will most likely be properly educated and remain devout Jews."

"Will it be a challenge to find an available scholar?" Ridge asked, grinning as a sleeping boy was jostled awake by the rabbi.

"Not too tough. Most will remain in the yeshiva until they're eighteen, or older. In all of Eastern Europe before the Holocaust, there were perhaps 35,000 yeshiva students. Today, in Israel alone, there are almost 50,000. The government obviously encourages these schools. They give grants to the families of the students; that tradition, and the high birth rate among haredi Jews, will keep the schools in business."

"And find those girls the right man."

"Of course." Alexsana grinned. They walked down several streets in silence, eventually making their way to the Western Wall of the Temple Mount.

"Ah, the Wailing Wall," Ridge nodded in recognition. "Maybe you can enlighten me...."

Alexsana nodded sadly. "It's as close as they can come to their God and an understanding of where he lives. So they stick prayers between the stones that Herod had placed there, and they pray that the Temple will be theirs again."

"By the looks of the Dome of the Rock, that's not likely to happen."

"No, especially after 176 pounds of gold has just been plastered over it, a gift from King Hussein. You understand the significance of this place?"

"Not as deeply as you do. And that's where you hope to

excavate Solomon's Stables — under the Haram, as Palestinians call it?"

"Yes. The Temple Mount is huge: the length and width of five football fields. Once it housed the grand Jewish temple. Or I should say twice. It was destroyed and rebuilt. People used to enter it from the eastern side, through the Golden Gate, or from the south end at the Triple Gate — you know, the ones we saw earlier, walled off, as we entered the Dung Gate?

"Behind the Double Gate is a staircase that Christ and his disciples walked. For centuries, erosion and filler, as well as political or religious differences, have kept scholars from exploring the structure underneath. The Crusaders used the caverns as stables. Thus, the name."

"The excavation is a big deal because no one has done it before?"

"Well, yes. To excavate anywhere on or under the Haram would be a dig of significance. Under the Dome of the Rock is the stone where Abraham is thought to have gone to sacrifice Isaac and where his hand was stayed. The Temple Mount itself held the two greatest temples ever built for Jews, one of which was attended by Jesus Christ himself. Today the Temple Mount, or the 'Haram el Sharif' as Muslims call it, holds two holy Muslim mosques, one of which is the El Aksa Mosque, a pilgrimage site for all believers. Directly under it and eastward," she said, gesturing toward the smaller dome, "is where I intend to dig. The work is bound to anger those who mistrust the motives of those considered a threat to the Haram."

"Especially the Hamas," Ridge said.

Ignoring his comment, Alexsana gestured for him to follow her. They quickly walked another three blocks and soon were standing in front of a store called "The Bookstore of the Temple Mount Faithful." The window appeared to be made of bulletproof glass, and protective bars could be seen inside. "Look at this picture," Alexsana said, pointing.

Ridge stared through the glass at the picture of Jerusalem, then whistled as he saw the importance of it. Someone had taken a photo, airbrushed out the El Aksa Mosque and Dome of the Rock, and added a computer-generated image of the Temple as it once had looked. He glanced up at Alexsana. "I bet this fuels the fire between Jew and Muslim."

They walked away from the window, past a coffee shop where men sat drinking dark liquid out of exotic-looking, long-necked pots. "That bookstore," Alexsana indicated, "has been firebombed several times and rebuilt. With a holy pilgrimage site on one hand and the passion, the calling, that Jews have to rebuild the temple, how can the two sides not battle?"

Ridge walked beside her, studying her face. "It all pains you, doesn't it?"

"I feel this is my homeland, despite my dual-citizenship with America. This is where my heart is. Even with the peace accord between Arafat and Rabin, the upheaval continues. I've had a Palestinian friend die in my arms, shot by accident, and I've seen Jewish children wounded in other street battles. It is an insane, wonderful, passionate place to live." Her eyes begged him to understand.

Alexsana glanced at her watch. "Oh my, it's almost four. I've got to pick up some food for dinner. My brother and a friend are coming over. Sorry, but I must go. I hope these last few days have been helpful."

"Oh, yes. Yes, they have. You've been a great guide, but I think I've only gotten a glimpse of what I'm seeking."

"True enough. There will be other days."

Impulsively, Ridge reached out and took her hand. "When?"

She smiled and gently pulled her hand from his. "Call me," she said evasively. "We'll find a time. Good-bye." With that, she walked away. Ridge stared after her for a moment, then forced himself to turn away as well. After glancing back over his shoulder several times, he finally gave up, stopped, and watched until she was out of sight.

February 13

Sam and his dark-haired companion walked through the winding streets of Old Jerusalem, down countless stairs worn smooth by centuries of foot travel. The streets were nearly empty as cool darkness enveloped the city, making the damp streets even chillier. They passed the building that once housed the Knights of Saint John, then the towering Lutheran Church of the Redeemer.

Absorbed in conversation, neither noticed the impressive buildings. Initially awkward, they soon got past their shyness and talked nonstop from the airport in Tel Aviv, catching up on their personal and professional lives. Passing the Church of the Holy Sepulchre, they entered the Christian quarter of the city, where Alexsana lived, and were soon knocking on her door.

"Christina!" Alexsana grinned and hugged her old friend. "It's so good to see you." She glanced over the brunette's shoulder toward her brother, wondering if it troubled him to see his old girlfriend. It had been five years since they had broken off their relationship, but she knew that Sam had had a hard time forgetting the woman. Then he had finally found someone special again. *It must have made his breakup with Lydia even tougher,* Alexsana thought for the hundredth time.

"How are *you?*" Christina pulled back to admire the attractive woman she had considered a little sister ever since their days at Columbia. "You look beautiful. And I hear that you're making waves as a biblical archaeologist — the Temple Mount, no less!"

"Well, we haven't started yet. And it doesn't outshine what you've been up to. Sam and I have been keeping track of you. We were so worried last summer when we heard over the BBC that you were tangling with Hobard. Suddenly my most scholarly friend is playing Pirates and Treasure Hunter. But wait…we have so much to catch up on! Please, sit down and Sam will get us something to drink. Dinner will be ready soon."

The two women seated themselves on Alexsana's couch as Sam obediently went to get them warm beverages. "Nice place!" Christina raised an eyebrow. "Spacious," she teased, looking up at the loft that had been made into a bedroom, then down at the narrow kitchen that stood beside the bathroom. The living room measured only about ten by fifteen feet.

"I was lucky to get an apartment with its own bathroom!" Alexsana exclaimed. "Could you see me traipsing down a hall to share one with five other apartments? By the time I get home, I want a tub all to myself."

"It's wonderful," Christina assured her warmly. "Cozy, but wonderful."

"It's all I really need, as often as I camp out at dig sites."

"I know the feeling. By the time I get home, I can't believe how much space is in a real bed and I usually stick to the three-foot space I'm allotted on a ship bunk. I've had dry-land quarters for the last year, and Mitch still can't get me to take more than that three-foot section of our king-sized bed!"

The two laughed, then quieted as Sam came in, suddenly aware that their conversation might make him uncomfortable. He and Christina had parted amicably, but even years after their breakup, things were still a bit awkward at times.

"I sure appreciate you having me over for dinner," Christina said, pushing a wave of dark brown hair over her shoulder.

"No problem," Alexsana assured her. She took a sip of hot tea from a locally crafted mug. "If I know my brother, by the time he gets you out to Caesarea, I won't have a chance to see you again. I assume you're only staying for a brief consultation visit."

"Afraid so. Mitch and I have a ton of work to do on *El Espantoso* at Robert's Foe, and we still want to search for *La Canción*. We're close — I can almost *feel* her when we dive in a certain harbor we're searching off the coast of Mexico. He'll have my hide if I stay too long, but realizes I can't pass up the chance to see another Greek mariner. Especially here."

Sam sat down in a wicker chair beside the couch, smiling. "It sounds like you finally found a man who can understand your obsession with work."

"Just a little better than you. The difference is that he's a sea lover through and through. Except for this Caesarea dig, I bet you'll spend most of your career deep in the sands of Israel." She looked at him fondly. "I have to admit, though, that our run-ins with Hobard made Mitch and me think long and hard. We both came to the decision that work would never come between us — that our marriage would be priority over everything else. We think God really worked through that whole, awful situation to show us what's really important in life."

Sam smiled at her frankness and nodded. "I agree, like we decided five years ago: a relationship marked by separations half-way around the world would not be a good idea."

Alexsana realized the conversation could become very uncomfortable. "I'm hoping to drag him away from Caesarea for the Solomon's Stable dig," she interceded.

"If she can convince Hoekstra," Sam said, knowing full-well that his sister could sweet-talk the older man into anything. Robert had been like an uncle to the two since they were toddlers; without kids of his own, he doted on them.

"Do you have the rest of your team pulled together?" Christina asked.

"No. I was given the news that I would be supervisor just a few weeks ago. Even with the peace process underway, Israel has been in even more upheaval than usual. I assume you heard about the Beit Lid massacre. If things don't smooth out soon, I might never get a chance to dig; you can imagine the uproar there will be once this news gets out."

"I wouldn't want to be you. So you'll pull them together once you get the go-ahead?"

"I've contacted four out of the twelve I'd like. I'm going to keep the team small, at least at first. So far, everyone I've contacted is busy on other projects. I just want them to get permission for a leave of absence once we get the 'all clear' sign."

"Do you think that because of the importance of this dig, they can all get out of their current assignments?"

"Of course, there will be the usual ruffled feathers here and there. But yes, because of this project's importance, it should be okay."

"You know my sister," Sam said. "Somehow everything always falls into place for Sana." His tone held a note of envy, but also one of pride.

"Except for finding love," Alexsana sighed. "Sometimes I think God will never decide it's the right time for me."

"Well, you are accomplishing good things for the Kingdom," Christina said. "Look at your work at Kinneret and Hazor — you've opened up whole new excavation sites."

"We really just scratched the surface," Alexsana said modestly. "The teams on those sites now are accomplishing even greater excavations. If I had my druthers, and if Solomon's Stables weren't looming on the horizon, I'd be at Caesarea."

"No doubt," Christina said, smiling. She sniffed the air delicately. "Something smells fabulous. What's for dinner?"

"Something light," Alexsana said, assuming her best stuffy, nasal "chef's voice." "A lovely baked chicken, spiced ever so delicately with rosemary, and pita bread with melted goat's cheese over fresh, garlic-marinated tomatoes."

Sam's stomach rumbled as if on cue, and the three laughed, each feeling like they were sharing good, old times.

February 16

Hundreds of miles away, in Damascus, Ridge and his cameraman, Steve Rains, walked into an upscale house in a finer part of the city. As they passed through a dark passageway, they called out so as not to surprise anyone. Suddenly, six guards in uniform rushed them, threw them to the wall, and began to yell in Arabic. Steve's camera crashed to the ground, and both he and Ridge winced at the sound of heavy plastic cracking and metal crunching.

"I'm Ridge McIntyre from CNN!" Ridge shouted as he was roughly searched. "I have an appointment with Fathi Shkaki!"

"Who is this?" a man asked loudly in rough English, pointing his Uzi at the base of Steve's skull.

"Steve Rains! My cameraman!" Ridge stared over at his friend, who looked as concerned as he felt himself. Steve's normally ruddy complexion was as pale as his blond hair.

One of the guards pulled their wallets from their pockets and reviewed their identification. He nodded at his companion. "Proceed. Fathi Shkaki is expecting you."

Steve bent and gingerly picked up his camera. After briefly examining it, he shrugged at Ridge as if to say, "With any luck, it will work." They passed through a room elaborately decorated in Middle Eastern fashion — with oriental rugs, brass lamps, spare furniture — then into a wood paneled library that smelled of stale cigarette smoke.

Across from them sat an obese, older man, dressed in a cardigan and wearing thick glasses. Nodding at them, he finished his conversation and hung up the phone. He then took a drag from his cigarette, held it for a moment, and forcefully blew out the smoke. "My friends from CNN. Welcome."

"Thank you," Ridge said, pushing the confrontation in the hall out of his mind. He and Steve had been through worse for an interview of this scale. "Do you mind if we tape this?"

Shkaki shook his head, and Steve quickly set up his camera. He turned to Ridge. "Looks like the damage is superficial. We should be okay." Ridge nodded. "Ready?" Steve asked.

"Ready."

"Rolling. Three, two, one.…" Steve focused on Ridge for the introduction.

"We're here with the Islamic Jihad leader, Fathi Shkaki, who lives in Damascus and has done so since he was deported to a refugee camp in 1988. Since 1989, Shkaki has been directing the Islamic Jihad from this city. The group is best known for its suicide attacks in Israel and the occupied territories."

Ridge paused uneasily as two guards silently entered the room, then forged on.

"Two days ago, an attack at the Beit Lid bus station resulted in the deaths of twenty soldiers and five civilians." Ridge glanced over at Shkaki, to make sure he was not overstepping his bounds, but the man was grinning and nodding his head, as if celebrating Ridge's words. Ridge felt a chill, but continued. "Although Shkaki disclaims direct responsibility for the attack, he *has* agreed to speak with us about how it might have been planned."

Ridge gazed steadily at the camera until Steve said, "…and cut." He then sat down across from the grinning terrorist and tried to ignore the smile he found to be so extremely distasteful. Steve refocused and began the count again. "And three, two, one.…"

"How do you plan a bombing like Beit Lid? How was the target chosen?" Ridge began quickly, warming to the interview.

"We send men to a potential target and study it carefully," Shkaki said, as if lecturing to a crowd of students. The man's English was quite good, Ridge noticed. He nodded, urging the man to continue. "Beit Lid was an obvious choice. At the appointed time, the *mujahedin* went from Gaza to Tel Aviv, and from Tel Aviv to the military bus station. They coordinated themselves: the first man was to enter the shop and detonate the bomb strapped to his body; the second was to stay outside, wait for the soldiers to run out, then rush into the crowd and blow himself up."

Ridge swallowed hard, his face devoid of emotion. "Did you order the bombing?"

"That is handled by our mujahedin in Palestine. It is not logical to give orders from outside. Of course I have contacts with the movement."

"Did you know in advance that the attack would take place?"

Shkaki grinned. "I cannot tell you that."

A muscle twitched along Ridge's jaw line. "How can you justify the killing of civilians, like the Hamas bombing that killed more than twenty in Tel Aviv last October?"

Shkaki remained unrepentant. "You have to ask our brothers in Hamas about that. Our orders are to attack Israeli military targets and settlements. But Palestinians face an organized army, and most of our own losses are civilians, not mujahedin. We do not intend to attack civilians, but what can I say?" he gave a slight shrug. "This is a war zone."

"What was your reaction to the Beit Lid bombing?"

"This was the biggest military attack ever inside Palestine, other than the Arab-Israeli wars," the man said, sounding noncommittal.

"You are pleased?"

"My people are pleased," he finally said smugly, his words sounding falsely humble.

Ridge held the man's gaze for a moment, then motioned for Steve to stop the tape. His stomach turned as he thought about the twenty young soldiers who had died at the bus station. Ridge had visited Beit Lid after the bombing that day and had observed rabbinate representatives scouring the scene for bits of human flesh; under Jewish law, the whole body had to be given a proper burial.

In contrast, he had also seen Palestinian women mourning their children, slain in a slew of bullets after Israeli soldiers opened fire on a crowd of jeering, rock-throwing youths. Since the enactment of the peace accord, over two hundred Palestinians and a hundred Israelis had been slaughtered. Rather than embracing a new understanding in the region, the two groups had proven themselves irreconcilable: many Palestinians refused to recognize Israel's statehood, or its power to establish borders, while thousands of Jewish settlers continued to build houses and communities in the occupied territories, eating away at already-decreasing Palestinian land.

Ridge met Shkaki's level gaze.

"Thank you for your time," he said tightly. He couldn't wait to leave and pushed away the urge to shiver.

"It is my pleasure," Shkaki said, grinning. "You Americans must understand. We attack because we are attacked. The Jews are simply more subtle in their war tactics."

Ridge and Steve quickly packed their things and exited the building. This time they were ignored by the hall guards. "You think you got that on tape?" Ridge asked under his breath.

Steve nodded. "With any luck, it'll be on *Headline News* tonight. Why don't you think about your recap? We'll film it once we're back in Israeli territory."

Ridge nodded and started the engine. He was anxious to get the long drive through Jordan over with. Jerusalem was looking better all the time.

Seven

February 17

Responding to an anonymous phone call he had received that morning, Ridge made his way toward the shops and vendor stalls near the Church of the Redeemer. There in the *suk*, he would meet his contact. As he walked the narrow street, covered by old arches and cloth canopies and founded on ancient stones, he ignored the vendors selling huge hammered copper pans, brightly painted Jerusalem pottery, leather bags, and fly-covered meats. Overhead, the dark afternoon skies were heavy with threatening rain clouds.

"Special deal, mister!" one vendor called.

"Every day a sale, American!" yelled another.

As Ridge kept walking, his mind constantly wandered to thoughts of Alexsana: where she was and what she was doing. He struggled to get her out of his mind and focus on the task at hand.

He passed a spice vendor, who was selling colorful bins of bright saffron, golden cumin, brick-red paprika, and dark green oregano. The combined aroma was powerful, and Ridge resisted the urge to stop. The vendor nodded sedately as Ridge passed, not needing to hawk his wares — everyone in the city needed spices and came to him at some point. Next to his stall stood a fruit stand, displaying brilliant red apples, huge pink grapefruit, and a luscious assortment of dried apricots, peaches, pineapples, and bananas. It was here that Ridge was to meet his contact.

The fruit vendor emerged from behind a large drape. "Ah, you need fresh peaches? Or perhaps some dried pineapple, just arrived?"

"I need a pound of dried apricots and two red apples," Ridge said evenly, as he had been instructed. "No, make that a pineapple and two peaches."

"Ahh. Yes, of course. Please, come. The best peaches are behind the large drape," the man said. The vendor pulled aside the cloth, and Ridge entered alone as the curtain fell behind him, blocking out the street market.

A second man sat at a tiny table inside the cordoned-off "room." Ridge instantly recognized him as the smaller guard from the Negev Desert. *Hamas*, Ridge thought. *I have my Hamas contact at last.* In the Old City, Hamas had recently been much more active than the Jihad. It was critical to Ridge's work that he observe first-hand the inner-workings of the fundamentalist group, and Khalil al Aitam had been less than helpful in this endeavor.

"I am Ridge McIntyre." He pulled out his wallet and set it on the table. "You are?"

"You may refer to me as Shehab Madi." The man glanced from Ridge to his wallet and back again. "I have news for you, worth at least two hundred American."

"Tell me your news, and I'll figure out how much it's worth."

"Two hundred," the man repeated calmly as he leaned back in his chair.

Ridge leaned forward and pulled a hundred dollar bill from his wallet. He laid it on the table. "One hundred now. One hundred if the news is worthy."

The small man grabbed the bill and flashed a tobacco-stained grin. "There is to be another bus attack. This time in West Jerusalem. I tell you so that you might be at the right place at the right time, not so that you might alert the world. It would make for a good news story to have a camera there at the right time, no? We want no interference. If you try to interfere, you will find yourself in an uncomfortable position."

"When and where?" Ridge asked tightly.

"Three days from now. On Habad street outside the Zion Gate."

"So soon after Beit Lid?"

"We owe them many Beit Lids. This has been planned for months. It will have even greater impact coming soon after the Jihad attack."

"There's certain to be civilians on that bus. Surely, Khalil al Aitam won't endorse such a mad attack...."

"Khalil will endorse whatever is necessary. This is a war." The veins in Shehab's neck stood out as his speech grew more and more passionate. "They think they can push us away...continue to build on our land...even take the Haram from us!"

"The Haram?" Ridge asked sharply, thinking instantly of Alexsana's involvement.

Shehab sat back, rubbing his eyes as if weary. "I will talk of that with you later. First we will see how you fare with the news you have. And how you pay for your information."

Ridge rose from his seat and threw another bill on the table. "How do I get ahold of you?"

"You don't," Shehab said, grinning again as he studied the new hundred dollar bill. "I will contact you."

Ridge left the suk and went directly to Alexsana's apartment, asking directions from people along the way. Finding her number at last, he knocked on the door and hoped that for once she would be home. To his surprise, she opened the door.

"Ridge!" She was obviously surprised to see him.

"Are you free for dinner?" he asked earnestly. "I need to talk with you about something."

Seeing the concern on his face, she nodded soberly and waved him inside. "Let me pull on a sweater. It's still cool outside in the evenings." We can eat over on Ben Yehuda Street. I've been craving French, and a rich CNN correspondent with a generous expense account makes for just the right dinner companion."

He smiled and watched as she walked up steep stairs and disappeared into the bedroom above. "Nice apartment," he said, loud enough for her to hear.

"It works well for me," she said, coming back down the steps while pulling on a deep green V-neck sweater over her T-shirt. "The dress code isn't strict at Ben Yehuda, but it's still cool outside in the evenings."

Ridge smiled. "Let's go."

They hailed a cab outside Jaffa Gate and the driver pulled into the chaotic one-way street traffic of West Jerusalem.

Around them, drivers changed lanes and honked constantly, as if each vehicle carried a mother in labor. Ridge and Alexsana's cab reached Ben Yehuda quickly, and the two found a secluded table at Chateau, Alexsana's favorite restaurant.

"So. I assume you've been busy since you haven't been leaving message after message on my machine," Alexsana teased quietly. She studied his serious expression, so different from his usual roguish, devil-may-care look. "Something's obviously bothering you, Ridge. What is it?"

A waiter came and Alexsana — noting that Ridge was irritated by the interruption — quickly ordered for both of them. "Bottled water and veal marsala, please. Ridge, I'm sure you'd like it, too."

"Fine, fine," he said, handing his menu to the waiter. "I'll go with the lady's suggestion." He tried a smile, but it came out rather crooked. Alexsana took it as a sign of fear and frustration. "I'm sorry," Ridge continued. "I wish I were taking you out as a date. But I'm afraid I have business to discuss."

"To tell you the truth, Ridge, a date would make me feel uncomfortable," Alexsana said with a relieved sigh. "I'd rather meet with you as a friend or a business contact."

He frowned at her easy rebuff. "Well, then. Let me cut to the chase. I met with a member of the Hamas today."

"Khalil?"

"No. Another man. Here's my dilemma. I need advice, and since you seem to be my most politically unbiased contact, here it is: my contact told me there is to be another bus attack. I can't tell you when or where. If you were me, what would you do with this information?"

Alexsana was unfazed by the news. "It could be true," she said, considering. "Of course, this puts you in the terrible position of choosing between reporting first-hand on the attack or trying to stop it. The report could also be false: a test to see if you truly are trustworthy, where your loyalties lie, which you fail if the Hamas finds out that you alerted the Israeli authorities."

"Yes, yes. And?"

"I assume you know when and where this bus attack is to occur."

"I do. *If* my contact told me the truth. Alexsana, I need your advice."

His pleading, honest look went straight to her heart. The way he treated her, spoke to her...everything he did made her feel respected and valued. As much as she wanted to keep her distance from the man, he drew her like few had. *I had better bury myself in my work soon or this man will have me, hook, line, and sinker.* She cast up a silent prayer. *Protect my heart, Father.*

She sighed and forced herself to concentrate on their subject instead of Ridge. "My problem is that I understand the pain, the passion each group feels. I know many moderates on both sides who want only to find a peaceful, godly solution. I also know many radicals who want only to destroy their enemies. That is not of God. If the Jews were attempting a forceful takeover, endangering lives, if the Palestinians were attempting to make a statement by blowing up a bus...in either case I would have to try and avert it."

"So you're the Switzerland of the Middle East," he said, nodding at the waiter as he poured their sparkling water into glasses.

"I suppose you could put it that way."

"Yet my job is to report the facts, not get entangled in the political goings on of a war-torn country. This isn't the first time I've seen impassioned people trying to tear each other apart. Check out Liberia on your next vacation, and you'll see what I mean."

"No, thanks. Israel is enough for me," she said. "When I go on vacation, I want it to be far away from the pain I see here every day."

He nodded again, studying her. "So, Switzerland, what should...what would..." he paused. "What would a Christian do in a situation like this?"

Alexsana stared into his eyes, wondering that he would bring up Christianity. *Maybe Jerome got to him after all....* "I believe that a true Christian would do everything in his power to save a Jew *or* a Palestinian from death," she said.

Ridge nodded again, thinking. "There's more."

"More?"

"My contact mentioned the Haram."

Alexsana's eyes narrowed. "The Haram? What was said?"

"Very little. He just intimated that his organization was aware that the Jews were trying to 'take it over.' Could he be referring to the Solomon's Stable dig? Could that be misconstrued as a Jewish plot?" Ridge leaned forward and covered her hand with his. "I'm worried for you, Alexsana. These people are dangerous. What if they try and stop your dig...any way they know how?"

She gently withdrew her hand and stared back into his eyes. "They can try. But this is the first time we've gotten permission from both sides to excavate. I have to try. Do you understand? I have to try."

Much later, Alexsana left Ridge at the restaurant, assuring him that she could see herself home. Needing advice of her own, she decided to stop by her friend Lydia's house. She knocked and held her breath, praying that the woman was home.

A pretty little girl opened the door, and Alexsana sighed. "*Marahaba*, Maria," she greeted Lydia's younger sister. "Is Lydia here?"

Maria nodded and left the door open behind her as she yelled up the stairs.

"Yes, yes. What is it?" Lydia called down, toweling her hair dry after an evening bath.

"It's me," Alexsana said, smiling up at the pretty Palestinian. "I need to talk with you in private."

"Sana! Come up! We can talk on the balcony."

Alexsana climbed the narrow, curving stairs and hugged her Christian sister. "How have you been?"

"Busy, busy. We've been working on a special order from the States." Lydia Nusseibah ran the Palestinian Christian Women's Needlework Shop and had successfully put hundreds of women to work creating elaborate weavings and needlepoint artwork for tourists and foreigners. The pay had helped to sustain many Christian families over the years, and the shop was heralded by many as a prime example of how a business should be run.

The two women seated themselves in iron chairs outside Lydia's bedroom, on a small balcony. Her view encompassed much of the Old City and, against the cold night's backdrop, the twinkling lights before them seemed comforting. "Will you be warm enough out here?" Lydia asked.

"Yes," Alexsana said, motioning down at her warm sweater. She could not hold it in any longer. "Lydia, I've been told there is to be another bus attack."

Her friend groaned. "Jew or Arab?"

"A Hamas attack outside the Old City."

"You are worried because it might delay your dig at the Haram?"

Alexsana shot her a sharp look. "I am worried because there has been enough bloodshed for one week. Have you not heard anything?"

"I am afraid not. But I will ask some friends and see if I can get some answers."

"Please be careful in your questioning. I got the news from a correspondent who would like to set up reliable contacts with the Hamas and others. If they get wind that it came from him...."

"I will make it sound as if I had heard it from a Hamas soldier myself."

The two women sat for a while in silence, sad and lost in their own thoughts. Lydia was the first to speak. "I had such high hopes last spring," she said. "I thought this would be it...that finally we would have a chance at peace. Instead, it is worse."

Alexsana nodded miserably. "Maybe we can stop some of the bloodshed this time," she said.

"Maybe," Lydia said. But her eyes held no hope.

Eight

❧

February 19

Alexsana rose early, bathed, and headed to the École Biblique to speak with Professor O'Malley, a renowned expert on the subject of the Temple Mount. He was also one of the few allowed frequent access to Solomon's Stables.

Alexsana entered the ancient monastery, which housed the school. As usual, the escape from the busy street outside soothed her soul. The complex consisted of a series of monastic buildings and crusader arches, built to stand the test of time. She walked directly to the library, a magnificent building that was heralded as one of the best biblical archaeology libraries in the world — and had once been the *only* biblical archaeology library in the world.

Walking under a stone arch, she studied the various familiar faces, already hard at work. As he had for years, Jean Baptiste sat in his corner, cutting up photographs of the Dead Sea scrolls and taping them together under a magnifying glass hooked to the cherry wood table.

In another corner, Marcel was nearly hidden behind a stack of nineteenth century excavation reports from

Megiddo, as he carefully combed the pages for information.

The others in the room were young monks, studying for exams. Professor O'Malley had not arrived, so Alexsana quietly drew out a chair, trying not to disturb the students, and stretched her neck in an attempt to release some tension.

The scope of knowledge covered by the volumes in the room astounded her, no matter how often she visited. Many of the books were ancient, bound in lambskin and adorned with ornate artwork. These volumes had been meticulously copied in broad script by French monks of centuries past. The library encompassed eight centuries of history related to biblical archaeology. Alexsana reflected on the countless days and nights she had spent there, researching one project after another. Her father, Samuel Sr., had started using her as a research assistant when Alexsana was only twelve. *I've probably spent years in here,* she thought, realizing why the place gave her such comfort.

The steady tapping of a cane on stone floors drew her gaze to the front door. There, as she expected, Professor O'Malley appeared. He greeted her enthusiastically, ignoring the troubled looks of his two older colleagues and the younger monks' glances of surprise at his loud, "Sana, my dear!"

Alexsana rose to hug him. "Thanks for meeting with me, Professor. And thanks for your time with Ridge. I think you really might have reached him."

"My pleasure. It's good to see you," he said, looking at her proudly. "I knew you'd be coming to the École soon when I heard the wonderful news. Congratulations, by the way, on being awarded the Stables."

"I never asked you: how *did* you find out about it?"

Alexsana teased, knowing full well that no important archaeological news made it past the professor's ears.

"Find out about it!" O'Malley looked shocked. "I'm the
one who recommended you! They wanted me, of course,"
he said mildly, "but I had to decline. Getting too old for a
dig, even something like the Stables. I've waited a very long
time to see what's down there beneath the rubble; I'm
depending on you for a grand tour, Sana."

Alexsana smiled, thinking of the several times the man
had led her down the stairs to peer at the small portion of
the caverns that could be seen. Her grin quickly faded as she
watched the man labor to sit down in a chair.

"What's this?" she asked lightly. "Getting too old to climb
the mount?"

He smiled. "Never too old for that, my dear. Never. These
bones will walk the hills of Jerusalem 'til my dying day. But
enough about me. Let's talk about the Haram. Where will
you begin?"

"Behind the Triple Gate. Then we'll move to the Double
Gate, taking out everything in between," she said, watching
for his reaction. "I want to excavate the stairs and rebuild the
arches to make sure the Haram won't come crashing down,
perhaps winning Islamic approval to excavate even further at
a later date."

The professor nodded, thinking about the wisdom of her
choice. "That would be a marvelous place to begin. To walk
the steps Jesus walked...." His eyes grew hazy. "Soon I'll
walk with the Savior, not just in the city he loved."

Alexsana drew in a deep breath. "Not before I take you to
explore the place you introduced me to," she quipped. "I'll
need all the knowledge you have in that head of yours before

I'm through," she continued. "So quit your talk of walking with the Master."

O'Malley smiled benevolently. "I'll hold out for a while longer, Sana. For a while longer. Now say a quick prayer with me, and let us examine your plans."

Despite the upheaval caused by the Beit Lid attack and the consequential takeover of an entire Old City block by right-wing Israelis, Alexsana was given tentative approval to begin her dig in four weeks. Her heart pounded at the prospect of all she had to do: obtain financing, assemble her team, and plan the process. Her first mission would be to secure her brother as her area supervisor. Few in Israel could match his architectural drawing skills.

She was just pulling her gear together to go see him in Caesarea when there was a knock at her door. Alexsana pulled open the door to the safety chain's length and frowned at her rapid pulse. *Ridge.*

Ridge quickly noticed her expression. "What? Did I choose a bad time? Should I come back later?" His voice echoed regret at his choice to show up unannounced.

"No, no," Alexsana mumbled through the crack in the door. "I'm just on my way out." *Thatta girl. Keep it businesslike.*

"Where are you heading?"

"Caesarea. I have to talk Robert into letting my brother Sam off the dig in a month. I want him as part of my team."

Ridge looked pleased. "Great! I've been called to cover a story in Tel Aviv tomorrow morning. Let me drive you up. I'd actually like to do a feature story on the Caesarea

Maritima dig sometime. It'd be a great chance to do the research."

Alexsana frowned again. She knew her heart was pulling her closer to the attractive man than was safe, but she unhooked the chain, anyway.

"If you'd rather not...." he began.

"No, no. I'm sorry, I've just got a lot on my mind." *You made a business deal with him, Alexsana. He's just trying to do his job. Stop reading things into his intentions.* "Are you coming back tomorrow afternoon?"

"Uh-huh. I still have to figure out how I'm going to handle the situation we talked about the other night."

She nodded. "Okay, then. But I have to get back tomorrow. I've got a lot of work to do here, and I can't afford to get stranded. Deal?"

"Deal." Ridge moved to wait for her on the couch, wearing a smile that was a mile wide.

Despite Alexsana's intentions to keep their conversation focused on CNN business, Ridge managed to draw her into more personal discussions all the way to Caesarea. As the city came into view, she sighed. "I love this place. The aqueducts...the amphitheater.... I think it's one of the richest, most exciting archaeological sites in Israel."

Ridge smiled, appreciating her fervor. He motioned toward the many people parking around them, heading toward the tourist grounds. "Even with the masses?"

She laughed. "Oh, yes. I think there's a spring concert tonight. Maybe we can crash it. The people give it a much more realistic feel, I think. With a little creative imagination

— if you squint your eyes — can't you just see them heading toward the amphitheater in Herodian dress to watch the gladiators?"

Ridge smiled again, and Alexsana momentarily felt self-conscious. When would she learn not to wear her emotions on her sleeve? But Ridge's smile continued. The moment passed, and she found herself relaxing under his warm gaze.

They made their way through the city, and Alexsana pointed out various landmarks, offering her own archaeological insights. As she was chatting amiably, Ridge impulsively slipped his hand around hers.

Alexsana stopped and pulled away. Her heart skipped a beat, then pounded double-time in reaction to her emotions. "Ridge, I need you to stop taking hold of my hand: here, at the restaurant...anywhere. We have a business relationship, and you're risking that by making me feel awkward."

Ridge frowned too. "I'm sorry, Alexsana. It's just that — I have to be honest here — I'm very attracted to you. More so than I've been to any woman in a long time."

Alexsana tried to regain her composure. She looked back up into his gray-blue eyes and concentrated on breathing steadily. "You are a handsome man, Ridge, and you've got a lot going for you. I'm very drawn to you. But I can't be with you."

Ridge's eyes opened wide. "Because of Khalil?" he asked incredulously.

"No." Alexsana shook her head. "Not because of him. It's because I want something that will last. Longer than what you and I can share." Alexsana lightly placed one hand on his chest.

His pulse beat quickly beneath her touch. Alexsana spoke

slowly, painfully. "I can't give my love to a man who does not share what I hold most dear. And that's *God*. Without that bond, I cannot begin a relationship." Her eyes begged him to understand. "Please respect that decision."

She turned and walked away, leaving Ridge to trail behind her.

Later, Alexsana couldn't help but eavesdrop on Ridge's conversation with Robert Hoekstra. Ridge asked detailed questions which pleased Robert to no end. "Well, I'm glad you asked that, Mr. McIntyre." Robert placed his arm around the newcomer who was so ready to listen. "Caesarea Maritima was built in approximately 30 B.C., during the Herodian period. We have been working on a variety of fronts here: an early Christian church, Herod's temple, Roman baths, the stadium, mosaics.... But most interesting to me is what lies beneath the breakwater, there: the harbor. She was the first artificial harbor ever built...."

Alexsana watched as the teacher-at-heart walked off down the beach with Ridge on one side and Jennifer on the other. Thankful for the breathing room, she turned and headed the other way.

"So what's up between you and Mr. CNN?" Sam asked as he ran to catch up with her, then easily matched her long stride.

"Nothing," Alexsana grunted.

"Nothing?" Sam sounded incredulous. "You arrive here unannounced and obviously brooding over something. You're barely talking to one another. What happened?" Sam's grinning face suddenly clouded over. "Did he try something?"

Alexsana sighed. "No, Sam. There was nothing. We're just trying to establish some boundaries while we work together."

Sam looked only partially satisfied. "Why work together at all if he bugs you that much?"

"Because he does hear some interesting news," Alexsana reasoned, as much to herself as to her brother. "He's already learned more than I anticipated."

"Like what?"

"There may be another bus attack on the horizon." Alexsana carefully left out Ridge's kernel of knowledge about the Haram.

Sam groaned. "When is it going to stop?" He ran his fingers through his hair and over his face. "I wonder if Lydia knows anything about it. She's got the best connections in the City."

His eyes grew sharper as he searched his sister's face. Samuel had loved Lydia for years, but her parents would not hear of her marrying a non-Palestinian, even one as dear to them as Sam. When things did not work out with her, soon after his failed relationship with Christina, Sam had sworn off women. But whereas he had managed to get over Christina, Lydia still haunted him.

"You saw her, didn't you?" he asked softly.

"Yes." Alexsana laid a gentle hand on his arm. "Come on, Sam. Don't dwell on it. I'm going to see her from time to time. She's my friend, too. And I thought that she might know more about the bus attack...that maybe she'd heard something and could confirm it. Who knows? Maybe Ridge was just set up. You know. They take his bribe money and then disappear."

"Why do I doubt that?"

"I know." Alexsana sighed heavily. "It's too easy to believe in people's basic depravity these days."

By evening, Alexsana had talked Robert into allowing Sam time off-site for the duration of her dig, with the stipulation that Sam would return to Caesarea when and if there were significant delays. After dinner, the entire Caesarea team went to the amphitheater for a sunset concert by the Tel Aviv Philharmonic. In the ancient, rustic setting, with the scent of the sea and the faint sound of lapping water between overtures, the Philharmonic's sound was glorious. Alexsana concentrated on the music, trying to avoid the sight before her as two rows down and to the left, Ridge whispered and laughed with Jennifer. The girl was on cloud nine, enjoying his undivided attention. Alexsana could almost hear his deep, resonant voice: "I'm attracted to you." She scowled. *Yeah, right. That's why you're flirting with the coed.*

Alexsana caught Sam's eye, who looked at her with an open question on his face. She turned away with a grimace. *Jealous. About a man you cannot and should not have. You've made the right choice, woman.*

She found herself wondering why it hurt so much. *Please, God. Give me some reassurance.* Alexsana could not find any consolation in her heart, although she knew she had made the right decision. She struggled to focus on the music, to be carried away in its melody.

The sound of Ridge's beeper brought her thoughts right back to where they had started. He rose, disentangling himself from the pretty girl, and climbed the amphitheater steps right beside Alexsana without looking at her.

Once away from the crowds, Ridge opened his cellular phone and dialed headquarters.

"McIntyre, where are you?" Jack's characteristically irritable voice crackled over the line.

"Caesarea. I'm due in Tel Aviv first thing tomorrow morning."

"Well, get your rear in gear and back to Jerusalem. There's been another bus attack. Fourteen dead. It happened seven — make that eight — minutes ago."

Ridge sank down upon the stone brick, assimilating the information. "But it's a day early," he mumbled.

"What?" Jack asked crossly. "I can barely hear you, McIntyre! Now get back here! It's no scoop, but we can at least give it some coverage."

"I'll head out right now." He hung up without saying good-bye and miserably hurried back down the steps.

Ridge's hot breath against her chilled ear made Alexsana squirm. She looked at him with irritation, but seeing his ashen face, turned her head again to hear.

"It happened, Alexsana," he mumbled hoarsely. "The bus attack. I'm leaving now. Do you want to come with me? You said you had to get back."

Nodding gravely, Alexsana turned to tell Sam and rose to go. Sam grabbed her hand, looking at Ridge with mistrust. "I can drive you home tomorrow after my shift."

Alexsana shook her head. "No good. I have an appointment with Professor O'Malley tomorrow afternoon. I'll see you next week for Ash Wednesday services."

Sam nodded and kissed her on the cheek. "Be careful, little sister," he quietly admonished.

Alexsana hurried away with Ridge, topping the stairs as the Philharmonic reached the crescendo of Ravel's "Bolero."

Nine

February 21

Ridge had found no solace in sleep. He was haunted by the knowledge that innocent people had died and he had known it was going to happen. Not that he could have done anything, he told himself. But the question ran through his head again and again: *Given the correct timeline, would I have done anything to stop it?*

He had made one live report on the evening of the bombing, and the visual images still turned his stomach forty-eight hours later. This time it was not only soldiers who had died. He was haunted by images of Steve's footage, taken shortly after the attack occurred.

A Palestinian woman, burned horribly herself, wailed not in physical pain, but over the dead body of her two-year-old son. A Hasidic Jew appeared in one corner of the camera frame, watching the woman as tears streamed down his face. Ridge shook his head. *So much pain. So much anger. So much need for healing.*

He sat in his hotel room, in shambles from weeks of living on the go, and thought about calling his brother. He needed to talk with someone, and his younger sibling was as close to him as anyone. But as he picked up the receiver and started to dial, he thought better of it. Philip would just tell him to buck up and handle it. Ridge wanted to talk it through, explore why he was feeling these things. Phil would not welcome that.

He hung up the phone and rubbed his face with a calloused hand. *What is happening to me?* Over the years, he had witnessed hundreds of similar attacks in war-torn countries. Why should it bother him now? His mind kept clicking back to one thought: Jesus. What would this man called Jesus do?

A true Christian would do everything in his power to save a Jew or a Palestinian from death. Alexsana's words rang in his head. As he thought about the Palestinian toddler killed by a bomb Arab radicals had planted, he suddenly knew: Jesus would have wept like that old Hasidic Jew. Ridge knew little of the Christ, but the image rang true to his mind and heart.

He picked up the phone and dialed.

A distracted voice answered on the fourth ring.

"Alexsana? I know you don't want to see me on a personal basis, but I really need to talk to someone. Please."

After momentary silence, she answered simply, "Come over."

Ridge breathed a sigh of relief. "Right away?"

"Any time."

Alexsana awaited Ridge's arrival. She hadn't intended to see him again outside of business. But his voice had changed her mind. It was so different. So sad...not full of life and bravado. For an instant she wondered if it had been a ruse to see her, but she dismissed the thought. The man was clearly in pain.

Ridge arrived twenty minutes later, his normally smooth hair in a tangled mass. Two days' beard growth revealed neglect. Dark circles rimmed his eyes. To Alexsana, he looked as if he might be ill.

"Come in," she said, touching his arm gently. "I have some tea on. I'll join you in a moment."

She brought in two Jerusalem pottery mugs, filled with steaming lemon tea. "Have you eaten?"

Ridge shook his head as he gratefully accepted the drink.

"No one can talk without energy to think clearly. Let me get you some fruit at least...." She was in the midst of rising when his voice stopped her.

"No, Alexsana. Please. Just sit down and talk to me."

She sank back down to the couch: quiet, waiting. The way he said her name made her shiver. She forced herself to concentrate on his reason for coming, and not his gray-blue eyes, or his well muscled forearm....

He took a deep breath and began. "As you might have guessed, I've been wrestling with the bus attack since it happened. I don't know what's wrong with me. I've had information like this before. In the past, my rule has been non-interference: just report the facts. It's gotten me to where I am today.

"But something's changed. I feel more responsible somehow. I couldn't have stopped the attack if I had tried, since it happened a day earlier than I'd been told. But I know I wouldn't have said anything, anyway." He looked up at her, the anguish plain in his eyes.

Alexsana was silent, sorrow evident in her own gaze. She waited for him to continue.

He rose abruptly and began to pace. "What keeps haunting me is what you said about Christ. How you said he would have tried to stop it. As I look at footage of the carnage, dead bodies strewn everywhere — and me there reporting on it with an appropriately grim face for the world to see — all I can think about is how phony I am. How utterly false. And how could the God who accepts an innocent two-year-old boy into heaven accept a liar like me?"

Ridge turned to stare out the window. "What is it about you that makes me tell you my deepest, darkest secrets?" he asked in a low voice.

"Oh, Ridge —" she began.

He turned back toward her, interrupting. "Why would God want me? Why would he be making me feel this way? I know it has to be him, because I've never experienced anything like this. After all, I'm 'Ridge McIntyre, CNN,'" he said in his best on-camera voice. "I'm supposed to be made of steel."

"No one is made of steel," Alexsana said softly. "Be glad you're not. Be glad that you have a heart God can reach. I told you Jerusalem is a city of passions. Like Jerome said, it will be here that you will make a decision about Jesus. What you're wrestling with is fundamental to the faith. Sin. Guilt. Grace. I'll try to explain it the best I can — but please know that I'm not a perfect witness. Jesus comes to us with open arms, whether or not we want or deserve him...he still paid the price. We only have to accept his gift of love."

She rose and stood beside Ridge at the window. Outside, a vendor hawked fresh flowers cut from the hillsides of the Galilee. "Jesus is real, Ridge. He walked in the hills beside

Lake Gennesaret among flowers like those you see out there. He died for you. For me. And he rose again. The key to God — and to the peace you so desperately seek — is in him." She thought for a moment. "We're approaching Easter, you know. This is a good time of year to explore what Christianity is all about. Come with me tonight."

"Where?" Ridge asked dully.

"To an Ash Wednesday service at the Lutheran Church of the Redeemer."

He gave her a blank look. "Ash Wednesday?"

"Traditionally, it's a day when some Christians remember how we're separated from God by sin and reconciled through Jesus. We're at the beginning of a season called Lent. The first Christians observed Easter and the days before it with a passion. For them, it was a season of penitence and fasting. Converts were prepared for baptism. Those who had been notorious for their sinful lifestyles were freely accepted back into the fold, reminding everybody about the message of forgiveness that Christ embodied."

She touched his shoulder in encouragement. "Everyone needs a time of self-examination. It's not all gloom and doom, Ridge. It's a message of hope and glory. But to get there, we first need to truly acknowledge where we stand: without Christ, away from God."

Ridge nodded, not yet embracing Alexsana's beliefs, but apparently finding comfort in her words.

Alexsana walked to a small table and picked up a well-worn, pocket Bible. "Here. This verse might help. I think it's in Job." She scanned the pages. "No...Joel. 'Even now, says the Lord, return to me with your whole heart, with fasting, and weeping, and mourning; Rend your hearts, not your garments, and return to the Lord, your God.'"

She paused. "In the old days, mourners would tear their clothing, crying in the streets in very public displays of sorrow. But God wants us to tear our hearts, open them to him, and him alone." Alexsana studied his face, realizing that she might have said too much, making him uncomfortable.

Yet she pushed on. "But here's the message of hope. 'For gracious and merciful is he, slow to anger, rich in kindness, and relenting in punishment.' It is a good time of year to think about Christ: who he said he was, and what that means for you today. You are standing on the land where he once stood." She spoke earnestly. "He offers peace and absolution, Ridge. You just have to accept it."

Ridge turned his gaze back out the window, saying nothing.

"Meet me there tonight, Ridge," she said, her eyes imploring him to come. "Go back to your hotel, take a shower, think about what I've said, and come. You risk nothing. Only a chance at salvation."

Ridge managed a faint smile and, lost in thought, left without saying good-bye.

February 28

Look out!" Ridge screamed, dodging another bullet. Drawing upon training received at a special CNN "boot camp," he dove and rolled over the dusty street. Loathing to give up his just-repaired camera, Steve Rains moved much slower. As Ridge turned, another shot rang out; a split-second later, Steve went down with a shot to the abdomen. The camera fell away, unnoticed.

"Steve!" Ridge yelled. His friend was fifteen feet away, directly between the source of the shots and the protective wall Ridge had found. "Steve!"

The man did not respond. Ridge scanned the dark, bombed-out building, searching windowless holes for signs of the sniper. To his horror, he caught sight of a gunman as he raised his gun again and fired. Ridge ducked and winced as Steve cried out again, this time shot in the leg.

"Oh, Lord," Ridge mumbled. "Don't let him die. And if my time is up, sorry about not getting back to you on the whole salvation thing." His words sounded flippant and unappealing, even to him.

Gritting his teeth, he ran, half-stooped, over to where Steve lay, nearly unconscious. "I'm gonna help you, buddy," Ridge assured him. "We're gonna get you out of here."

Another shot was fired. As Ridge automatically bent lower, the bullet sang past his head. He could feel its path as if it had singed a mark along his forehead, temple and ear. The slug struck the ground behind him with a dull thud. As if in a dream, Ridge acknowledged that he had narrowly escaped death.

"Get out of here, man. Send in the marines," Steve managed to grunt out.

"No way. I'm getting you to the hospital." Ridge's body was taut with adrenaline; he shrugged back the fear that threatened to set him into massive trembling. Ignoring Steve's moans and quiet swearing, Ridge pulled at his friend's arm, lifting the man over his shoulders and back.

Three more bullets sang past his ears as other snipers joined the game. He had carried Steve almost to the wall before he felt the shot. The impact of the bullet stunned him. He felt no pain, but looked down to see blood spreading over his shirt.

Ridge passed out before he could even determine the location of his wound.

March 1

Ridge woke up in a hospital bed to find Steve sitting beside him, grinning like a kid on Christmas morning. His friend was in a wheelchair and wore only white hospital-issued pants, revealing a white bandage around his abdomen. "I suppose I owe you some flowers or something," Steve said.

Ridge raised a hand, feeling as if he were moving in slow motion. He rubbed his eyes. "Just tell me you got some footage of the whole thing."

Steve grinned. "Some award-winning shots *before* I was hit. But better yet — you won't believe this — the camera fell, rolled, and came to rest as I was hit again. Caught the whole thing, at least from the waist down. Then, enter you, the News Junkie Stud. It caught part of our little escapade: the third bullet, barely missing you as you leaned over me, then you picking me up and carting me away like some fairy godmother." Steve grinned. "Unfortunately for the censors, your princess was not so grateful."

Ridge managed a faint smile, remembering Steve swearing in pain as he carried the man to safety.

"You caught it all on film?" Ridge asked incredulously.

"Well, not *all* of it. Even seeing our legs with the audio gives me the willies, and I was *there*."

"That's it? You couldn't get me carrying you to safety *and* taking a bullet for you in the process?"

Steve raised his hands and shrugged. "Hey. I'm good. But not that good."

"Well, I suppose it'll have to do. What'd headquarters say?" Just speaking sapped his energy. He struggled to stay awake.

"They're thrilled. Our footage, such as it is, has been played on every network and on countless feeder stations. The world is waiting for Ridge McIntyre to regain consciousness. Our story made the front pages of the *LA Times* and *The Washington Post*."

"No kidding?"

"No kidding. You're a hero." The man stood with some

effort, bending down to jokingly give him a smacking kiss on the cheek. Ridge grimaced and pulled away. "You're my hero, man. Thanks for saving my life." Steve sat back down and wheeled away toward the door. "I'm glad you made it, too. The bullet somehow missed any vital organs when it passed through. You lost a lot of blood, man, but you're gonna make it. Oh, and by the way, headquarters will be sending a full camera crew to do a 'bedside interview' with the News Junkie Stud this afternoon, once they find out you're conscious."

"Great. Just great. And quit calling me that," Ridge muttered wearily. But Steve was already gone. Ridge traced the bullet's path, where it had passed along his head. The second had apparently passed cleanly through his body. He remembered his prayer. *Hey, God, guess you have some business with me yet, huh?*

His thoughts turned to Alexsana, and the words she had spoken on Ash Wednesday a week before. Too ashamed to show up at church, he had not gone to services that evening. Consequently, he had not seen Alexsana since. He had delved into his work, wanting to forget the whole thing, but that single bullet had brought it all back.

March 9

Alexsana could feel the excitement and tension in the city as Christian pilgrims entered Jerusalem by the hundreds in preparation for Palm Sunday and Easter. It had been a long while since she had seen Ridge — nine days since his accident — and she frowned at the way she had last spoken to him. *I'm not a perfect witness,* she thought, remembering her disclaimer. *That doesn't even begin to describe your lame attempt, Alexsana Roarke. There the man was, ready to hear the gospel for the first time, and you bombard him with so much information, you scare him off forever.*

Alexsana tried to tell herself that she only cared because she wanted to show others the importance of faith. But she could not deny the truth: she missed seeing the handsome man. *Protect my heart, Lord,* she whispered the now-familiar petition. *I don't want a man who doesn't want you.*

Alexsana had heard about his escapades in Lebanon over the BBC. The audio tape of his encounter with the sniper in Beirut made for sensational audio footage. Even without a television, Alexsana knew that Ridge had nearly lost his life.

She had fought the desire to travel north to see him in the hospital, telling herself that she had no right to be there…to say nothing of the fact that he had not called in weeks.

He obviously did not want to see her.

March 16

Shopping in the suk, Alexsana had just negotiated a price for a luscious assortment of red, orange, and green peppers for a marinated salad when she recognized a voice in her ear.

"Hi there, Doc."

She turned, feeling a blush creep up her neck and hoping that it did not show. "Ridge! Are you okay? How long have you been back?" Her words sounded forced, trite, and she fought off feelings of guilt for not having looked in on him.

"I've been back about a week," he said, obviously uncomfortable as well. Alexsana could not help but wonder as he turned to the fruit and vegetables before them, picking out some apples and pears.

"I —"

"How have —"

They both started talking at once, stopped and laughed, then began speaking simultaneously once again. Both dissolved into laughter, which broke the tension like a welcome rain.

"Ridge, I want to apologize," Alexsana tried again. "I think I came on too strong about the faith and all."

"No, Alexsana, don't apologize," he assured her gently. "The truth is, it's all I've been thinking about — and running away from — these past weeks. It wasn't you —"

"Oh, you don't have to say that," Alexsana ignored his assurances. "I know myself. I can be so tuned into something, I don't even stop for breath. I'm just so in love with my faith and want others to know it that when I get the chance, I'm rather like a freight train."

Ridge looked down at the lovely woman in front of him. "I could never see you as a 'freight train,' even when you're giving one of your impassioned speeches." His look was tender and intimate.

Alexsana's blush deepened.

"I'll say it again. Don't apologize. Your words were well-meant, and they reached me in a way I can't describe. I know that you are nothing but honest. And I apologize for not calling you after that day. You probably thought you drove me away, but I just really needed time to think about what we had talked about."

Alexsana pushed aside the desire to ask where that process had left him. She nodded in understanding, discussed fair prices with the vendor for more vegetables, then turned and paid the vendor while Ridge completed his shopping.

Ridge turned back to the fruit, pretending to be particularly interested in the health of green bananas while she fumbled with her change. As she turned to go, he glanced up at her with a smile.

"Well, Ridge," she faltered. "I'm glad you're up and well. Really."

He nodded at her. "And I'm glad I had the chance to apologize to you for not calling."

"Well, um...I'll see you."

"I hope so," he said with feeling.

As she turned and left, Ridge once again found himself watching her as she disappeared into the crowded suk.

March 31

Ridge stood at the top of the Mount of Olives, between Bethany and Jerusalem, where he and Steve were covering the Christian processional that celebrated Palm Sunday. Group after group passed behind him, singing in French, Greek, Italian, and countless other languages as he made his report.

"From Jerusalem, this is Ridge McIntyre, CNN," he finished.

Steve shut off the camera and swung it away from his eye, flinching at the pain in his side. "Great story, man," he managed. "Especially poignant with the pilgrims behind you."

"Yeah," Ridge said absently, searching the crowds behind Steve. "I see that you're still hurting. Better get some rest before they call us out on another assignment."

"Yeah? What about you?" Steve returned.

"Stitches came out yesterday. I'm fine," Ridge said with forced bravado.

His eyes quickly left his friend's as he spotted Sam and Alexsana coming toward him. They were a part of an English-speaking group, singing hymns as they passed. When Alexsana's eyes met his, they smiled into his soul. Ridge's heart skipped a beat.

"May I join you?" he asked, as they passed without stopping.

"Certainly," Alexsana said throwing a smile over her shoulder as they passed him.

Ridge turned to Steve.

"Should I follow you and get some more footage?" his friend asked.

"Nah. I think I want to do this on my own, not for the world to see. Want to come?"

"No, thanks. Think I'll go grab a sandwich and some R 'n' R as my colleague suggested."

"Okay," Ridge said, hurriedly. He watched as Alexsana walked farther away down the winding road that led to the Garden of Gethsemane. "Catch you later!" he called over his shoulder, hurrying to catch up with her.

As they walked, Sam and Alexsana taught Ridge the tunes to some Easter hymns, smiling encouraging smiles as he joined in. Several were vaguely familiar to him; most were completely new. Between songs, the pilgrims chatted quietly or said nothing, and Ridge was caught up in their contemplative mood. Gradually, among the untrained but fervent voices, he grew more at ease and concentrated on the photocopied words before him.

Most of the songs were somber, a few celebratory. As he reflected on Alexsana's explanation about Palm Sunday, he decided the mixture of tunes was fitting. Jesus had ridden into Jerusalem upon a donkey, down a path much like this, with hundreds of people laying palm branches and their cloaks before him as if he were king. Yet he had ridden knowing he was to give the supreme sacrifice: his life.

Long after the group had gone on to another song, a verse from an African-American spiritual echoed through Ridge's head. *"Were you there when they nailed him to the tree? Were you there when they nailed him to the tree? Oh, sometimes it causes me to tremble, tremble, tremble. Were you there when they nailed him to the tree?"*

His mind whirled with the thought of it. Feelings of anger rose in his heart at the injustice of it; feelings of unworthiness swept through him as he contemplated Alexsana's explanation: that it was for him, as much as any other, that God had sent Jesus to die.

Alexsana's sweet, earnest voice brought him back to the hymn that the group was now singing. When it ended, she looked up at him curiously. "Ridge," she said quietly. "Remember when you were about six years old and you wanted a bike with a banana seat or a race car model or whatever?" Ridge nodded, feeling a little guarded in the face of her odd question.

She stopped and held him by the forearm, an urgency present in her expression and actions. People filed around them like a stream around a rock. "Remember when Santa Claus came and you got that bike and you said, 'I believe in him. I believe in him!'?"

Ridge gave her a funny little smile. "I think I knew the

truth about Santa by the time I was six."

Alexsana sighed. "Okay, then. How about when you read *Peter Pan* — I mean *really* read it — so that you were so deep into the story, you could see yourself flying with Wendy. Or maybe you were even Peter himself. All you needed was a little magic fairy dust, and you'd be flying. Flying!"

Ridge nodded warily.

"You believed. You *believed*." The words left her lips in a hushed, awed manner. She stared into his eyes, and Ridge knew it was a moment he would never forget. He saw what she was after. There, on the hillside of Bethany, across from the City of David, Ridge understood.

"You're speaking of a leap of faith," he said in a hushed, sure voice. "Believe it, and you'll fly."

"I know it's just a fairy tale. But it's a perfect illustration of what it means to choose faith." She took his hand. "Come."

Ridge walked with her, lost in thought. They joined Sam, who waited for them at the bottom of the hill, and together the three made their way to the Church of All Nations, where people had begun to gather.

"All glory, laud, and honor, to you Redeemer, King. To whom the lips of children made sweet hosannas ring. You are the King of Israel And David's royal Son, Now in the Lord's name coming, Our King and Blessed One." Alexsana's face shone as she lost herself in the words of the song. To Ridge, she seemed more beautiful than anyone he'd ever known — both inside and out.

He joined her on the last verse, his deep voice blending sweetly with her own soprano. "To you before your Passion, They sang their hymns of praise. To you, now high exalted, Our melody we raise."

They fell silent as they entered the gorgeous cathedral, officially named the Basilica of the Agony, but built with funds from sixteen countries and therefore dubbed the "Church of All Nations." Above them towered a magnificent ceiling made of twelve domes and arches on top of marble columns. Each dome displayed a royal blue background adorned with delicate paintings of olive trees and marked with Latin phrases. Far beneath the arches, the pilgrims gathered: silent, praying.

Alexsana pulled at Ridge's sleeve, and he bent over to hear her whisper. "Jesus told his disciples to sit here while he went away to pray. We stand here to remember that moment and what is to come." Ridge watched as many kneeled or found a wall to lean against, their hands over their faces. Some wept. Some smiled, raising their hands in silent worship.

He closed his eyes, feeling awkward at first. But in the midst of all those people, somehow silent in a building that would resound with the echo of a falling pin, Ridge felt peace. He prayed, imagining himself at the feet of an enthroned Christ in heaven. That was one of the few emotions he could identify. *Peace.* Then: *Understanding. Security.* His heart leaped with excitement and appreciation.

"I am unworthy, Father," he prayed silently. Suddenly, he could visualize Jesus' face looking down at him with nothing but love. "I am unworthy," he repeated, shaking his head.

"I have made you worthy," came the words, spoken, not verbally, but straight to his heart. Tears sprang to his eyes as Ridge thought of all his past sins, the way he had lived his life, how he had virtually ignored God until this point.

"I am sorry, God…my Lord. I am so sorry." Slowly, he

sank to his knees as a flood of emotions ran through him like an ocean tide. His mind called him to stop, and rise, but his heart told him to stay.

"Is this how you speak to me, Father? Through my heart?" No answer came as clearly as those first words deep within him, but Ridge understood. Silently, he concentrated on feeling God's presence, praying for the first time with pure pleasure.

A woman's voice rang out through the grand cathedral, beginning quietly in Italian and building to a crescendo at the end of the verse. The group she had come with joined in the second verse. Most people in the room recognized the famous hymn, "Beautiful Savior," and as the Italians finished, the Greek group beside them continued the song in their own native tongue. The French, German, and English groups followed suit as the crowd listened, contemplating their faith that was shared around the world. Ridge rose to stand beside Alexsana and Sam, and tears streamed down all three of their faces.

"Beautiful Savior, King of Creation, Son of God and Son of Man! Truly I'd love Thee, Truly I'd serve Thee, Light of my soul, my Joy, my Crown. Beautiful Savior, Lord of the nations, Son of God and Son of Man! Glory and honor, Praise, adoration, Now and forevermore be Thine!"

As the chorus ended, the crowd filed out of the church silently, each person lost in his or her own thoughts. Outside in the bright spring sunshine, Ridge turned to Alexsana, his eyes and face shining.

"I felt him, Alexsana. I saw him. I spoke to him." He grinned widely, and Alexsana reached up to hug him, smiling in return.

Ridge held her fast. He felt alive. Free. Excited beyond measure.

Alexsana gently pulled away. "I'm so glad, Ridge. I'm so happy for you," she said.

Sam clapped him on the back. "Congratulations, my friend. It's the best thing that will ever happen to you."

"I know," he said to both of them. "I know!"

Eleven

April 5

L ydia reached across the restaurant table and squeezed her friend's hand. "So, he accepted the Christ!"

"I believe he did," Alexsana smiled. "But my heart tells me to be careful still. I don't want to find out it was just a passing fancy or that he was caught up in some kind of an 'emotional high.' She tried to keep her voice light, but her face revealed her depth of feeling. "Oh, Lydia, I hope it's real! Because I think he's terrific."

"And he is obviously interested in you."

"I think so," Alexsana hedged. "But I've put him off several times. Maybe he's given up."

"No, I do not believe that is possible," Lydia said in her very proper English. "Once one comes to know my friend Alexsana, one cannot get her out of one's mind. I have seen many men fall by the wayside. But I have seldom seen you in such a state. You are in love."

Alexsana's eyes grew wide. "Love?"

Lydia smiled smugly, her dark eyes crinkling in the corners. "Love."

"Oh, I don't know...."

"Yes, you do," Lydia insisted. "Your heart pounds when he is near...you look for him in the suk...you wonder if it is him when the telephone rings...." She studied her friend. "I am right?"

Alexsana blushed. "Perhaps," she admitted shyly. "But I'm too old to have feelings like that!"

Lydia laughed and said mockingly, "Yes, thirty-one is quite old. But your heart is young." She grew serious. "God has been preparing you for a long time." Her smile faded as she looked away, lost in thought.

Alexsana sobered, too, as she studied her friend's beautiful features: olive skin; delicate, long bones; dark eyes the color of melted chocolate; and thick, lush eyelashes. When the two had attended school together in Ramallah, Alexsana had wished she could trade in her stock American looks for more exotic features, like those of her friend.

"You are thinking of your own love now, aren't you?" Alexsana asked gently. Lydia and Samuel had been apart two years. Lydia obviously hadn't fared any better than her brother.

Khalil, Sam, Lydia, and Alexsana had grown up together at the Ramallah school. The four had been inseparable, venturing into Hezekiah's tunnel at night or the catacombs that only locals knew about. They had remained unaware that politics caused many to view their friendship as distasteful.

As they grew up, understanding more about the real world with each year that passed, Khalil had pursued both Lydia and Alexsana. Although the dangerous element to their relationship made for potential "Romeo and Juliet" encounters, both girls saw the flirtations as idle explorations. After leaving school, each knew that Khalil would never be anything more than a friend. And he had gradually seemed to accept it as well.

When Sam returned to Israel after spending eight years at college and grad school, he rediscovered his friendship with Lydia and, several years later, something more. The two dated secretly, aware that her father would not approve, but certain that they could convince him when the time came.

That time came soon, yet neither could convince the elderly patriarch that their union was right. Despite his long-term friendship with Samuel Roarke Sr., his commitment to educating his daughter among other bright scholars, and his solid devotion to the peace process and international relations, Lydia's father wanted his daughter to marry a Palestinian. The episode tore the families apart.

"I was so sure that Father would come around," Lydia said to Alexsana, her eyes welling up with tears. "I thought that he would relent if I respected his decision but showed him I was miserable."

Alexsana reached across the table. "Oh, Lydia, I'm sorry. All this talk about Ridge has brought up sad memories for you."

"No! Don't be sorry. I am happy for you," she said, smiling through her tears. "But I am sad for myself. And for Samuel. Oh, how I miss him!"

Alexsana smiled ruefully across the table. "He misses you, too," she said in a low voice.

Lydia swallowed hard. "Is he seeing anyone?"

"No. The only one he 'sees' is a certain tall, beautiful Palestinian named Lydia. There hasn't been anyone else. He's still hurting."

Lydia looked away and shook her head. "Am I being foolish? Should I simply defy my father and follow my heart?"

Alexsana thought carefully before speaking. "Only you can decide that, my friend. Jacob is a wonderful, loving, terribly stubborn man. If you defy him, you must be ready to walk away from your whole family. He might accept your decision, later. But he might not. You'd really have to be ready to say good-bye."

Lydia sighed. "I have a lot to think about again. As you said, we are not schoolgirls anymore, but grown women. And seeing you in love — yes, in love — awakens in me those feelings for Samuel I have tried to bury. Do not let me pour water on your parade —"

"Rain on your parade."

"Rain on your parade," Lydia smiled. "I am so happy for you. You watch. Your love will prove himself to you. I know it."

"Thank you for your vote of confidence, Lydia. I hope — with all my heart, I hope — that you and Sam can find each other again some day," Alexsana said earnestly. "You'll know where God is calling you when the time comes."

Ridge called that morning after five days on assignment in Jordan.

"Good! You're home," he said when she answered.

Alexsana smiled at the sound of his voice, thinking of Lydia's words. "Yes, I am," she said, trying to keep her voice cool. "I'm trying to pull some things together for my presentation. I have to show Abdallah and Abba Eban that my plan of action is in order. We're already a month behind schedule. They're close to giving me the go-ahead after stalling for a while; I just need to take care of some last-minute details."

"If you really wanted to wow them, I should take you to headquarters in Tel Aviv," Ridge offered. "They have a computer system that could help you create a three-dimensional presentation."

"Oh, thank you, but no," Alexsana said smiling. "They've agreed to let me lead this dig because of personal and professional reasons. I don't need to 'wow' them with computer-generated programs."

"Listen, I have to cover the Via Dolorosa processional at nine, but what are you doing this afternoon?"

"My presentation, mostly. I don't think I'll go to Good Friday services. After I get some work done, I'd like to walk through Jerusalem alone, away from the crowds and think about Christ's last walk."

Ridge ventured hopefully, "You want to be all alone?"

She smiled again. "I could use the company of a certain CNN correspondent, if he'd like to join me."

"He would," Ridge said quickly.

"Then meet me at the Jaffa Gate at two."

As he walked toward Alexsana, Ridge tried to discern what he found so appealing about her. It was more than a physical attraction; seeing her stirred his heart. He wanted to know her, inside and out. And he wanted their relationship to be something God smiled upon: a surprising, new concept for him.

He wanted to take her in his arms, lift her up, and swing her around in celebration of being together. But there was no legitimate reason to touch her, and she might shy away if he were to be so bold. He would have to keep his emotions in check, or perhaps lose her forever. Ridge approached her, smiling a soft hello.

Alexsana greeted him in the same manner.

"Many walk the Via Dolorosa on this day," she said, motioning for Ridge to walk beside her. He quickly matched her step. "But that's only the traditional route that the Crusaders popularized. To me, this route seems like a more logical choice: it runs from the palace of Herod, or 'David's Tower,' rather than from the Antonia Fortress. Scholars believe that Pilate probably stayed at the palace, and not the fortress as the Crusaders thought."

Ridge nodded and looked at her curiously. "What do you think about when you walk this path?"

Alexsana was thoughtful. "To be honest, on most days, I don't think about Christ's last walk. Usually, I'm thinking about how I'm running late, or a certain aspect of my dig. Occasionally, the wonder of it hits me. But only on Good Friday do I set out to simply walk his walk."

Ridge nodded. He seemed genuine in his search for knowledge.

"Jesus was tried by the people and sent out to be crucified," Alexsana went on. "His clothes were taken, his body whipped and bludgeoned by jeering passersby. All the while, he dragged his cross down the street. It probably weighed close to a hundred pounds. He went from king to criminal in the eyes of the people. Still, he went forward: innocent, but willing."

Ridge walked beside her in silence. Their pace was slow, contemplative. He did not intrude on her thoughts; indeed, he was lost in his own. All along the street, vendors sold olive wood trinkets that were spread out across the ground on brightly colored, woven scarves, or on small, portable tables. Tiny crucifixes. Manger scene ornaments. Miniature camels. There were fewer vendors on the street than usual, for many had gone to the more lucrative Via Dolorosa to capture the attention of pilgrims from places like Moscow, Cairo, Bombay, and New York.

As they neared the Church of the Holy Sepulchre, Alexsana stopped and watched as hundreds of people filtered through the giant doors. "I'm sorry," she said. "I don't think I want to go in. It's difficult enough to imagine Golgotha as it was without tons of people around."

Ridge nodded. "I've been inside. I know what you mean. Jesus seems more simple than what that place conveys — shrine upon shrine."

Alexsana shrugged. "People have to worship God in the way that touches their hearts. In that Byzantine church, you see the evidence of fourteen hundred years of adoration for Christ. Some people express that adoration in gifts of artwork or ornamentation. I lose sight of him inside there; others see him for the first time."

Ridge smiled at her in understanding. "So your walk is over?"

"For today," she nodded. "Would you like to join me, Sam, and my father this Sunday?" she asked hopefully.

"I would love to. It just depends on my assignments."

Alexsana looked surprised. "You don't even get Easter off?"

"I get those days off that are slow news days. A good reporter never rests. I can get the occasional leave, but I have to arrange it at least a week in advance."

Alexsana forced a tight-lipped smile, trying not to let her disappointment show. "Well, if you do end up being available, we are going to a sunrise service on the Mount of Olives, then to a brunch hosted by U.S. Ambassador Hughes."

"Sounds like it could be a news story," Ridge said, thinking fast.

She smiled. "It could be. There's usually some United States congressman or other dignitary who attends. It could be an interesting angle for your ongoing story: 'Holy Week in the Holy Lands.'"

Ridge looked shocked. "Have you been watching?" he teased.

"Sam told me. No television, remember?" she said with a grin.

Ridge sobered and unable to stop himself, reached out to caress her cheek. "Now how can I be interested in a woman who doesn't even own a television?"

CHAPTER

Twelve

❧

The Mount of Olives
April 7, Easter Sunday

Ridge was interviewing U.S. Congresswoman Snyder as Alexsana and her family arrived. He smiled over at her briefly, but remained distant from the gathering of about forty that congregated on the small hilltop platform. To the east, one could look out on the hills of Jordan; to the west lay Jerusalem.

Alexsana was dressed in a beige linen suit, ivory silk blouse, and cream high heels, an odd choice for her. Sam laughed and reached out to steady her as she tripped again. "Are the heels a new fashion statement or a ploy to draw the attention of a certain CNN correspondent?"

Alexsana pursed her lips. "I bought these long before I met Ridge," she said.

"But you never wore them."

"Nonsense. Leave your sister alone," their father piped in as he moved to join them. "I think you look stunning, dear. Your mother would be quite proud of you." He leaned closer. "And I look forward to meeting your young man," he said. "Your brother has told me all about him."

Alexsana smiled fondly at her white-haired father, his figure hunched over from years of working in tight quarters. His first love had always been archaeology; after his wife's death twelve years earlier, it was all he talked about or did. Alexsana and Sam rarely saw their father. For him to express interest, or even be aware of a man in whom she might be interested, was overwhelming. She hoped Ridge would make a good impression.

As the sun rose behind the Jordanian hills, the congregation listened quietly to the minister's brief prayer, then joined him in singing one of Alexsana's favorite hymns: "Jesus Christ Is Risen Today." Even while singing and celebrating the resurrection in her heart, Alexsana could not keep her mind from continually straying to the reporter somewhere behind her.

"I'm going to go join them," Ridge said as Steve filmed the gathering of people.

Steve kept shooting. "All right. This is some great footage, with the sun rising and all. Congresswoman Snyder's publicist is going to love us."

"Yeah." Ridge sounded distracted. "You coming?"

"Nah. I'll stay back here." Steve switched the camera off and lowered it from his face. "Hey, are you after God or just a girl?"

"Both, I think," Ridge said nonchalantly, heading toward a certain beautiful blonde in heels.

On the third verse, Sam moved aside to let Ridge stand between him and Alexsana. Ridge joined in singing, sneaking a peek at Alexsana. The service progressed quickly; afterward, the group began to move toward waiting taxis.

"Can you both come to brunch with us?" Alexsana asked Ridge, including Steve in her invitation.

"Press usually isn't invited to shindigs like that," Steve said, who had joined them after the service.

"Oh, I think the ambassador would be happy to have you. You'd probably just need to check that camera at the door."

"No way," Steve protested. "I don't go anywhere my camera isn't wanted."

"Then I'll meet up with you later," Ridge said to him, without taking his eyes off the woman in front of him.

"Sure," Steve said easily. "Happy Easter, Dr. Roarke."

"Happy Easter, Steve." Alexsana said. "If you change your mind...."

"Yeah, I know where to find you."

Sam Sr. took to Ridge in much the same way Robert Hoekstra had, pulling him aside and filling him in on his current dig. Against her wishes, Alexsana found herself lost in a crowd of old friends and political allies, talking about her own upcoming dig. She found it hard to extricate herself, and it was two hours before she was finally able to look up her father and Ridge.

Spotting Samuel and Ridge on a garden bench, she poured two cups of punch and took them outside. Pleased, both men accepted their beverages.

"Your dad has just been telling me about his dig at Tel Dan," Ridge told her. "It sounds as intriguing as Caesarea."

"But not as intriguing as what that daughter of mine has going in Jerusalem," the jovial man said.

"Papa is always somewhere interesting," Alexsana informed Ridge. "Have you two eaten?"

Ridge nodded. "We grabbed a plate on the way out. But we've been too absorbed in our conversation to go for seconds. How about you?"

"A bite here and there. I was talking too much to put food in my mouth. Think I'll just grab a sandwich at home...." Her eyes invited his next question.

Ridge took his cue. "Are you heading out?"

"In a moment," Alexsana said. "I just want to thank our host and then I have some work to do. We begin in three days!"

Alexsana's brother came up behind her. "Three days! I wanted a vacation before we started!"

She laughed. "Then take it now, big brother, 'cause we've got a window of opportunity I can't pass up."

"She's a tough trail boss," Sam said, raising an eyebrow at Ridge as if in warning.

"Thatta girl," her father said, reaching out to pinch her cheek. "You know where to find me if you need some extra help."

"Thanks, Papa. Happy Easter," she said, embracing him fondly.

"And to you, too, my girl. Nothing like a fine Easter day and a look at his children to make a man happy."

"You know you could see us more often," Sam chided him.

"I know it. I get so involved on site, it's tough to leave."

"As always," Alexsana ribbed him.

"I hear you, my girl. I hear you. Your mother would have my hide if she were here to take it."

"Just know that we'd like seeing more of you, Pops," Sam said.

"I'll work on it, Sam. Now you two be good. And Ridge, it was good to meet you. Take care of that daughter of mine."

Alexsana's eyes grew wide then she scowled at his comment. "I don't need some hotshot reporter to take care of me," she announced primly, turning away and moving toward the ambassador's wife.

Ridge turned to her smiling father. "Don't worry," he said conspiratorially. "I'll take care of her."

As Ridge and Alexsana stepped out of a taxi outside the Damascus Gate, a second car drove by with a man hanging out the window, Uzi in hand. Lifting his arm, he sprayed the air above them with bullets. Around them, women screamed and people scattered as Ridge pushed Alexsana down behind the taxi.

The gunman drove away, tires squealing.

Above them, the taxi driver snickered quietly as the taxi motor purred.

Ridge rose, angry. "That was funny?"

There was no laughter in the man's eyes. "Consider that a warning," he said, looking not at Ridge, but at Alexsana. "Hamas will not tolerate a Jewish plot to destroy our holy mosque."

Her eyes narrowed as she realized that the driver was a part of the attacking party. "It's not a plot! The dig is purely academic!" She brushed herself off, ignoring the rip in her skirt. She took a deep breath, refusing to sound defensive in her reasoning. "I only intend to study the passageway and stairs. In fact, I plan to strengthen the foundation."

The driver laughed again sardonically. "You will not be warned again, Alexsana Roarke. You have been a friend to many Palestinian nationals, but you are now a pawn of the Jews."

Ridge moved to grab the man, fury plainly written on his face, but Alexsana stopped his hand. "Wait! Let me take care of this." She turned back to the driver. "Tell Khalil al Aitam that I will be willing to talk with him at any time," she said calmly, hoping to bring a measure of control into the crazy situation. "I will dig, but I want it to be under peaceful circumstances. Abdallah al Azeh himself will be overseeing the process."

"Abdallah al Azeh is a fool," the driver spat out, then sped away, leaving black skid marks on the golden limestone street.

Thirteen

Alexsana turned and strode angrily through the gate, burning with fury that someone should attack her. Ridge ran to catch up.

"You're not thinking of moving forward with the dig," he began.

"I most certainly am," she said, pausing to pull off a broken heel, then tossing both shoes in a nearby trash can. She walked forward barefoot, and Ridge smiled in spite of himself as he watched her plod ahead. "Leave it to you, McIntyre, to fall in love with a pig-headed archaeologist," he mumbled.

"Don't you see," he tried as he caught up with her again, "that this is what Shehab was talking about? They *honestly* see your work as a threat to their precious mosque. You're in danger! Your whole team is! I bet the only reason those bullets went above your head and not into it was because of Khalil."

"Khalil told me himself that he could not protect me. In fact, it was probably he who sent the gunman to warn me.

The nerve!" She turned to walk again, flushed with anger.

Ridge grabbed her arm. "Alexsana. Perhaps they have reason to expect a Jewish plot."

Alexsana stopped struggling and frowned. "What are you talking about?"

"I'm saying that I have heard about The Temple Mount Faithful, or Kahane. From you. From others. You know as well as I do that they want the Temple Mount back. Your excavation would give them a prime opportunity. Are you absolutely sure that Abba Eban is not a part of — or at least sympathetic to — their group?"

She pulled him toward a nearby wall at an attempt to speak privately. "What are you saying?" she said angrily. "That my dig is all a Jewish plot?"

"At least consider it! You're a smart woman! Think it through."

"Nonsense!" Alexsana sputtered. "Approval to dig comes simply as a result of the peace process. This is an unprecedented opportunity. I will not believe that it's all because of some crazy plan to blow up the Temple Mount. There's going to be Waksf soldiers all around us — *us*, a bunch of nerdy archaeologists. How could we possibly tear down such a massive structure?"

"You plan to excavate the stairs behind the Triple and Double Gates. Once you get in, a well-placed bomb...." Ridge suggested.

"McIntyre! Ridge!" Steve Rains hurried up to them, favoring one side as he lugged the weight of his ever-present camera. "I heard there was gunfire. Do you want to film a report?"

Ridge grimaced, but nodded. "Will you wait here?" he asked Alexsana.

She looked away: angry, confused, and lost in thought.

"I'll be right back," Ridge told her. "I'm going to have to make you part of the report," he warned. "I'm sorry, but it's my job."

"Whatever," she said noncommittally.

"I'll be right back," he repeated, then joined Steve outside the Damascus Gate. "Let's keep it short," he said, gathering his thoughts.

"Righto." Steve held several fingers in front of the camera. "In three, two, one...."

"Easter has heightened the religious tension that plagues Jerusalem," Ridge said into the camera. "Between the thousands of pilgrims in the city for the Christian Holy Week, the Muslim fasting period of Ramadan, and Passover, the emotions of all three major religious groups have reached a fever pitch. Last week, a known member of the Kahane led a group in overtaking an entire city block in the Christian quarter, at the time owned by a Palestinian.

"This week, gunfire continues to erupt in and outside the city, this morning just outside the Damascus Gate, which you see behind me," he said, gesturing over his shoulder. "The apparent target: archaeologist Alexsana Roarke, leader of the proposed Solomon's Stable dig under the Temple Mount, which is scheduled to begin this week. Miraculously, no one was injured. One can only hope that as spring fades into summer, emotions will settle. From Jerusalem on Easter Sunday, this is Ridge McIntyre, CNN."

"...and 'cut.'"

"Great, Steve. Thanks for coming out. Now, I've got to get back to Alexsana...."

But when he turned, she was gone.

134

Alexsana looked up to see Ridge standing in her doorway, his face a mask of concern. It was obvious that her apartment had been ransacked. Inside, the furniture had been turned upside-down, the pictures pulled from the walls. Her filing cabinet had been emptied, leaving her paperwork scattered.

"Alexsana?" he asked. His face registered fear when he did not see her right away. "Alexsana?" he called, louder.

"I'm here," she said meekly, staring at him in a daze from her place on the stairs.

His face relaxed when he spotted her. Quickly, he went to her and pulled her into his arms. "Are you okay? Was there anyone here?"

"No. They were long gone," Alexsana mumbled. She rested one hand on his chest and closed her eyes, drawing comfort from his proximity and the feeling of his strong arms around her.

Ridge stared over her head to the wall beyond, spray-painted with red Arabic lettering. "What does it say, Sana?" he asked gently.

She shut her eyes again, wishing away the words that were embedded in her head. "It's just an idle threat."

"What does it say?" he insisted.

Alexsana swallowed and moved away from him. "Enter the Haram and you will die," she translated, willing her voice to sound confident, uncaring. She bent down and shuffled through several stacks of drawings that had been slashed. As she expected, her Solomon's Stable pictures and notes had been taken.

She looked up at Ridge. "Don't worry, al Azeh called. The

dig is 'temporarily on hold.' He said he's worried about my safety and that of the team, as well as the ramifications. He wants to wait a couple of weeks, let it all die down."

Ridge took a deep breath. "I know this is crushing news to you, but I can't help but feel relief that you won't be taking on all of the Hamas this week."

"Your report won't help me to get the dig back on track," she said, beginning to fume as the shock wore off.

Ridge's eyes grew wide as understanding dawned. "Is that why you left? What did you expect me to do? Not tell what I know? I'm a reporter, Alexsana. I told you I'd have to mention you. I was right in the middle of a terrorist warning toward one of the most prominent archaeologists in Israel. What would you have me do with that information?"

Alexsana ignored his explanation. "I knew I shouldn't get involved with a journalist...."

"Whoa!" Ridge protested. "Wait a minute! If you're suggesting that I'm using you somehow...."

"Maybe you should leave." She stared stonily at him. "I have a lot to do around here, and I don't feel like company anymore."

Ridge's mouth dropped slightly. His eyebrows knit together. He seemed unwilling to leave, but Alexsana's expression invited no argument.

"Fine," he said angrily. "Good-bye, Alexsana. Happy Easter." He maneuvered his way out of the room and slammed the door behind him.

Alexsana sank to her knees and gave into the tears she had not wanted him to see.

April 8

The next morning, Alexsana was trying to calm her brother down over the phone when she heard a knock at the door. She opened it to find Ridge waiting hopefully with an armful of flowers.

Cradling the phone between her shoulder and ear, Alexsana waved him into her tiny home, which had been set to reasonable rights. She took the flowers from him with a half-smile and motioned for him to sit down on the couch.

"No, Sam. I can't do that.... Hey, if they wanted me dead they could have had me yesterday. It was a warning, that's it." She crossed her eyes at Ridge, letting him know that his report had gotten her into trouble.

Ridge smiled sheepishly at the playful sign.

"No. No!" Alexsana protested into the phone. "Sam, when we get the go ahead again — and we *will* get it — you'll be around to help. We'll discuss it then. Things can radically change in a week around here...you know that."

She listened for several seconds, then said, "Fine. I understand your concern. Tell Papa I won't do anything he wouldn't do. And leave me alone until I call you."

She hung up the phone, sighed, and turned to face Ridge. "Look, let me say that I overreacted yesterday. I know you were just doing your job."

Ridge shook his head. "I'm sorry it had to involve you...and that I obviously got you into hot water with Sam."

Alexsana laughed. "He's just overdoing the big brother bit. He'll get over it."

"Maybe he's right," Ridge ventured.

She eyed him warily. "About what?"

"I'd guess that he's attempting to talk you out of excavating the Stables."

"If he were in his right mind, he wouldn't even try," Alexsana said stiffly. She tried to sound confident. "Everything will be fine. The City just needs some time to cool off."

"Ever since this peace process began, the City — and the entire West Bank — has gotten hotter and hotter," Ridge said. "Not cooler. I'll admit, emotions are at their peak because of Easter and Passover and Ramadan, but it's more than that. Gaza City is a mess. There was another shooting this morning, and the Palestinian police arrested hundreds, trying to regain some control."

"Why aren't you there on assignment?" Alexsana asked, placing the flowers in a vase of water.

"I got a few days off," Ridge said casually.

"A few days off?" Alexsana looked at him in surprise. "I thought you never got a break."

Ridge shrugged. "I requested a few days off. Officially, I'm looking for feature pieces. But really, I just wanted to see if I could whisk you away to the Galilee and Masada."

Now Alexsana really was dumbfounded. "I thought you had to request time off a week in advance."

Ridge smiled smugly. "Maybe I did."

"What?" Alexsana protested. "And you didn't give me advance warning?"

"I thought if I gave you too much time, you'd have second thoughts."

She smiled and then looked at him skeptically. "How long would we be gone?"

"Three days."

"And where would we stay?" she asked skeptically.

"I've booked rooms at the Peniel Guesthouse on the Sea of Galilee and at that resort on the Dead Sea."

Alexsana laughed. After all she'd been through, an escape from the City sounded wonderful. And the opportunity to get to know Ridge better was irresistible. "You booked two separate rooms?" she queried.

He pretended to be shocked and hurt at her insinuation. "I may be new to the faith, but I *am* an honorable man, Alexsana."

"Of course," she said, sounding as if she'd never doubted him, then continued, "Two *separate* rooms in *each* hotel?"

He sighed. "Two. Scout's honor. And I'll even submit the bill to CNN if you'll be my guide and help me find some good feature stories."

She pretended to consider his offer. "Hmm. That'll cost you meals, too."

"Done," Ridge said, looking pleased. "When can we go? My bags are packed."

She threw him a merry grin. "Give me ten minutes."

Ridge and Alexsana drove east with the top down on Ridge's company Jeep. Alexsana leaned back in the seat, loving the feel of the wind in her hair. It was too noisy for discussion; they simply enjoyed being together.

Half an hour into their journey, they turned north on Highway 90 and Alexsana shouted out bits of trivia as they passed several sites. Most notable was the Jordanian border to their right, marked by a tall, barbed-wire fence that was patrolled by soldiers. On the Israeli side, the ground was covered by a twenty-foot strip of groomed sand. "So they can tell if anyone has crossed!" she yelled in explanation.

They passed groves of luxurious palm trees, bright green against the red-gold desert rock. Ridge stopped at a roadside stand to purchase some of their dates and Alexsana laughed when he told her how much he had paid for the ripe, brown, sweet fruit. "Tourist," she taunted.

"Next time, I'll send you to negotiate prices," he threatened, pulling back onto the road.

"It'd save CNN thousands," she replied.

As they passed Jericho, Alexsana informed Ridge that it was the oldest continuously inhabited city in the world. "Seven thousand years!" she shouted. "Check out the monastery on the Mount of Temptation — there's a rock there with two indentations on it. The Greek Orthodox monks say that's where Jesus knelt for forty days and nights during his battle with Satan."

Ridge nodded, waiting to see where Alexsana was headed with this information.

"Maybe you could do a story on the remote monasteries of the Middle East," she suggested. "There's St. Catherine's on Mount Sinai, this one, and another remarkable one called St. George's in the Wadi Kelt, a valley outside of Jerusalem."

He smiled at Alexsana warmly, presumably contemplating the story idea and then the woman behind it.

Alexsana looked away, suddenly shy in the face of what seemed to be his growing infatuation. *Is it infatuation, Lord? Or love? Please show me the truth of it soon,* she prayed silently as the Jeep ate up the rolling, smooth highway.

Half an hour later, they reached the fertile valley that surrounded Lake Gennesaret, more commonly known as the Sea of Galilee. Rolling green hills banked the massive lake;

nearby, cooperative farms, or *kibbutzim,* blanketed the valley floor. Carefully irrigated crops brought the arid ground to life.

She directed Ridge to turn left at a sign written in Hebrew, and they quickly wound their way through a prospering kibbutz, on up to the top of a western cliff. He pulled to a stop, looking at her with a question in his eyes.

"Come on," she said, laughing. "I didn't show you up here just so we could park."

"Too bad," he quipped as they hopped out of the Jeep.

"You have to see this view," she said, ignoring his comment with a smile.

"Right." He followed Alexsana up a narrow dirt path to the hill's crest, casting furtive glances at her as they climbed.

When they reached the top, he whistled and said admiringly, "It's gorgeous." The water was met by several valleys, each filled with farms laid out neatly in squares of various shades of green. The lake met the graceful hills at their base, the color complementing that of the fresh spring grass.

Alexsana drew in a deep breath. "It's one of my favorite views in Israel," she said. "And it's such a perfect day!"

She was pointing out a landmark to him, not watching her step, when she tripped, then twisted and tried to correct her balance. Ridge was right there to catch her. She laughed sheepishly as he took her in his arms and held her firmly.

"Ridge," she began, placing her hands on his chest.

"Alexsana," he answered, his voice low.

She tried again. "Ridge...."

He silenced her half-hearted complaint with a kiss.

Surprised, she pulled back, breaking their embrace, but then to his surprise, leaned forward and returned the kiss.

He grinned, then picked her up, twirling her around as she shrieked. "Ridge! Ridge! Put me down!"

He did as he was told, but kept on grinning. "I finally got a kiss from the great archaeologist, Alexsana Roarke!" he shouted to the valley below. He turned back to her and looked tenderly into her eyes. "Do you know how long I've wanted to do that?"

"Well, you're lucky you waited until now, mister," she threatened, pointing one finger at his chest. "Because I wasn't ready."

"What made the difference?" he asked, sobering.

"Well, for one, I see you in a whole new light now that you've become a Christian. Besides that, I just know you better. I don't make a habit of kissing men I don't know."

He nodded, appreciating her standards and values. Drawing her close, he looked beyond her to the view of the Sea. "So this is the Galilee?"

"Yes. Across that valley, on the northeast shore of the lake, is Tabgha, where it is said that Jesus fed five thousand with five loaves of bread and two fish. The little fishing village you can just make out beyond Tabgha is Capernaum, where Jesus centered his Galilean ministry. That was where he healed the paralytic who was lowered down to him through the roof by his friends."

She pointed down below them. "Those caves were used by Jewish zealots. They hid there, trying to escape the Romans who sought to kill them. Eventually, they were found and, by repelling down on ropes, the soldiers murdered them all."

"Like at Masada," Ridge said soberly. "How many famous massacre sites are we going to see?"

"Israel is full of them," Alexsana admitted. "You'll see Gamla tomorrow. It is beautiful now, two thousand years after the carnage. I think it's important to remember where people lived and died, don't you? I mean, the forces that shaped their lives were powerful: the passion of faith, the fervor of government, the blind hatred of a people at large. By exploring how others expressed those feelings, I feel as if I understand myself better, and my world."

Ridge nodded. "That's what makes you a great archaeologist," he murmured.

"What?" Alexsana pulled back and looked at him curiously.

"It's what makes you a great archaeologist," he repeated. "You fall so deeply into the lives of the people you research, you're able to really know them." He looked out at the valley below.

"I've spent the majority of my professional career trying to stay emotionally detached," he said. "I visit a subject long enough to understand and report, but briefly enough so as not to become too involved. That way, I don't sway the report. But maybe the journalistic code is a mistake. How can I report how things truly are if I don't let myself become involved, like you would if you were excavating one of those caves?"

"The trick would be to represent both sides equally," Alexsana said. "Undoubtedly, you'd sway one way or the other, as you said."

Ridge shook his head. "But don't you see? I've spent more than ten years totally absorbed in my work, scratching the surface of the deepest passions of the world. Now suddenly, it's as if my eyes are open wider. There's more meaning in everything around me. I want to know what drives people. I want to understand. To *feel*."

He reached out and held Alexsana's face tenderly between his palms. "Don't you see, Alexsana Roarke? You've led me to a Savior who loves me. And in doing so, you've opened my heart to love, true love." He paused, searching her eyes with an intense gaze. "You've also opened my heart to someone else."

"Who?" she whispered, knowing the answer.

"You," he said, and kissed her.

This time, her lips awaited his.

Fourteen

❧

Alexsana and Ridge explored the west side of the huge lake all afternoon, stopping at the excavation of Peter's house in Capernaum and at an ancient synagogue in Chorazin. Their evening was spent in the gardens outside a chapel on a hillside north of the lake, built to commemorate Jesus' Beatitudes. From a seat in the surrounding rose gardens, they enjoyed a spectacular sunset on the water as Ridge read Christ's words.

He opened Alexsana's pocket Bible to where she directed and read aloud to her. "'Blessed are those who hunger and thirst for righteousness, for they will be filled. Blessed are the merciful, for they will be shown mercy. Blessed are the pure in heart, for they will see God.'"

Dusk quickly lapsed into night as the couple talked about themselves, their lives, their faith, and Israel. Finally, at two in the morning, they turned in for the night. Separating in the hallway at their guesthouse, feeling as if parting physically hurt in some way, they said goodnight with a brief, tender kiss.

At eight-thirty sharp, Alexsana heard a quiet knock at her door.

"Ridge?" she called out sleepily.

"Yes," he answered eagerly, his voice muffled. "Good morning!"

"It's not good until ten!" she protested. "Come back later!"

"No way. You're on CNN time, lady. I'll see you at breakfast in thirty minutes."

Alexsana groaned mournfully, but did as she was told.

A short time later, Alexsana met him in the spacious living room, looking fresh and pretty in a bright yellow blouse, white Bermuda shorts, and Keds. Her legs were beautifully tanned, and Ridge struggled not to stare as she came toward him.

"You look like you've been primping for hours," he said appreciatively, rising out of a wing-backed chair to greet her. "Not like you were rudely awakened half-an-hour ago."

It was a gorgeous spring day, and the sun streamed through the plate-glass windows behind him and onto the wood floors below.

She smiled shyly. "Ready for breakfast, you workaholic?"

"After you."

They dined on freshly baked scones with homemade jam, scrambled eggs, and fresh-squeezed orange juice, a specialty of the guesthouse. Alexsana ate like she hadn't eaten for days, suddenly aware that Ridge had distracted her from her appetite.

Ridge grinned over his coffee cup as she took a second helping of eggs. She caught his gleeful glance and immediately felt defensive. "What? We have a big day ahead of us."

"Right," he said, raising his eyebrows. "It's smart to eat a big breakfast."

She took a spoonful of eggs and poised the ammunition to flick it at him.

He raised his hands. "Truce! Truce!"

"Eat another scone," she said firmly.

"Taskmaster," he teased. They smiled, enjoying their temporary truce, and silently mulled over the relationship they were building as they flirted across the table.

Their morning was spent in the Golan Heights at Gamla, just beyond the rusty tank and jeep wreckage that remained from the war of '67. All around the verdant hillside, wildflowers sprouted in vast sheets of purple cosmos, yellow sweet peas, and red poppies.

They left the black basalt stones that made up the remains of the Jewish stronghold and synagogue, and headed south.

At a public beach on the Dead Sea, Ridge and Alexsana stopped and changed into swimsuits. "Be very careful to not get the water in your eyes and mouth," she warned as they walked across the beach. "At eleven times the saline of normal salt water, it'll sting like everything if you do."

"Gotcha. No water fights."

Alexsana looked at him with alarm. "*Definitely* no water fights."

Holding hands, they waded into the dense salt water. They laughed as their feet left bottom, yet they stayed effortlessly afloat. Ridge leaned back and kicked his feet up, laughing harder than he had in years. "Look!" he called, placing his hands behind his head. "It's like I'm in an inner tube on the river! Except there's no inner tube!"

She giggled.

Ridge laughed so hard he lost his balance and flipped over, inadvertently splashing water in his eyes and hers, too. Both blinked as they were temporarily blinded by the stinging liquid.

"Ridge?" she called out.

"Alexsana! I can't see you!"

"I can't see you either!" Alexsana said, helpless as she lapsed into fits of giggles. "Ridge! Come here! Come grab my hand!"

He followed the sound of her voice, like a child playing a game of Marco Polo.

"Ridge?" she called again, worry creeping into her voice when he did not respond. Though there were few ways to drown in such a buoyant waterway, the lack of sight unnerved her. "Ridge!"

Her last call solidified her location for him. He grabbed her around the waist, pulling her backward. She shrieked and splashed, narrowly missing his eyes with another wave.

He laughed and picked her up in his arms. "Just taking my damsel in distress ashore," he said.

"Great," she said, relaxing a bit. "But my hero is as blind as a bat."

"That's true," he admitted, releasing her in the shallow waters. "Perhaps we can stand for a minute while we wait for our eyes to clear. I don't know about you, but it makes me feel more secure."

Ten minutes later, their vision was back to normal. They waded out of the water and immediately showered under spouts of cold, fresh water, rinsing off the stinging salt that coated their bodies.

From the Dead Sea, they drove south to Masada. In the face of desert heat without a hint of breeze, they elected to ride the tram to the top of the mountain butte, rather than climb the famous "snake trail." Alexsana pointed down to the path as they sailed past, high above. "There's another good feature story for you," she said.

"What's that?" he asked, searching the steep hillside below.

"The Israeli soldiers climb that path each year in a parade of lights, commemorating the deaths of those Jews who held out on Masada against the Romans."

"That'd be a sight to see," Ridge said reflectively.

"It's very dramatic," she mused.

At the top, they entered the remains of what was once Herod's winter palace and later a Jewish fortress and compound. After three years spent building a ramp to reach the Jews, the Romans found that once inside, there was no one to capture; after surviving the long siege, the Jews had cast lots and killed each other with knives, rather than surrendering to the Romans.

"Their defiance is legendary," Alexsana said. "It inspired the motto you see in graffiti throughout Israel: 'Masada shall not fall again.'"

Together, they explored the giant underground cisterns that had supplied the Jews with water over the years, the complex series of houses that were built to accommodate Jewish lifestyles, and the remains of the Herodian palace, steam baths, and beautiful mosaic floors and columns.

"It's astounding," Ridge said. "To think of them all here. Herod, at one time. Refugees, at another. Conquerors with no captives later. Coming from a country that's only two hundred years old, that much history is overwhelming."

"Welcome to my world," Alexsana said with a grin. Her hair had dried slicked-back after her seaside shower, emphasizing her big blue eyes.

Ridge took a deep breath. "Thanks for letting me be a part of your world." He pulled her to a stop by a Masada fortress wall bordering the Dead Sea, then put his arm around her and looked out toward the blue-green waters.

"That's *another* story idea," Alexsana began, looking at the Sea. "Due to evaporation and diversion of the water from the Jordan River by both Jordan and Israel, the Dead Sea is shrinking at an alarming rate. There have been ambitious, hugely expensive pipeline projects proposed...."

Ridge turned her toward him and silenced her with a kiss. "And you call *me* a workaholic," he said, tenderly stroking her cheek. "I have enough story ideas for a month's work. Let's enjoy a romantic moment, shall we?"

"We shall," she declared happily, kissing his dimpled chin, then rested her head on his chest as the sun's last rays filtered through the mountains behind them, casting deep shadows on the desert and sea below.

Fifteen

❧

April 11

I've enjoyed being away! Thank you for inviting me!" Alexsana shouted, pushing back tendrils of hair that had escaped from her braid and were whipping about in the wind.

Ridge smiled and nodded, but remained silent.

Alexsana noted the growing crease in his brow and reached over to play with the curls at the base of his neck. When he looked over, his face clearly expressed his concern.

Ridge pulled off the road and took her hand in his. He sighed heavily. "I realize that by taking you away, I was trying to protect you as much as get to know you. Now all I can think of is that I'm taking you right back into the danger zone, while I will probably be sent out on assignment. There's no way I can keep you under lock and key."

"You couldn't do that, anyway," Alexsana said gently, lifting her chin. "I have a life to live, and I won't hide away just because some threats have been made."

He turned to her, his frown deepening. "But Alexsana,

you can't just treat these warnings like idle threats; messing with the Hamas and Jihad is serious business. They believe this is a holy war. They blow up entire busloads of people; why would they hesitate to kill one archaeologist? You can't consider yourself exempt anymore. People like Khalil — who were once like family to you — most certainly consider you the enemy."

She leaned her elbow on the door and cradled her forehead in her hand. "Do you think I'm naive?" Her stomach churned as the tension between them mounted.

"In some ways, yes." He paused, thinking. "It's just that your passion for your work blinds you to reality."

"I am well aware of my world," Alexsana said defensively. "I've grown up here."

"Yes, but maybe growing up here has made you calloused. You think you're untouchable. But your flesh is as soft and vulnerable as the next person's. One bullet could end it all, and that makes me frantic to try and protect you."

She turned toward him in the seat. "I understand what you're saying, Ridge. But *I'm* not the one who was shot while on assignment. Don't you see? Your work is just as dangerous, if not more so. My family has ridden the wave of Israeli politics for years. In some ways, that protects me." She grabbed his hand. "I hear what you're saying. And I appreciate your fear for me. I'll take precautions, okay? But don't ask me to give this up."

Ridge's cellular phone rang, interrupting their intense gaze.

Grimacing, he flipped open the receiver. "McIntyre here."

"We're on assignment," Steve said without preamble. "Where are you?"

"Ten miles outside of the Old City," Ridge said tiredly. "Where are we headed?"

"Gaza. The team they sent has only been doing a mediocre job. They want Mr. Ratings out there ASAP to draw back some viewers from the networks."

"How long, do you suppose?"

"If we leave today: three, maybe four days. Depends on what's happening."

"Okay. I'll grab some clean clothes at the hotel and meet you there in an hour."

"I'll be there."

Ridge sighed and clung to the steering wheel as if it might somehow sustain him. He looked over at Alexsana, who waited silently to hear the news. "Suddenly, my life has gotten more complicated, Dr. Roarke. Infinitely more interesting, but much more complicated."

Taking comfort in the fact that the dig was still more than a week away, placing Alexsana temporarily out of danger, Ridge dropped her off at the Damascus Gate.

"I think I can manage it from here," she said. "You need to get to your hotel. Steve will be waiting."

He looked with consternation from the gate to her. Then, giving in, he lifted her chin with his strong hand and kissed her softly. "Please, Alexsana, be careful. You become more important to me each day. If you won't take precautions for yourself, do it for me, okay?"

She reached over and poked him in the chest. "And you do the same. Going to Gaza isn't exactly like going to Honolulu."

"Deal." He kissed her once more, briefly, then hopped in the Jeep. "I'll call as soon as I'm back. I don't think I'll have much opportunity to contact you from there."

"That's fine," Alexsana tried not to let her disappointment show. "I enjoyed being with you. I'll be praying for you," she said softly.

"And I'll try my hand at doing the same for you," he promised, his smile returning. "Until later...."

"Until then," she said. Knowing they would stand there for hours if she did not make a move, Alexsana smiled, turned, and disappeared through the gate.

Alexsana was surprised by what awaited her at the apartment.

"Sam!" she said, pleased to see her brother, but not anticipating a visit from him. Although he had a key to her apartment, he had his own flat on the other side of the city. "What are you doing —" her voice broke off as she saw the reason for his visit.

In the kitchen, Lydia hummed and stirred a steaming pot, apparently unaware that anyone else had arrived. "Oh, no," Alexsana said. "Or should I say, wow!? What is going on?"

Hearing the sound of Alexsana's voice, Lydia turned with a taster spoon still in her mouth. Looking embarrassed, she dropped the spoon and moved toward Alexsana to explain.

"We couldn't wait any longer," Sam said. "We've been apart for over two years now, and when we saw one another in the suk today, we knew that nothing had changed." Lydia came to stand by his side and he put an arm around her. "We're still in love and always will be," he said confidently, smiling down at the woman he adored.

"And I made a decision that I would say good-bye to my family if they could not accept it," Lydia said. "I'm hoping Father will come around. But if not, you will have to be my family now."

Alexsana nodded soberly, her smile slowly growing. "I'm so happy for you both. It's been torture to watch you spend this time apart, knowing you were still in love." Her face took on a faraway look as she wondered how often she and Ridge would have to be separated. *I suppose that means I think we're in love, too,* she thought. *Please Lord, help me to keep some perspective in my crazy life.*

"And where have you been?" Sam asked. "I'm sorry to just barge in here, but I couldn't reach you on the phone, and I thought it would be better to meet here than to have Lydia come to my apartment."

"Of course," Alexsana said. If Lydia were seen entering a man's home — even under the most innocent of circumstances — her reputation in the tight-knit Palestinian community could be demolished. "We went to Galilee and then down to the Dead Sea."

"'We'?"

"Ridge and I," she said nonchalantly, setting her backpack down on the sofa beside her. But she could not keep the grin from her face.

"Uh-oh," her brother said. "Something tells me we're not the only ones head over heels in love."

Alexsana ducked her head, smiling. "I'm not sure it's love yet, but I'm sure getting pulled in."

"You will be a beautiful bride!" Lydia exclaimed.

"Whoa!" Alexsana laughed. "Hold on! I just said I didn't know if it was love."

"But your eyes, your face, tell me something different," Lydia said confidently. "I've seen it on my own in the mirror. If you do not know now, it's only a matter of time until you do."

"You're a romantic, my friend," Alexsana said.

"And I think she's right, little sister," Sam said. "Are you sure he's right for you?"

Alexsana hesitated. "I'm not sure of anything. All I know is that he has come to Christ, and that I think he's wonderful!"

"Does he find you to be the same?" Lydia asked.

"I think so," Alexsana said sheepishly. "If only love could be as buttoned down as archaeology!"

Five days later, Alexsana unexpectedly received the go-ahead to proceed at the Haram. She had her team of twelve assembled and in the city within two more days. The group worked quietly, trying not to draw attention to themselves — or to their mission — as they explored the outside of the Double and Triple Gates, continued research at the École Biblique, and arranged for delivery of needed equipment.

April 18

As the muezzin's plaintive cry called the Muslim faithful to prayer, Alexsana and Sam made their way onto the Haram and around the El Aksa Mosque. Al Azeh himself unlocked the steel door and let them into the tunnel that led down to Solomon's Stables.

Even from below, they could hear the high wail of the prayer call, and Alexsana shivered in the darkness. The muffled sound — though one she had heard since childhood —

lent an eerie feel to the blackness that surrounded them. Sam worked quickly, setting up several lanterns. Their bright light illuminated the huge archways that supported the weight of the Temple Mount above them. At one time, the entryways had consisted of nothing but archways covering a staircase that led the people into the temple. But over the centuries, deterioration and hysterical overprotection had led people to fill in many caverns with rock and cement, leaving few of them clear.

Alexsana and Sam planned to explore the tunnels for several hours, then emerge into the crowd when the next prayer time was called, hopefully escaping the notice of the many Muslims who gathered at the mosque each day. "I wish Professor O'Malley could be here," Alexsana said, forcing herself not to whisper.

"He would've drawn too much attention," Sam said. "There isn't a Muslim on the Haram who doesn't notice when the prof comes to explore."

"If he can get away with coming here, why can't we?" Alexsana complained, thinking of the graffiti written on her wall. Even with two coats of white paint over it, the red lettering still showed through.

"The professor has always come to look, not to dig," Sam reminded her. "But they don't like him coming down here, either, even though he's done so for years."

"Sometimes the paranoia gets to me," Alexsana said, flashing her light around one massive Herodian block.

Sam set up the last lamp and stood to face her. "You're absolutely sure that no one on the team has connections to the Kahane."

"Oh, come on, Sam," Alexsana sighed in frustration. "You

know these people as well as I do."

"Yes," he admitted. "But even the most stalwart person can be swayed by the right sum of money — and it'd be worth a lot to the Kahane to destroy the Haram."

"I can't let myself think that. I'd have to watch every team member every second. They'd feel the tension; it would affect our work."

Sam did not relent. "I think you and I need to keep an eye out for danger signals. Let's not be naive, Sana; let's be careful. The stakes are high enough as it is without a bomb planted in a rocky alcove...."

She raised her hands in surrender. "All right, all right. We'll keep an eye on everyone. But let's be subtle about it, okay? Now, let's get to the task at hand while we have the time. Where do we start?"

High above them, past many layers of stone, a man looked from the doorway to his companion as they bowed and prayed. "You saw them," he whispered in Arabic.

"I did," the man stated, not looking at him.

"It was Alexsana Roarke and her brother? You're sure?"

"It was them, Shehab," the man said, afraid to see the other's eyes. The voice was frightening enough.

"Khalil will have to act now," Shehab said. "No more warnings. They must be stopped."

Deep in the Negev Desert that night, Shehab met with Khalil.

"You saw them yourself?" Khalil asked, his voice devoid

of emotion. He was glad for the cover of darkness that hid his upper lip — covered with sweat — and forced himself not to wipe it away.

"I did. My companion saw them enter the tunnels, given access by al Azeh himself. We hid after prayer, then watched them emerge five hours later when prayer was called again, using the cover of our own holy time to do their dirty work," Shehab spat out.

Khalil ignored the man's assumption. "And you wish me to act."

"*I* wish you to?" the man's voice rose in intensity. "*You* should wish to do so! What keeps you from entering the woman's apartment tonight and slitting her throat yourself? Why do you not take charge? It is unlike you to act this way. Have they bought you off? Or does the woman have your attention in other ways?"

Khalil whirled, a growl on his lips as he swiftly nabbed Shehab's throat between his powerful fingers. He pulled the smaller man's face close to his own. "Never again will you question my authority, or my loyalty to the Hamas," he growled. "I am well aware of what I must do. You will wait for instruction."

Shehab backed away, bowing. "Give me the chance, Khalil," he said ingratiatingly. "I will take care of the Roarke woman once and for all. Let me prove myself to you and the Hamas by this holy act. Let me protect our holy mosque."

Khalil turned away, frowning. "You will await my orders," he repeated.

Shehab bit his lip. "As you wish," he said dully, and disappeared into the black, starless night.

$\mathcal{S}ixteen$

❧

April 19

Ridge swallowed hard, facing his informant, willing himself to remain impassive. "You are so sure that you will be successful that you are claiming Hamas responsibility *before* your task is complete?"

"I am. To know our target and receive an American 'scoop' — is that the word? — will cost you five hundred American."

Ridge laughed, hoping he did not sound nervous. "Five hundred? This must be big news indeed." *Please God! Please let us not be talking about Alexsana.* But instinctively, he knew. He could almost place the words in Shehab's mouth.

"It will be good information for you as well. If you do not know, your own life is at risk."

Ridge's sinking feeling grew. "How's that?" he said, playing dumb.

"Where is the money?"

Ridge pulled out his wallet and counted out three hundred dollars. "Two more if the news is as worthwhile as you say."

Shehab nodded. "I would stay away from Dr. Roarke if I were you. I know you have been seen with this other source of yours. It is not good for your health."

"Why?" Ridge leaned forward urgently. "She is not working on the Haram. The dig has been postponed."

"Apparently, they have been given permission to proceed," Shehab said, grinning. "I myself saw them enter the tunnels, like black spies, not two days ago. They will soon begin. But I will stop them."

"How?" Ridge asked, again willing himself to sound uncaring, like an uninvolved journalist, simply collecting information for a story.

"I will kill her," Shehab announced proudly.

"And why don't you think that I will try and stop you?" Ridge could not keep the pitch of his voice from rising.

"Warning her would be unwise, Mr. McIntyre," Shehab threatened. "If you get in the way, there will simply be two dead instead of one. What is the sense of that?"

Ridge squelched the urge to grab the man by his throat. "Perhaps I have feelings for this woman," Ridge ground out. "I might feel the need to protect her from you."

Shehab frowned at Ridge's reaction. He had not anticipated such strong sentiment from a journalist. His eyes narrowed. "This is a war, Mr. McIntyre. She is not innocent, but a pawn of the Kahane. If we do not act, they will take the Haram from us. If you are involved, you choose a side. And if you choose Dr. Roarke's side, you will not live to see tomorrow."

You will not live to see tomorrow. They plan to act tonight. Ridge had to find her. He stood and threw two hundred dollars on the table. "Thanks for the scoop, Shehab," he said mildly. "It will make a great story." He turned and forced himself to calmly walk away.

Shehab flashed a yellow-toothed grin and watched as Ridge disappeared into the suk's crowd.

Ridge ran to the École Biblique, praying that he would find Alexsana inside. He felt weary, suddenly aware of his lack of sleep and the weight of his worry for his love.

He asked an elderly monk how to get to the library, then ran forward, ignoring the man's protest that visitors must not intrude on the sanctity of the compound. Ridge burst into the library, unintentionally slamming the heavy, ancient door as he came through.

"Sam! Thank God!" he said between gasps for air.

Samuel looked at him, confused, as did Professor O'Malley and six others from the team. In front of them lay stacks of books and piles of notes. Behind them, a photo of the Haram was projected on the wall and beside it, an illustration of the Temple as it once had looked.

"Where is your sister? I've tried reaching her on my cell phone all morning!"

Sam frowned and checked his watch. "She might be outside the Double Gate at this point. She was going to —"

Ridge's heart sank. "She's outside the city walls?"

"Well, yes. If she's where she's supposed to be."

"Come on!" Ridge yelled over his shoulder. "I'll explain on the way!"

"Wait here," Sam said to the team. "I'll be back." He tried to sound calm, but Ridge's serious, frantic look made his heart pound.

Alexsana closed her notebook and rose from her perch on a three-by-nine foot Herodian stone. From outside the Haram, she had sketched the Double and Triple Gates with renowned architect Benjamin Shachaf, making plans on how to excavate beyond them.

Ben had left an hour earlier, but Alexsana chose to stay, relishing the tingling anticipation of beginning the dig. When she closed her eyes, she could see the stairs as they once were: a series of steps and landings that encouraged worshippers to enter slowly, reverently. She imagined the people reaching the temple, washing in the ceremonial *mikvehs*. Outdoors, the steps spread over two hundred feet in length to the Double Gate, which led to the grand Temple one hundred feet above. She raised her head and shielded her eyes from the intense sunlight.

"Father God, let me show the world what Jesus would have once seen. Let me show them a little more about his life, his ways. And let me do this for your honor, not my own."

As she prayed in the peaceful quiet, a shiver suddenly ran down her spine and broke her concentration. She opened her eyes and looked around, but saw no one.

Rising, she packed up her things and picked her way down to the asphalt-covered highway. Forty feet from the Dung Gate, a car screeched up beside her.

Alexsana turned, frozen by surprise, but did not run. She was surrounded in seconds by black-masked assailants, who pulled her into the back seat of the car.

"No!" she shouted, kicking and struggling to get away. "No! Help! Help me!" she cried before a man pulled her toward him, covering her mouth.

The car screeched away just as Ridge and Sam reached the gate.

Spotting her notebook and backpack on the pavement, and catching sight of the escaping car, they knew exactly what had happened.

Frantically, Ridge looked one way and then the next, searching for empty cabs. But there were none to be found. *No one would be willing to pursue the kidnappers, anyway,* he thought grimly. He set out after the car in a dead sprint, willing his body to go faster and faster.

But they were too fast. In seconds, the car had outdistanced him by half a mile. Ridge watched helplessly as it disappeared into the winding streets of a neighboring Palestinian village. Sam reached his side, panting as hard as Ridge, and stared after the car.

"Call the...police," Ridge gasped, pulling his cellular phone from his pocket. "Tell them your sister...has been abducted...by men in a...beige BMW." His head felt thick, his thoughts garbled, as fear choked him.

"License plate...number?" Sam asked hopefully, gasping for breath.

"No. I don't think...there was one," Ridge panted.

Sam stared at the despondent man for a moment, then clasped Ridge's shoulder. "We'll find her."

"Yeah," Ridge swallowed hard, his face distraught, angry. "But will we find her alive?"

Alexsana struggled against the men who held her, knowing that it was futile, but needing to try. Wearying of her fight after only five miles, the assailant in the front seat turned with a syringe in hand.

"No!" Alexsana said. "You don't have to give me that! I'll be quiet." She forced her body to relax, trying to demonstrate that she would cooperate.

"We do not only want you quiet," the man said in Arabic, leaning over the seat as one of the guards pulled her bare arm forward. "We want you blind."

Alexsana winced as the syringe entered her arm and the yellow liquid hit her system. She began to pray that it would not kill her. But before she could finish her silent cry, unconsciousness enveloped her.

Alexsana awoke twenty-four hours later, her mind fuzzy and her head aching as if from a migraine. She tried to sit up, but then slumped back against the bed. The afternoon was stifling hot, especially with the closed windows, yet Alexsana felt sick at the mere thought of standing to reach the dirty panes.

She raised her arm to look at her watch and discovered that she had been dressed in traditional Bedouin attire. Her long dress was made of heavy, black cotton, and was hand-stitched with brightly colored patterns of reds and purples. She touched her face. A complex veil of coins, teardrops, and other metal ornamentation covered her forehead, nose, and mouth, exposing only her eyes. The black veil had been sewn to the edges of another cloth that covered her hair.

Wearily, she struggled to make sense of her surroundings. She did not remember being abducted; indeed, she could barely recall her name. A man entered the room.

He was handsome in white formal clothes that flowed softly as he walked. His white headdress was secured with a black, twisted cord. The man knelt beside her bed. "Sarah," he said over his shoulder, speaking Arabic. "Please open that window."

He took Alexsana's hand and stared into her watery eyes. "Alexsana. Are you awake? Can you hear me?"

Khalil. Her thoughts began to focus. *Khalil!* She tried to make a sound, but her mouth would not function.

Khalil patted her shoulder as Sarah brought her a glass of water. Gently, he lifted Alexsana to a sitting position and pulled aside her veil while the woman lifted the cup to her lips.

Alexsana drank thankfully, suddenly aware that her mouth and throat were parched. "Khalil...." she whispered.

"Shh." As tenderly as he had raised her, he lowered her back to the cushions. "Please, Sarah. Leave us for a moment."

The woman bowed and backed out the door as she was bidden. He turned to Alexsana.

"I do not know how clearly you can think. I am sorry you were drugged. It was the only way. It is safer if you do not know where you are. An assassin was on the move. If you had remained in Jerusalem last night you would not have lived."

"But you...." she tried.

"Listen to me, Alexsana," Khalil said urgently. "Yes, I knew about the danger. I discouraged the assassin, but men loyal to me reported that he planned to defy my orders and act on his own. Our people had seen you enter the Haram and Solomon's Stables. We knew then that you had been given permission to proceed. My men will not listen to reason. Too many want you dead. I cannot control them all in this matter. I sent four friends who trust me implicitly to collect you. Even they do not know where you are now, or what I plan to do with you."

Alexsana raised a hand to her aching eyes and rubbed as the coins on her forehead clanged like church bells in her drugged ears. She struggled to make sense of his words.

"You feel terrible. I can see that. But you are alive!" He rose and paced the floor. "I could not let them kill you. You are too important to me. And although you are a stubborn woman, I still count you as a friend."

He turned back to her. "I must go now. I am expected at a dinner party tonight and must punish Shehab for acting against my orders." He grinned at the prospect. "You are in the house of my friend. He and his family will care for you until I can decide what to do."

He bent and kissed her forehead below the coins. "I will be back as soon as I can, Alexsana." Quickly, he strode through the door, never hearing her feeble call. Feeling incredibly weak, Alexsana let unconsciousness claim her once again.

The next time Alexsana was awakened, it was by two women. She had no idea what time it was or how long she had been in the house of Khalil's friend, but she did realize that the narcotics were slowly wearing off.

The women raised her to a sitting position, then fed her broth and water and tea. When she had finished, they held on to her arms and pulled her to her feet, smiling as she took several unsteady steps.

"I have to call my family," Alexsana said to the older

woman, whom she assumed to be the wife of Khalil's friend. In her groggy state of mind, Alexsana spoke rough Arabic, but it was good enough for conversation.

The woman shook her head. "We have no phone here. You are to wait until Khalil returns. You are our guest."

"I am in hiding," Alexsana corrected. "Where are we?"

Her hostess paused. "We are not to tell you that. Khalil warned us that you are a clever woman and that you would try to return to Jerusalem if you got your bearings. It is not safe for you, or for us. We are trying to help."

Alexsana sighed and sat back down on the bed, examining her image in the mirror the girl handed her. With her blond hair hidden, she looked like a traditional Bedouin woman, although a little pale. If anyone were to come near, and if Alexsana averted her gaze, they would not recognize her as a Westerner.

"He leads the men who want to kill me, but then rescues me," she muttered in English. "So what am I supposed to do now, Khalil?" She shuddered at the thought of what Ridge and Sam must be going through. Did they think she was dead? She had to get back to the City. But how?

Seventeen

April 22

"S pare me the flak, Steve," Ridge snapped. "Just find someone else to do it. Someone at headquarters can certainly report that she's missing."

"Yeah, but the audience would eat it up. Your girl, kidnapped. Why not let them in on it? The world would go nuts, just like when you saved my tail in Lebanon. Come on, Ridge."

"No. I'm not going to exploit my relationship with her to gain some ratings points."

"Even if it helps you gain political backing? She's out there, Ridge. She's alive. You need U.S. pressure to help locate her and bring her home. Then you need more American pressure to make sure she stays alive when that stubborn girlfriend of yours goes ahead with the Solomon's Stable dig."

"Who's to say she's still alive?" Ridge growled, his face revealing his fury. "How can you push me on this?"

Steve was unfazed. "Shehab hasn't come back to you since he told you of his mission three days ago, right?"

"Yeah. So?"

"Wouldn't the greedy jerk be back to spill the details and get more money, rather than simply fade into the woodwork? Besides, it's not Hamas style to let something like this pass unnoticed. They'd want to exploit their control over the preeminent Dr. Roarke by showing video footage." He lowered his voice. "Think like they would think," he instructed. "Wouldn't they at least show her body if she were dead, to tell the world that they have the upper hand? As a warning to others? As a further declaration of war?"

Ridge sank into a chair, realizing that he became more exhausted by the hour. He looked at Steve with hope. "You really think she's alive?"

"Oh yeah, she's alive."

"Let's shoot that report."

Ridge's phone rang off the hook for the four hours after the footage aired that evening. People called from all over the world — experts on terrorism, government officials, resourceful viewers who called to extend their well wishes. Much later, Ridge gave into a fitful, dream-laden sleep.

He awoke in the early dark hours of morning to a sound in his room. Sitting upright, he listened carefully, the blood pulsating in his ears. Another creak to his right. Close. He whirled his head, but stopped as he felt the cold flint of a knife blade at his throat.

"You warned her," Shehab growled.

Ridge swallowed hard. "I did not."

The knife pressed harder. "You would have warned her if you could."

"I told you as much," Ridge said through gritted teeth. "I love the woman."

"Fool!" Shehab growled, pressing harder. Finally, he eased the knife away and stalked over to the desk at the window. He turned and watched Ridge warily.

Ridge briefly closed his eyes, then rose from the bed and turned on his bedside light.

Shehab whirled, revealing a black eye and a broken nose. He rushed over to the bed and pulled the plug from the outlet.

Ridge waited, dead still.

"No lights," Shehab growled. "I am not to be seen."

"You are not to be seen? Or you don't *want* to be seen with that shiner? Where'd you get it?"

"No questions!" Shehab cried. "I have come here to find the woman. Where have you hidden her?"

"I told you, I would have warned her, but she was taken before I reached her."

"You saw this?"

"I…. Wait a minute." Ridge could hardly believe what he was hearing. "Are you saying somebody else nabbed her? It wasn't the Hamas?"

Shehab paced silently.

"Then who has her?"

Shehab sighed. "It is of little consequence to me. Perhaps the Kahane jackals have hidden her away. As long as she is far away from the Haram, I am satisfied."

"She is not involved with the Kahane," Ridge insisted.

Shehab snorted. "Impossible. You think they would ignore such an opportunity? Even if she is not overtly involved, one of her team is." He strode to the door, a dark

171

shadow in the dawn light. "If you have lied to me, I will be back. And the knife will not remain clean."

April 23

Alexsana drank the strong brew, thankful for the caffeine jolt and hoping that the coffee would help clear her senses. Four days after having been drugged, she still suffered from the effects. As the women left with her lunch dishes, she moved to the living room window. Outside was a huge Bedouin tent, traditionally used by the wealthy for entertaining, despite the modern amenities available indoors.

She sighed heavily. She could be at any one of hundreds of encampments located across several deserts. If only she could get outside, she might be able to recognize some landmarks.

"Looking for an escape route?" a deep voice asked her.

She whirled. "Khalil! I have so —"

He walked toward her. "You are beautiful in the dress of my Bedouin friends. Very enticing."

"Khalil." Alexsana pulled away her veil in an effort to make him focus. "I appreciate that you've tried to protect me, but I must get home."

"Impossible. If you are seen by a member of the Hamas, you will be killed."

Alexsana kept her gaze level, testing him. "Rescind your order."

A pained expression crossed Khalil's face. "I did not order your death warrant. I have told you. I can no longer control the various factions within our group in this matter. There is too much being accomplished for me to risk my station.

Simply trying would make many of my men question my wisdom and authority."

"Yet four of them agreed to come and collect me," Alexsana accused.

"There are some devout believers who trust me beyond the scope of others," he admitted. "They have no idea what I plan to do with you now."

"If you can convince them that you have your reasons, then you can convince others," she tried.

"No, Alexsana," Khalil said, regretful. "I cannot. If I had seen any other way in the first place...."

"Khalil, please. I can't stay here forever!"

"No. Just a few months."

"A few months! You must be joking! I have an excavation to lead!"

Khalil grabbed her arms, digging his strong fingers into her tender flesh. "You must give it up! Do you not see? It is your only chance!"

Alexsana struggled under his grip. "It is my only chance to prove, once and for all, that I am not a pawn to either side. I must show that I am a professional archaeologist who simply wants to excavate a site. I will make it stronger, Khalil. I *will*. The Haram will be safer when I'm done."

Khalil released her and walked away, shaking his head. "I might be able to believe you. But there are too many who are ready to fight at a moment's notice. Hysteria and mob mentality already run rampant in Palestine. You do not think this will be a spark to dry weeds?"

Alexsana rubbed her arms, realizing that he had not meant to hurt her, but feeling angry anyway. She swallowed hard. "Perhaps if I delay the dig a while...."

"You must cancel the dig and stay out of sight. In a while, tensions will ease. You may be able to live in Jerusalem again. But not now. You must stay hidden. If you refuse to do this for yourself, *I* will keep you safe."

"You have no right!" Alexsana protested. "I am a grown woman! This is kidnapping!"

He reached out to touch her cheek. "It is an effort to keep you alive."

She slapped his hand away. "No. No more, Khalil. I must make my own choices," she said. "I appreciate what you've done. You probably even saved my life. But I need to take care of myself now. There are others who need to know that I am okay."

"Like Ridge McIntyre?"

Her eyes flew to his face, and Khalil closed his own in silent defeat. He turned away. "You are in love."

"Yes," Alexsana admitted softly. "Have you spoken to him?"

Khalil nodded. "He called this morning. He obviously knew that Hamas had not abducted you. He wondered if I knew who had."

"And you said?"

"I told him that it was not Hamas. How could I know who had done such a thing?"

"You couldn't have hinted that I was alive?"

"It is imperative that no one — especially a CNN journalist — know that I am hiding you, nor that I know that you are alive."

Alexsana turned to the window, tired of arguing. "I cannot, I will not stay here, Khalil."

"You are a hundred miles from civilization, Alexsana," he

broke the news quietly. "To run would be to sign your own death certificate." He left the room without another word.

Following Steve's directions, Sam found Ridge in a corner of the Church of All Nations, staring at the ceiling. The reporter looked wrung out, exhausted, echoing the image Sam had seen in his own mirror that morning.

Sam slid to the floor beside Ridge. "We're doing all we can," he assured him.

Ridge turned to him. His eyes were sad. "Shouldn't I be comforting you?"

Sam shrugged. "I guess I've known Alexsana longer than you. She's strong, Ridge. Stronger than most women I know. And she's alive. I'd know it somehow if she were dead."

Ridge looked unconvinced. "I've seen people disappear in Guatemala, Peru, Liberia, Pakistan, Lebanon. People who never come back. I've seen their families try to grieve and get over it, but they never really do because they don't have a body to bury and say good-bye to."

"Ridge. You can't let yourself think that way. I can't let myself think that way."

"I'm sorry," he said helplessly. "I shouldn't be saying such things to you. You're her brother; you have your own issues to deal with."

"Not as many as the man who has fallen in love with her."

Ridge looked at him sharply. He hadn't been in love since his freshman year at college. There had been too many places to go, too many women to date, too much of the world to see for him to settle down.

Letting himself finally explore the concept of love again

had been a monumental risk. He'd attributed his ability to try to God. But had God led him down this path just to crush his heart?

He looked back up to the ceiling, studying the contours of each dome. "I guess I am in love. All I can see is her face. All I want to hear is her voice. All I want to do is hold her —" his voice broke, and tears sprang to his eyes. He felt humiliated by his unaccustomed lack of control. "I'm sorry...."

Sam placed his arm around Ridge's shoulders in a brotherly fashion, feeling the journalist's body shudder as he gave way to silent weeping. "Don't be. I know how you feel." They sat for several minutes, sharing the silence and the memory of standing together with Alexsana in that same sanctuary just weeks before.

"I can see her, almost feel her here," Ridge said.

"That's because God is present, and he's with her, too," Sam said confidently. "He'll keep her safe."

Eighteen

April 26

Within a week of her arrival, Alexsana had persuaded her Bedouin hosts to let her get out, stretch her legs, and help shepherd the large flock of sheep and goats down from the hills each night. She reveled in the opportunity to get out, and worked on perfecting her plan to get away. Khalil's friends meant her no harm. They sincerely believed her life was in danger and that they were helping to keep her alive. But she had to get back to Jerusalem. To check on the status of the dig — now hopelessly behind schedule — her team, and Ridge. If she were in danger, Alexsana feared that the rest might be in peril, too.

She climbed higher, reaching up to pull herself onto a large boulder in spite of her troublesome long skirts. There. Beyond the hill was a highway that led north, most likely toward Tel Aviv or Jerusalem. Alexsana turned and hurried down the slope toward the shepherd boy.

In a few days, she decided, *I'll gather some supplies and begin my journey home.*

Sam watched his father pace the floor in front of his living room couch.

"I tell you, boy, I've gone to every man I have ever spoken to, and none of them could tell me a thing! Imagine living in a country where no one of political influence can tell you what his men have been up to. Somebody took my girl, and I'm bloody well going to find out who did it."

"But, Pop," Sam reminded him, "you just said you've gone to everyone you know."

"I'll go to them all again! And a few I don't know! I'll bother them so much, they'll beat the bushes and find out the truth just to get me out of their hair."

"Pop," Sam protested weakly. "Sit down before you work yourself into a heart attack. Tell me who you've gone to so we can compare notes and make a concerted effort on this next round."

Still muttering to himself, Samuel sat down beside his son and took an agitated sip of coffee.

Speaking in a quiet, soothing voice, Sam compared notes with his exhausted father.

Lydia came out of the kitchen, carrying a tray of fresh coffee. She sat beside the professor and patted his back as he shook his head at his son's words. "No, Sam. I don't think you should go to Khalil."

"It's the only thing that makes sense. Ridge called him, but Khalil may share with an old school chum what he might never tell a journalist."

"Your school days are far gone, son. Khalil is a powerful and dangerous man. I've been told that certain members of the Hamas were out to kill Alexsana. He probably issued the order himself," he said bitterly.

Sam looked doubtful. "I can't believe that. Khalil might kidnap her, but he could never have issued an order for her death. We were like family!"

But Sam remembered his words to his sister, uttered on the beach at Caeasarea Maritima. He'd issued his own warnings about Khalil, shared his own fears regarding her denial of what the man had become: a general in an abhorred, unidentified army. Leader of the Hamas.

He raised his hands to his father in surrender as Samuel's face reddened. "I know. He's not family anymore. But he might possibly be the only link to Alexsana we have left."

On a temporary leave of absence while he searched for Alexsana, Ridge was only too happy to drive Sam to Khalil's hideout. If it helped in finding Alexsana, he was willing to do anything.

Khalil was not happy to see them. He whirled in his robes, his face betraying his emotions. "You dare to bring someone here — you dare to come yourself — unannounced? I could have you both shot!"

"Khalil —" Sam began.

"Quiet!"

Sam frowned. He knew Khalil no longer considered him a brother, but why was the man so furious? Simply because Ridge had exposed his hideout to another? No, there was more to his anger, Sam was sure of it.

"Because of you, I will need to relocate," Khalil fumed. "You were to come here only if I summoned you. Who knows who might have followed you."

"I'm sorry," Ridge began. "It's just that we're still searching for Alexsana...."

"I told you on the phone when I was informed you wished to speak with me," he said, turning from them. "I do not know where she is."

But Sam remembered a time when they had been exploring Hezekiah's tunnel and were caught. Khalil had lied to cover their actions. His tone now was the same as it had been then.

"Ridge, please. Take a breather, will you? I need to talk to Khalil alone."

"No!" Khalil turned on them. "Both of you! I want you both out!"

"Khalil," Sam tried, "if you ever valued our friendship, give me five minutes. If I don't get what I want in those five minutes, I'll walk out of here and never return."

A pained expression crossed Khalil's face. "Very well," the man said wearily. "But he goes," he said, pointing to Ridge.

Ridge eased out of the tent, knowing that Sam was very close to discovering the truth.

As the gray goat skin flapped down behind Ridge's back, Sam rose and walked toward Khalil. "Please. As the brother I once had, answer me. We've been told that the Hamas is out to kill her. Is she dead?"

Khalil studied him again, pain clearly visible on his handsome features. "No, Samuel. She is not dead."

Sam looked at the ground, shaking his blond head. "Thank you. I knew she could not be dead. I would have known it if she were."

"You two were always kindred spirits," Khalil said, sitting down on the luxurious cushions. He sighed. "Sit. Sit, my old friend."

Sam did as he was bidden. "Please, is there anything more you can tell me?"

"If you give me your word it will not be on CNN."

"Done. Ridge would promise anything to know. You have my word."

Khalil paused, considering his friend. He spoke at last. "She is safe. I did not issue an order to kill her. But there are others who will act without my direction. Too many of my men knew of your visit to the Haram and the impending dig." He gave Sam an accusatory look. "In order to head off a potential murder of a woman I once loved, I sent four trustworthy friends to collect her —"

"— outside Dung Gate," Sam finished for him.

"Yes."

"Where is she now?"

"In safekeeping."

"That's not enough, Khalil!" Sam protested. "We want her! We can protect her!"

"Nonsense. Who can protect the woman better than I? I am the one who sees both sides."

Samuel sighed. "You know you can't hide her forever. And when she comes back, she'll come out swinging. There's no way you'll keep her from the Haram; you know that. And I can't keep her from it either."

"You must," Khalil insisted fiercely. "I am giving her time to calm down, come to her senses, walk away. If I release her and she ignores the warnings of those who feel she is a pawn to the Kahane, I can do nothing more."

"Tell them the truth, Khalil. I'm in this project with her. There's no one involved in a plot to bring down the Haram. I swear it!"

Khalil exhaled in exasperation and rose. "You have lived

in this land too long to be so naive," he said derisively.

Sam rose too, fighting to control his anger. "I swear it. She's honestly going to make the Haram's foundation stronger."

"And when neither of you are looking, a Kahane or Mossad agent will slip in and place a plastic bomb in a crook here or a crevice there."

"No!" Sam would not accept it.

Khalil strode forward stopping inches from his face. "How can you stand there and deny it? You know how things work here! You cannot have eyes in the back of your head!" He turned away. "It is not you, nor is it Alexsana I mistrust. It is the doors you are opening. But the men of the Hamas do not know you as I do. There are too many who believe that *you* are Jewish spies."

Sam sat down, feeling beaten. "Then what are we going to do? You can't hold her forever. Deep down, you know she won't turn away from this opportunity when she gets free. I can't stop her, either. If Alexsana has the go-ahead from both Eban and al Azeh, she'll move forward with or without me."

Khalil turned, and looked at Sam with a piercing gaze. "Then you had better remain very close to her. If she excavates, does indeed strengthen the foundation, and exits the Haram without causing damage, she'll win many Palestinian friends — even in the Hamas and Jihad. But emotions are running too high. I am afraid she will not survive the dig itself. Do you understand me, Samuel?"

Sam stared back at him for several seconds, his mouth set in a grim line. "I understand." He cast about for a point on which to pin his hopes. "Maybe your boys will forget about her," he tried hopefully.

Khalil looked grim. "It is not likely."

Nineteen

❧

So you're telling me that the leader of the Hamas has spirited away your sister — actually has her hidden somewhere without his followers' knowledge — and I can't say a word to the world?"

"Not if you want her to live. There are many in the Hamas who would perceive Khalil's action as traitorous and torture him until he revealed her location."

"You and I both know he would die before he told," Ridge argued.

Agitated, Sam took a corner too fast, throwing both men to the edge of their seats.

"Look out!" Ridge yelled. "Getting us killed won't help your sister!"

Sam screeched to a stop and pulled over on the narrow shoulder of the highway.

"Look, do you think this is a good place to stop —"

"Ridge!" Sam interrupted. "Stop. Don't you see? I know this is an incredible scoop for a reporter, but you're more in love with my sister than Khalil ever was! Think about her safety! Do you have a choice?"

Ridge stared at the dashboard. "I am thinking about her safety," he said slowly. "Without pressure from U.S. officials, triggered by media attention, she might never be found. Without U.S. pressure, she might not survive another night in Jerusalem once she *is* found."

"You don't know Alexsana well enough yet," Sam argued. "You can be sure she'll escape wherever Khalil has hidden her. And she'll be knocking on my door the next day, asking if the team is ready. My sister is the most determined woman I know."

Ridge sighed. "We've gotta stop her."

"We can try, but I really don't think we can succeed."

"Then we'll have to protect her from herself," Ridge began. "Maybe Khalil's right. If the only way to keep her safe is to hide her away someplace —"

"If she comes back — make that *when* she comes back — you can do your story. Wait for God's timing, Ridge. Listen to his voice, not to your own fear. If you do so, you endanger Khalil's position of authority and, consequently, her safety. If they figure out Khalil was behind the kidnapping, they might go after all his friends, looking for her. Right now, she's out of sight and, hopefully, out of mind."

"And when she comes back?" Ridge asked.

"We'll have to keep her whereabouts hyper-secret. Maybe Khalil will find a way to deal with the assassins by then." Sam's voice held little hope.

"So what you're telling me is that there is little or no chance that I'll ever get to broadcast this story," Ridge said.

"Not unless we all survive and make it to the end. Then

you can fill the world in on the juiciest saga to hit the Old City in years."

May 2

Alexsana felt badly about ditching the sweet young shepherd boy, but she saw no other alternative. Khalil had not been back for a week. Few visitors came to his friend's home. Freedom was up to her to claim.

She crossed the rocks and climbed down the side of the hill, making her way toward the highway, which she judged to be about half a mile distant. Alexsana reached the pavement just as the sun set and breathed a sigh of relief. She paused and drew out the bottle of water which she'd strapped to her leg beneath her skirts, and drank deeply, sweating beneath the heavy clothing. Even in the cooling darkness, the temperature still hovered at around sixty degrees.

Alexsana looked each way, wondering how often traffic passed. Banking on the fact that she was in the Negev Desert and that Jerusalem was due north, she began to walk, praying that her hosts — or captors — would not come after her before she obtained a ride. She frowned and rubbed in irritation at the silver coins that stuck to her damp forehead.

She frowned as a Palestinian farmer passed her, then pulled over three hundred yards distant, apparently waiting. Middle Eastern women were not often seen traveling alone. She had banked on the Bedouin tradition of "taking care of their own" in getting a ride. Still, pulling off the hoax would take some work.

As she approached the decrepit old truck, Alexsana kept her head down, averting her eyes to avoid discovery. She moved to the passenger door, not daring to look in the vehicle, and awaited the driver's greeting.

"Woman, what causes you to be on the road at this hour?" the man said, his voice full of reproach. Few respectable women would be found in such circumstances.

"I have lost my husband to illness," she mumbled, hoping to hide any trace of an accent in her Arabic. "My son is ill, and I hope to find relatives in Jerusalem who will help me."

She waited, holding her breath. The seconds crawled past as he studied her, thinking.

"You are not a woman of ill repute?" he asked suspiciously.

"No! By Allah I am not!"

"Get in," he groused.

Alexsana started to open the door, but his angry voice startled her, interrupting her action.

"In back, woman. I do not know you and will not be seen with you beside me."

She nodded humbly, walked quickly to the back, and climbed up through the open tailgate. Alexsana bit her lip and tried to avoid animal excrement as she looked for a clean place to sit. The truck lurched forward.

Sighing, she collapsed into a relatively clean spot of hay, staring back at a goat who observed her dolefully. He chewed his cud and looked away as the truck picked up speed.

"Well," she whispered to her hairy companion, "I guess we're on our way."

The truck approached Jerusalem late that night. The city walls were lit by the reddish glow of lanterns, giving it a foreboding, impressive look. "Drat," Alexsana muttered, wondering how she would maneuver through the city without being apprehended by Israeli patrols. It was late for a Bedouin to be out, and she had no identification.

The driver stopped outside the Damascus Gate. "Get out," he yelled back at her.

Alexsana jumped down, and her heart pounded as the man drove away. "Okay, God," she murmured. "It's just you and me." She approached the gate with purpose, walking as if she had nothing on her mind but thoughts of getting home.

Keeping her head down, she walked through, incredulous when the card-playing guards neglected to demand her I.D. She had just dared to take a breath, silently thanking God that he had apparently covered her with an invisible shield, when one man barked after her in Hebrew.

"Wait a minute! Get back here. You know we need to see I.D. after sunset." He turned back to his cards smugly, wearing an expression of utter power.

Alexsana kept walking, pretending that she had not heard. She gauged the distance to the nearest corner. If she could gain another few yards before they realized she was making a run for it, she might have a lead that would save her from being shot.

"Hey!" the guard yelled casually, still distracted by his card game. He looked over his shoulder after playing his card and repeated his command in Arabic. Playing another card, he muttered an epithet against Bedouins. He finally rose as he realized the woman had not stopped or returned.

His companion cursed softly. There would be trouble with the sergeant if news of this got out. What if the woman were wearing a bomb? Certainly, she was up to no good.

The first guard set out after her while the second radioed for backup. She turned the corner just as he raised his gun and yelled another warning.

Alexsana gathered her skirts in her arms and ran hard, turning first one corner, then the next, until she had reached a familiar, old Muslim alleyway. She stopped in a small alcove, panting and praying that she had lost the young soldier. When she had caught her breath, she crossed the narrow alleyway and, drawing on childhood memory, jumped and caught the crossbeam of a sturdy overhang. She swung to gain momentum then, at the height of her arc, released her grip and landed atop the broad, cloth overhang like a circus gymnast.

She lay there, fighting off an insane urge to giggle, but remaining deadly still as the guard ran past three feet below her. He stopped at the corner and swore while Alexsana prayed that the old canvas would not give way.

After what seemed like an eternity, the guard removed the radio from his belt loop and made a connection with his companion at the gate. "She is harmless. I let her go," he lied, then left the alley, muttering.

Alexsana listened as his footsteps faded into the dark night. "Thank you, Father," she whispered, looking up into the starry Jerusalem sky. Then she clambered onto the rooftop and made her way toward Lydia's house.

Reaching the Nusseibahs' building, Alexsana took a deep breath and dropped to the wrought iron balcony below.

She knew she would find Lydia at her parents' home. The

woman had made peace with her father after threatening to move out and live with Alexsana. Seeing her determination, her father had allowed an uneasy cease-fire to take place, buying time as he tried to figure out another way to dissuade his daughter.

But in his heart, Jacob knew he would not succeed. And in his mind he acknowledged that if Lydia had to marry an American, there could be no better than Samuel Roarke, Jr. This is what Lydia and Sam had surmised. Jacob Nusseibah was not the type to abide by lengthy conversations, particularly when regarding his daughter's future. But by allowing her to continue living in his house, he communicated his grudging consent.

Alexsana eased open the door and slipped into Lydia's bedroom. Her friend sat up, alarmed. Alexsana smiled and hushed her, saying, "Lydia, it is me! Back from the dead!"

"Alexsana!" Lydia leaped up and pulled her friend into a quick embrace. She drew back, switched on a lamp, and looked her over. "You are very beautiful as a Bedouin woman. How did you get here unnoticed?"

"I drew some attention," Alexsana admitted. "But I got here easily enough over the rooftops. It was like old times! Suddenly I was twelve years old and sneaking over to spend the night with you."

"You are blessed that they did not stop you. After the bus attacks, security has become tighter and tighter. I do not know how much longer we can endure this 'peace process.' But enough. Where have you been? Samuel went to see Khalil. He told your brother that you were safe, but he would not tell him where you were."

"And Sam let it go at that?"

Lydia glanced guiltily away. "He took comfort in the fact that Khalil was sure to place you somewhere safe. Your absence from the City also gave the Hamas time to cool off and Khalil time to gain better control of his men."

"Did Ridge know?" she asked quietly.

"Yes, he went with Samuel to see Khalil. They did not know where you were. Khalil would not tell them," Lydia said.

"Khalil can be so stubborn," Alexsana admitted grudgingly.

"Yes. Are you all right? Were you treated well?"

"I'm fine, fine," Alexsana said, dismissing her friend's concern. "They'll see they can't stop us. We are going to move on the Solomon's Stable dig. Unless we've been delayed again."

"I haven't heard anything like that from Samuel. But is it wise —"

"Good," Alexsana said quickly. "Let's get some sleep. I'll need your assistance tomorrow."

Twenty

May 3

Alexsana made her way to the Lutheran Church of the Redeemer, quietly requested access to the bell tower, then raced to the top. There, Ridge waited for her as Lydia had instructed him. He paused at the sight of her in Bedouin costume, then quickly moved to take her in his arms.

"Ridge —" she began.

"Shh," he silenced her. "Let me just hold you for a minute. I was so afraid that you were gone forever." He pulled back, holding her away from his body so he could see her, searching her face. His gaze was intense. "I couldn't find you. I tried. You know that, right?"

"I know," she said softly, moving closer to him again.

Ridge kissed her hair and said, "I ran all the way here this morning after Lydia told me where you'd be."

She backed up again to study him. Dark circles ringed his eyes. He appeared to have lost several pounds. "Oh, Ridge, I'm sorry." She embraced him again. "I know it must've been as tough for you as it was for me."

"I'm sorry I couldn't find you. I really am. But maybe it was for the best."

"For the best!" She looked incredulous. "How do you figure that?"

He cradled her cheek in his hand. "It was for the best because I finally figured out something very important. I realized that I'm head over heels...totally, completely. Alexsana Roarke, I'm in love with you."

Excitement flooded through Alexsana, and she gazed at him in wonder. "I must confess, I doubted I'd ever hear those words from you."

"Why is that?" Ridge sounded only slightly surprised.

"I just didn't think the News Junkie Stud of the Year would ever commit to one woman," she said with an impish grin as she played with his shirt collar.

"I think I knew it when I saw you in Khalil's tent that first afternoon. I wondered what an American woman was doing there, and I admired how you handled yourself with him. You had obviously snubbed Khalil — the head of the Hamas — just before I entered. I thought, 'Now there's a woman with gumption. That's the kind of woman I want to find.' You haven't proven me wrong."

Alexsana smiled broadly and hugged him. "I've been so afraid to give in to my feelings for you," she admitted.

He pulled away. "Say it, Alexsana. I want to hear those words, if you're ready to say them."

She smiled again, feeling uncustomarily shy in the face of his need for her love. "I love you, Ridge McIntyre."

A broad smile spread across his face. "Enough to be my companion for life?"

Alexsana drew in a long, slow breath. "Is that a proposal?"

"Yes. It is."

Alexsana studied him carefully. "We've only known one another for a few months. You're really ready to settle down with one woman for the rest of your life? Because I could never handle it if you had an affair. I want you, and only you, Ridge. Can you say the same thing about me?"

"I'm sure, Alexsana. Maybe I once had a reputation as a ladies' man, but now I want you, and only you, for the rest of my life. I want to marry you and never let you out of my sight again."

Alexsana frowned and pulled gently away. "I wish you hadn't said that."

Pain and confusion crossed Ridge's face. "Are you saying you don't want to marry me?"

Alexsana turned to him, her blue eyes wet with tears. A lump formed in her throat as emotions flooded her heart. She swallowed hard, trying not to let her voice tremble. "Oh, Ridge, I do. But what do you mean when you say things like you're never going to let me out of your sight again? That's impossible. I love my work. I'm going to go on digs across Israel and beyond. Your work will take you around the world. Is it even possible for us to be together?"

"Of course it is! We may have to make some concessions," he admitted. "Give up an assignment here and there to be together. But won't it be worth it?"

Her eyebrows arched into a question. "Give up an assignment? Are you speaking for you or for me?" she asked suspiciously.

"For both of us!"

"For instance...."

"For instance, this Solomon's Stable dig."

"Oh, no," she mumbled in frustration. "I thought that's where you were leading. I'm not giving it up, Ridge. I'm not. No one is going to bully me out of it. Not the Hamas, and not you. It's a chance of a lifetime." Even as she spoke, Christina Alvarez's words came to mind: "...*work would never come between us; our marriage would be priority over everything else.*"

Alexsana pushed away the unwanted memory and turned to face Ridge. "You're as bad as Khalil! He wanted to marry me to keep me out of trouble, and now you're trying to do the same thing!"

"No, Alexsana. I'm not —"

"You are!" she protested, almost in tears. "I want this, Ridge! I want it as badly as you wanted to be awarded the Middle East news region! Can't you understand? You risk your life — practically every day — to pursue your dream. Most often, I don't have to take such risks. But this time, I do. It's just as important."

"But, Alexsana," he argued desperately, "there are a lot of men in the Hamas who want to kill you."

"Enough! I don't interfere in your work, Ridge. Stay out of mine." Alexsana turned away, not wanting him to see how sick their argument made her.

"Fine," he sighed in resignation. "I'll leave you to your work. I had better check with my office, anyway. I guess there's no reason for me to stay on leave anymore."

Alexsana glanced at him as he turned to go. "Ridge, I —"

He stopped her. "I think we've said enough for one day, Alexsana. Your brother should be here any minute. I'll leave you to discuss your excavation plans, and I'll pray that you get in and out of the Haram alive." He hurriedly exited the tower. Alexsana stood still and watched him leave, stoically holding back her tears. She swallowed hard, ignoring the lump in her throat, and resolutely awaited her brother.

Twenty-One

May 4

S am did an excellent job of notifying the entire team, and by the next afternoon, Alexsana found herself addressing them in the library of the École Biblique. The Bedouin costume was a helpful disguise, so she continued to wear the clothing which Lydia had washed and dried. She had told Lydia the whole, messy Ridge story the previous evening through her tears.

Alexsana's eyes were swollen, but clear, as she excitedly discussed excavation plans with the team. The group Sam had assembled was a skeleton crew; because of the death threats, Alexsana was hesitant to include more members of the team.

Rivca Weingarten, the team photographer, sat to her immediate right. Beyond her stood Helene Yefet and Sari Nasan, the "pottery readers" who would collect, sift through, and catalog any pieces of significance. Area supervisors Sam and Abu Khadim, both world-renowned for their experience, would watch over and direct the progress of the dig. Professor O'Malley served as an advisor. Old friends and experienced excavators Moshe Barazani and Haidar Iban would assist Sam and Abu Khadim in directing the fifty or more day laborers who would be doing the bulk of the work.

The last two people present were construction engineers Abraham Lott and Kamal Khalidi. These two men would be responsible for excavating the massive stone and rebuilding the Haram's infrastructure. Team members had been chosen carefully to equally represent both Jew and Muslim factions.

Alexsana stood and leaned over the table, resting her hands on the solid mahogany structure. She nervously felt along the scratches carved by students over a period of two hundred years. "Okay, ladies and gentlemen," she said, looking around the group. "I'm hoping we can finally begin this project. I think we have the political pull and financing set up to begin next week. With the peace process faltering, I'd like to treat this as a salvage dig; I want us all to think 'fast and furious' when it comes to the Stables."

She rose and circled the group like an excited professor lecturing on her favorite subject. "Now, although this will be a salvage dig, it is imperative that we not allow our work to compromise the Haram. We will excavate, create temporary reinforcing, excavate some more, then build in cement support piers. We will concentrate primarily on the area around the Double and Triple Gates. We plan to leave the Temple Mount stronger than when we began. I want us to be in and out within two months."

One of the construction engineers laughed in surprise, then quickly quieted when he saw the determination on her face.

"Abe, you have a problem with that plan?"

Abraham Lott sat back and took up his own defense. "I want to see this happen as much as anyone else. But you plan to excavate a space that measures approximately 2500 square feet. Plus we're talking about digging through nearly four stories of rock to get down to it. How can we get in, give you archaeologists time to study each level as needed, and get out in two months' time?"

Alexsana nodded, acknowledging his concern. "I know it's a lot to ask. But we have little choice. You must realize that we're in the center of a political hot spot. A Muslim uprising is bound to happen. No doubt, you've noticed my wardrobe choice these days..." Alexsana smiled ruefully as she indicated her flowing black robes and headdress. "My life has been threatened. Yours probably will be, too. You'll each need to examine your desires and priorities and decide for yourselves how important this is to you. I can't be responsible for your lives. It has to be your choice to work on this dig.

"What you stand to gain is incredible experience working on a site no one ever dreamed would be accessible. The trick is, our window of opportunity is closing. If we are to get down to the stairs that Jesus Christ walked and see if there's anything else of significance below, we need to do it quickly. You all know the political temperature is rising around here. I'm afraid they'll decide peace in Israel is a pipe dream at best and shut down this dig before it starts. We have no choice but to move fast, before we're shut out forever."

"But what if in our haste we miss something pertinent? What if we blast right through exactly what we seek?" Haidar asked.

"That's where our two construction engineers come in,"

Alexsana assured him. "We know that the stairs beyond the Triple Gate were partially filled in with rock and mortar after the Crusaders left. Judging from the exposed steps, we can approximate the depth of the remaining stairs and quickly dispose of the filler material.

"If you remember from our notes, excavating east of the Triple Gate would be a waste of time. The Crusaders used it as a quarry during construction and it's not likely that we'll find anything of importance there. So we'll move down and west, watching for the original arches — which we can, again, approximate in distance — speeding up our excavation process.

"Our pottery experts here," she gestured toward Helene and Sari, "will not be examining every shard we remove. They'll be sifting through the removed rock, checking to make sure we're not missing anything big. The rest of the rock will be placed directly outside the El Aksa Mosque; we can sift through it later. We're racing toward the original structures first; we'll examine the filler material at a later date."

Alexsana gazed around at the excited, nervous members of her team. "I know this method is highly unorthodox and somewhat antiquated. But you all must understand: this is our only chance at a site that might be closed again for a hundred, two hundred years, or more. Maybe forever."

The group nodded collectively and she looked at her construction engineers. "Abe and Kamal can tell you how we're going to go about it." She sat down and listened as the two men explained to the group how they would enter the Haram on the southeastern end, making a hole in the floor big enough to allow two miniature bulldozers and a small crane to enter and exit with ease.

"Is there any other way we could enter without being so exposed?" Sam asked. "That's practically the worst place on the whole Haram. With us so close to the mosque, every Hamas and Jihad member in the country will want to take potshots at us as they leave worship."

"That's true," Alexsana said. "Yet if we go in from the southern side, we'll have less control in knocking out walls. We could wipe out something vital, and be all the *more* exposed. We'll just have to depend on the security teams to make sure no one enters the Haram with a weapon."

"Far fewer people will get near us there than outside," Abu said, "And we won't be throwing salt on an open wound by tearing open the Haram's outer wall."

Alexsana nodded. "In the end, it might be much cleaner to go in from the top and use a crane to lower the equipment. Should we proceed on this track?"

Everyone nodded. "Excellent," she smiled confidently. "I'll leave you to figure out the logistical details while I secure final financing and get the nod from the powers that be. We'll need security forces, and that will take some finagling. I'll plan to meet all of you on the Haram in three days' time. 7:00 A.M., sharp. Security passes will be sent to you by messenger. If any of you feel that you must drop out because of the obvious risks, please notify me immediately." She smiled at each one. "Shalom and marahaba, my friends."

"You're not going alone, Sana," Sam began.

She turned to him with a pointed stare. "Yes, I am. The world will shortly know what we intend, and who's in charge. My disguise might throw them off for a while, but I cannot hide forever."

Across the Nablus Road from the École Biblique, atop a two-story building, Shehab and four of his men waited for Samuel Roarke and the others to exit. Intelligence reports told them that the team was proceeding with the dig, with or without Alexsana. It did not add up for Shehab; Alexsana had been carefully chosen to lead the dig. To hand it over to her brother — who had experience, but not as much as his sister — would require at least one meeting between Abba Eban and Abdallah al Azeh. Yet the two had not been seen together.

Shehab frowned as the Bedouin woman who had entered the École Biblique compound that morning emerged. He made a low sound in his throat and nodded, indicating that two of his men should follow her. Maybe the woman knew something, perhaps even the whereabouts of Alexsana Roarke.

Alexsana kept her head down as she made her way through the Damascus Gate and back into the Old City. She dared not look around, for fear of discovery. Although her blond hair was covered, her light skin might have given her away in the bright daylight. Remembering the veil, she drew the cloth across her mouth and cheeks, leaving only her eyes exposed. She then buried her pale hands in the folds of her skirts and walked quickly by two men who casually watched her.

Don't think you're going to pick up a new girlfriend, buckos, she thought. Her mind turned to a more intriguing man, Ridge. Would he ever forgive her? She berated herself for the way she'd handled the situation. Her chest felt tight as she thought about the conflicting desires of her heart: Ridge and Solomon's Stables. *Why must I choose, Lord? I don't feel you leading me to one over the other. Where are you?*

She turned the corner, lost in thought, and bumped directly into the chest of a very large man. He grabbed her by the shoulders. Alexsana glanced up, then, catching herself, back down. But he had already caught sight of her bright blue eyes, wide with surprise. Grinning with the excitement of discovery, he pulled away her veil and roughly turned her around so that his companion could get a good look.

"Recognize this one?" he asked his companion in Arabic.

The man grinned, looking her over. "Shehab will be pleased. Bring her."

Alexsana acted on instinct. She quickly threw a knee to the second man's groin, doubling him over, then brought her heel down on her abductor's toes. Both backed off momentarily. Alexsana never paused.

Running furiously, she first turned one corner and then another, heading directly to the suk. Disappearing into the crowd was her only chance, yet there was little time to blend in. Her pursuers could not be far behind. Alexsana chose a nearby dress shop, and, with a few hurried words and a few well-placed shekels, gained amnesty in the makeshift dressing room for five minutes. She grabbed two dresses on the way in, throwing one over the curtained door to make it look as if she were changing. No respectable Muslim man would give the door more than a glance.

She backed into the far corner, praying that they would not even enter the store. An urge to giggle washed over

Alexsana. She thought about her pursuers madly rummaging through women's clothing, looking for her.

Incredibly, no hand came to rip the curtain aside and drag her, screaming, into the street.

Alexsana left the store after purchasing a new headdress and veil, leaving the old clothing behind. Feeling safer on the rooftops than the streets, she climbed the stairs at the corner and made her way to Lydia's house.

Twenty-Two

May 5

Just before dawn, Alexsana and Lydia awoke to the sound of someone pounding on the front door. Frowning, Alexsana flew out of bed and into her clothes, preparing to flee out the window if necessary. Lydia put her hand out in a calming gesture, indicating that she would find out who dared to awaken the household at that hour. However, before she could act, both women heard Ridge's voice, raised in agitation as he spoke to Lydia's father.

Relief flooded through Alexsana as her heart cried for her to go to him. But in the face of his anger, she stood, frozen.

Lydia went to the top of the stairs. "It is all right, Father. Please, let Mr. McIntyre come up to the drawing room."

Grumbling, Jacob allowed Ridge to race past him and up the stairs.

"Where is she?" Ridge asked Lydia, bypassing any pleasantries.

"I'm here," Alexsana said quietly from Lydia's doorway.

Ridge turned and stared in relief, admiring Alexsana openly. Then he shook his head, as if trying to remember the reason for his abrupt visit.

"Can we talk?" he asked gruffly.

Alexsana's face fell, hope for reconciliation dying in the light of his harsh manner. "Here," she said, indicating a small library to the left of Lydia's bedroom. She steeled herself for what he had to say.

Ridge followed her into the library and frowned as they sat. "I had a visitor this morning," he said abruptly.

Alexsana looked at him, openly curious. "Who?"

"Another contact from the Hamas," Ridge said grimly. "He told me Shehab's men very nearly had you in their hands yesterday. He gloated, saying that Shehab spotted you leave the École Biblique and, on a hunch, had you followed."

"That was his whole scoop?" Alexsana scoffed, sounding more courageous than she felt. "I hope you didn't pay him for such gibberish."

"Alexsana!" Ridge signed in frustration. "Are you telling me that they didn't chase you through the suk? That they didn't nearly grab you?"

"Ridge, I'm sure his story was exaggerated," she hedged.

He shook his head, sighing. "So, it's true. You were almost taken again. And this time you wouldn't have been under Khalil's protection."

"We've been through this," Alexsana tried helplessly. "There is a small faction within the Hamas who want to harm me. But they're not going to! Look at what happened yesterday. They had me in their hands, but I fought them off. I can take care of myself," she said bravely. She fought to make her facial expression match her even tone.

Ridge rose and paced. "Don't be a fool, Alexsana. You're too highly educated and too knowledgeable about the ways of the Middle East to be so naive. No one is invulnerable here. Not even you!"

Alexsana lowered her head and closed her eyes. "All right," she admitted. "I realize that. I do. If it will make you feel better, I won't go anywhere alone, okay?"

Ridge stared out the window, silent. She felt miserable that he was so concerned for her and miserable that they were not together when each was so clearly in love with the other.

"Ridge, I —"

"Save it, Alexsana." He would not even look at her. "You can't convince me that this is a sane decision. That you really have to…" He paused and looked at her as if a divine revelation had just hit him. He came and knelt beside her, his expression softening as he took her hands in his. "What if…. What if I asked you not to do it?"

"Don't ask me, Ridge. Please. Don't make me choose." She looked at him tenderly. "I am in love with you. You know that, don't you? You might be too angry to care about that fact right now, but I still do. If you'll just hang in there, we'll get through this dig. It is undoubtedly the most volatile excavation I've been involved with. But Ridge, don't you see? What if I face all these roadblocks because there's something truly wonderful down there? What if Satan is using these men in the Hamas to keep us from discovering a find that is sure to glorify Jesus?" She stood and paced, realizing that this possibility was what pushed her to pursue the dig, even in the face of danger.

"There might not be anything down there but stairs. But even so, those are stairs that Jesus and the disciples walked. Maybe it will encourage someone, somewhere, to see those simple blocks of stone unearthed. Who knows how God works? You know he speaks to each of us in different ways. This is my chance to really make a difference."

"And make a name for yourself." His tone held none of the venom his words bespoke.

"No, Ridge," Alexsana said gently, refusing to give in to anger. "At first, I admit, I was glad for the opportunity. For a while, this dig will place my name front and center in the archaeology community. But when I was stuck in that Bedouin camp, it became clear to me what I seek.

"My original prayer was for this to glorify my God, not me. I've seen that I can be delayed, kidnapped...possibly even killed. But still those stairs remain, a solid reminder of God's power which withstands the tests of time. I'm still here. I truly believe God wants me to see this through."

Ridge frowned again. "How am I supposed to argue with that? You're telling me this is a divine call? That God spoke to you like he did to me in the Church of All Nations?"

She shook her head. "It wasn't a grand, spiritual realization; it's more like a sure, quiet stream...a pull that tells me that I'm following God's path. Sometimes God speaks in lightning bolts, fast and furious; at other times, his voice is as quiet and steady as a hummingbird's beating wings."

Ridge looked helplessly at her. "You know more about God than I...."

"Please, Ridge," Alexsana said, urging him to rise with her.

He let Alexsana draw him to his feet, then pulled her close. "I'm so afraid, Sana. I don't want to lose you."

"I know. I know." She rested her cheek against his broad chest. "But God is in this with us. He's watching out for us. If he weren't, I don't think I'd be standing here right now. He has a plan for each of our lives. Exploring the Temple Mount may be one of his purposes for me. I can't walk away. Do you understand?"

"I think so." Ridge pulled her away from his chest and held her at arm's length, studying her face as if he wanted to memorize each curve, each dimple, each freckle. "Please, Sana. Promise me you'll take more precautions. You're right: I can't be around to protect you all the time. I'll trust in God to take care of you. But I think he also wants us to use common sense. Try to stay one step ahead of these men; outsmart them. I know you can. You're a wise woman.

"And I'll do my part. I'll finally broadcast my story that you're alive and well and proceeding with the dig. Hopefully, some pressure from the U.S. will help dissuade the radicals who are pursuing you."

Alexsana grinned, realizing that he was reluctantly bestowing a blessing on her project. She wondered if there might be room in his heart for both her and her career, after all. "Thank you, Ridge," she said quietly. "I want you to be careful, too. You're sent to danger zones even more often than I."

"Agreed," he said, smiling at last and pulling her close once again. "And now, may I kiss you? I've been wanting to for days."

"Please do, Mr. McIntyre," Alexsana smiled back at him. "Please do."

Twenty-Three

❧

May 6

Responding to Alexsana's invitation, Ridge made his way to the Temple Mount, feeling as though his feet were cushioned by air. He absently fingered the press passes she had sent via messenger. "If Nike could package this feeling," he thought, "they'd double their profits!" He eagerly anticipated seeing Alexsana. Perhaps they might even have a moment alone. Then, he could ask her to dinner....

"McIntyre!" Steve yelled from the checkpoint where he waited, camera in hand. As he neared, Ridge realized that the security guard would not let Steve in.

"No cameras," the guard said in heavily accented English before Ridge could say a word.

"I am a journalist from CNN," Ridge said in sloppy Arabic. "I have a pass," he said, switching to English. "See my pass? Steve has one too." Both men held their clearance out to the guard. Although he obediently examined them, his expression remained one of determination.

"You may pass. No cameras. Leave here."

"No way, man," Steve said, gesticulating broadly. "This

baby is brand new. It's like a part of my body. I don't go anywhere without it."

The guard shook his head again, unmoved by Steve's dramatics, while Ridge struggled to figure out a way beyond the impasse.

"Ridge!" Alexsana yelled from the top of the ramp that led to the Temple Mount. Then, noticing their dilemma: "Let them by!" she commanded the guard in Arabic. "*And* their equipment. They have been cleared with security passes!"

"No picture of mosques," the guard grumbled. He then stood aside, realizing he had little choice in the matter.

Ridge and Steve hurried past. "Maybe we can film your intro in front of the Dome of the Rock," Steve said under his breath. "You know: give the audience a sense of locale."

"Good idea," Ridge agreed. "Let's see what Alexsana has in store for us, first, though." He smiled at her as they approached.

"She'll have to make it fast," Steve said. "Headquarters called. We need to hit Tel Aviv this afternoon. They want us to interview some American businessmen about the peace process and how it's affected financial matters."

"This afternoon?" A pained expression crossed Ridge's face as visions of taking Sana to the Seven Arches for a celebration dinner turned to mist.

"Yeah. Right away. What's wrong, man?"

"Nothing." Ridge turned and greeted Alexsana with a subtle kiss on the cheek. She smiled into his eyes.

"Hi there. Hi, Steve. I'm waiting on two members of my team. I'm hoping they haven't had second thoughts."

"Can't say I'd blame them. Anyone integral to your ground breaking today?"

"No. One area supervisor and a pottery reader. We have an extra of each of those," she said, grinning. "But we're still a skeleton crew. If they've decided against working on the project, I'll need to replace them." She quickly scanned the Wailing Wall square, hoping to spot her team members. Her radio suddenly crackled to life.

Alexsana grabbed it from her hip. "I'm here, Sam," she said into the receiver, then listened to his voice through the static. "Gotcha. We'll be there in a second. And — Oh! I just saw Sari and Abu Khadim passing the checkpoint. Just a few more minutes, and we're on our way."

After the arrival of her last two team members, Alexsana led the group around the El Aksa Mosque. Two hundred yards beyond it, they stopped at a big, orange fluorescent "X" painted on the two-thousand-year-old stones. Behind them stood a small, top-of-the-line crane, a forklift, and two miniature bulldozers.

Ridge smiled at her. "How did you manage to get that crane up here?"

"I told you," she said brightly, "God is going before me. There's no way I could get one of those up here without attracting a ton of attention. Fortunately, it's been stuck up here for months. It was left after the Dome of the Rock's roof was resurfaced. The owner went bankrupt and the creditors haven't arranged for pickup. It was easy enough to arrange rental time. The forklift and mini-bulldozers were airlifted in last night at 2:00 A.M.," she said, nodding in the direction of the equipment.

"Outstanding, or what?" Sam grinned. He turned to Alexsana. "Ready to break ground, Sis?"

She nodded. "Just about. Let's say a quick prayer." She

grabbed Ridge's fingers with one hand and trapped Steve's with the other before he could protest. Around them, the entire team joined in, forming a circle around the "X." Sam quickly asked God to bless them with safety and wisdom.

With a nod from Alexsana, Abe and Kamal spoke to ten men who were waiting with jackhammers, and the ear-jarring digging began. The men worked for over three hours around the edges of a Herodian stone that measured three feet by six feet. Finally, the clamp of the forklift was attached to the edges of the stone, and it was lifted out easily. The men stepped back to let Alexsana and Sam peer into the darkness.

Lying on their stomachs, Alexsana and Sam let their eyes slowly adjust to the dim lighting. Then Sam let out a whoop of joy that echoed throughout the cavern below. Flashlight beams confirmed that they were right on target, having narrowly missed one of the supporting archways.

Alexsana rose and brushed herself off. "Well, Steve, here's your exclusive. You have five minutes to film whatever you can see down there. Ridge, could I speak to you for a moment?" She gently drew him away from the group of workers.

"Pretty exciting day for you, Dr. Roarke," Ridge acknowledged. "I appreciate the exclusive."

Alexsana looked up at him hopefully. "That's what I wanted to talk to you about. I need you to hold off on airing it for three days. That will give us time to get down there and see what we're after, before attracting worldwide attention."

Ridge eyed her doubtfully. "You really think the media isn't going to find out this is happening? The whole Temple Mount is closed to nonworshippers. Tourists are furious.

Besides, I announced to the world last night that you'd been found, alive and well and as stubbornly set on moving forward as ever."

"Well, okay, I know chances aren't good that we'll remain invisible," she allowed. "But you and Steve are the only media representatives I'm granting a security pass. If the story breaks, you'll still have the only inside coverage."

Ridge gave her a grim smile. "You're asking me to risk my scoop. Steve and I have to head out to Tel Aviv today on assignment. We'll be gone for at least twenty-four hours."

Alexsana looked away and sighed. "I need this, Ridge. I let you in because I knew I could trust you."

"All right, all right." He raised his hands in defeat. "No low blows, please. We'll film our story and leave it at headquarters. If someone else somehow gets onto the story, Jack will air our coverage. Deal?"

She smiled at him gratefully. "Thanks, Ridge. I want this handled right. Just think, after a few more days, you'll have prize-winning footage to accompany the story; right now it's just a vision."

"Fine, fine. You don't have to sell me. This is your gig, and I'm here by special invitation." Grinning, Alexsana turned away. Ridge shook his head as she returned to the team to discuss their next move. "See you tomorrow, love of my life," he mused, wondering about a woman who could persuade him to delay a story of worldwide importance yet again.

Twenty-Four

&

May 15

Alexsana and Ridge saw little of one another as the days sped by. Ridge's plans for a romantic dinner never materialized as Alexsana worked sixteen hours a day to keep things moving and appease the powers that be. Ridge himself was called to do a report on the 1967 Six Day War at Golan Heights and the temptation for the Syrians to do battle there again. From there, he and Steve were sent to Gaza to do a story on Palestinians who cross Israeli borders for work.

Ridge and Steve managed to return to the Haram three days later. As they eagerly compiled their story, Ridge prayed that no one would scoop them. He knew news would travel fast.

He was right. Before long, the team's work below the Temple Mount had made both the national and international news. Crews from the three primary U.S. networks and stations around the world stood outside the Haram entryway. Like birds of prey, they waited to speak with Alexsana or anyone else they could get their hands on. They cast Ridge and Steve envious looks as the men showed their passes and threw smug smiles over their shoulders before entering the work site each day.

Although they immensely enjoyed their notoriety and special privileges, by day nine Ridge could not wait any longer to show their inside footage. "Please, Alexsana. Let us air what we've got," he urged. "It won't be long until someone sneaks in here after paying some guard off. Let's do it right."

Alexsana placed her hands on her hips and looked at the ground, considering his words.

Ridge studied her. "You look fabulous," he whispered so only she could hear. Alexsana threw him a look of surprise. "I know, I know. You're into business right now. But every time I see you, I can think of nothing but personal matters. Like making you my wife." He grinned as a slow blush crept up above her crisp white collar, obvious even beneath her rich tan.

"Business, McIntyre. Business for now," she said firmly, doing her best to hide a smile. "Let's go get Steve and shoot your final footage for the opening segment. I think I have just the thing for you today."

Ridge followed her to the hole in the Temple Mount floor, where it had been widened. A metal ramp — studded for traction — led down to the cavern far beneath them. Alexsana spoke with Sam, then, tossing Ridge a wide grin, disappeared down the ramp. He followed, motioning for Steve to get everything on tape.

With one eye glued to his camera, Steve switched on the lamp as the natural lighting faded. Deeper and deeper they descended. Ten feet. Twenty. Thirty. Ridge sucked in his breath as they reached bottom, forty feet below the surface.

There, a waterfall of light cascaded downward, and they were so deep that the sounds of men talking above were muffled. Dust pervaded the light, giving it the appearance of a physically tangible beam. Archway after archway spanned overhead, creating a magnificent wall of support.

Steve lowered his camera and simply stared. "It's like stepping back in time," he said reverently.

Alexsana smiled like a proud parent. "We're directly behind the Triple Gate, which the priests used to enter the temple. They probably used these caverns to store oils, wine, flour…anything they might have used in religious ceremonies."

She gestured for the two men to follow her deeper into the section of supporting arches, then stopped at the base of one column. Steve filmed while Alexsana pointed out tiny holes at the corner, then she moved on to show them identical marks on another column. "From Crusader times," she supplied. "They attached metal rings to which they could tie their camels or precious horses."

They moved further east. "Here, there are thirteen rows of vaults, thirty feet high, with eighty-eight piers. The temple once stood on the Haram foundation, forty feet above us." She looked into the camera. "Here," she said, pointing out a large stone at the base of the nearest pier, "are Herodian stones — easily identified by their masonry technique and dimensions."

She waved one arm upward. "There, you can see the smaller stones that represent the rebuilding undertaken during the Crusader period. This arch system supported the entire southeastern end of the temple. With the Royal

Portico right above us at one point, you can see why they were vital.

"The rest of the temple is founded upon bedrock. When earthquakes occur through this region, this section rocks and rolls more than any place else on the mount." She smiled as Ridge and Steve looked nervously upward.

"What?" Ridge asked defensively, catching her look. "So I don't want tons of the Haram coming down on me. Does that make me a coward, or smart?"

Alexsana looked at him with laughing eyes, but moved on, continuing their tour without comment.

May 17

Alexsana's jubilant mood soon came to an end. Abe and Kamal had reached a deadlock in their debate about how to best fortify the arches and subterranean structure. The team could not move forward until the construction engineers gave them direction. The impasse dragged on for days.

By the end of the week, Abraham and Kamal refused to even speak to one another. Frustrated, Alexsana paced back and forth, wringing her hands.

"You need a break," Ridge said. "Let me take you to dinner."

"Where?" she asked.

"My treat, my surprise," he said mischievously.

His tone helped ease Alexsana's irritation. Perhaps a romantic excursion was exactly what she needed. "Sounds good," she agreed, smoothing back her hair. "Please take me far, far away."

"Can we make it a night?"

She looked at him pointedly, a sanctimonious expression on her face.

He held his hands up in a gesture of innocence. "Separate rooms, separate rooms."

Her look softened. "That'd be wonderful. Can you at least tell me what to pack?"

"Casual, comfortable clothes," Ridge said mysteriously. "Think layers."

"Okay," she said hesitantly. "Pick me up at seven?"

"I'll be there."

At seven-thirty that night, Alexsana forced herself to stop pacing and sat down to wait. She had been looking forward to spending time with Ridge. How could he be late when he had made such a big deal about their getaway?

The old, black phone rang, disturbing the quiet of the apartment. Instinctively knowing it was Ridge, she picked up the phone reluctantly.

"Alexsana, it's Ridge," he said, sorrow evident in his voice. The line crackled, and he sounded half a world away.

"Where are you?"

"I'm on a plane to Egypt. Someone just tried to assassinate the prime minister. They missed. But I'm going there to do a live report."

"Oh," Alexsana said quietly. Both were silent for several moments. Then she began, brokenly, "Is this how it will be for the rest of our lives? Barely seeing one another, or separated by nations...."

"Alexsana, aren't you being a little melodramatic? We've been out for dinner every night this week. I know it's been crazy, that our time has been rushed. But it won't be this way all the time." He paused, then said with conviction: "I'll change jobs if it comes right down to it."

Alexsana gasped, stunned by his words. "You'd do that for me?"

"And only for you." Even from a distance, the warmth in his tone sent a slow blush up her neck.

"How can you be so sure?" she faltered. "How can you talk about tossing aside your career, as if you don't care?"

Over the line, she heard Ridge sigh. "Look, I can't talk much longer. But hear me, Alexsana Roarke: I'm in love with you. No career is more important than you are to me. That is my pledge to you. I've found the most wonderful woman in the world, and I'm not going to let anything come between us."

She struggled to find words. No man had ever made her such a priority. No man had ever made her feel so treasured.

"I love you, Ridge," she said, passion evident in her voice. "Come home in one piece." She looked in a wall mirror and happily placed the hat he had purchased for her on her head. She smiled at her reflection and wistfully wished he were near.

"Rain check on whisking you away?"

"After what you just said, Ridge, no rain check is needed."

Twenty-Five

⊱❧⊰

May 23

For several days, Ridge and Steve covered the events in Cairo, where rioting had broken out in the streets. Following these demonstrations, a key White House correspondent went into the hospital for emergency surgery, and CNN headquarters temporarily assigned Ridge to Washington to cover a meeting between the Syrian president and North American leaders.

On the TWA flight to America, Ridge plugged in his portable computer and modem. After keying in the word "Jerusalem" to check up on events at the Temple Mount, he grew pale as he read an exasperatingly short report filed by the UPI news service:

JERUSALEM/23.May/0730
Today, under the leadership of biblical archaeologist Alexsana Roarke, excavation teams continued to delve beneath the Temple Mount in Jerusalem while demonstrators numbering over three hundred raged outside. A crew of approximately sixty men and

women, wearing bulletproof vests, were escorted by armed guard onto the Temple Mount, which is closed to tourists for an unspecified time period. The crew is working to uncover the stairs that once led to the temple from the Kidron Valley: stairs which many believe were once walked by Jesus Christ.

Demonstrators maintain that the Temple Mount, known to Muslims as the "Haram," should not be tampered with, fearing Jewish plots to destroy their holy mosques and rebuild the biblical Temple of old. This, despite the fact that Dr. Roarke was given joint approval by Abdallah al Azeh, head of the Waksf and Islamic Affairs, and Abba Eban, head of the Israeli Antiquities Authority. Eban could not be reached for comment, but according to a source close to al Azeh, the Palestinian official stands by his decision.

Ridge clasped his hands together to still the uncontrollable shaking. *Armed guards. Bulletproof vests.* He checked his watch. The report had been filed less than an hour before, right after the teams had entered the Haram. Headquarters could not have known about the events before calling him to Washington and would certainly send him directly back to Jerusalem to cover the story unfolding there.

Steve read the report over his shoulder while Ridge leaned back, closing his eyes. The cameraman swore under his breath. "Any way we can get the pilot to turn this plane around?"

"It's not likely," Ridge said. "But you better believe I'm going to be on the next flight back."

Ridge and Steve arrived at the Haram thirty-two hours later, unshaven and sorely lacking sleep. Ridge reached the excavation site just in time to see Alexsana and Sam emerge from the gaping hole. Spotting Ridge, Alexsana hurried over to give him a quick hug and kiss. "Ridge! I was so worried about you!"

"I left messages on your answering machine," he said desperately. "I've been going nonstop since we last spoke."

"I haven't been home," she said. Her voice was grim. "I've been sleeping in a safe house supplied by the Israeli government."

Ridge rubbed his aching eyes. "Won't that make you seem all the more biased, politically?"

"I've got little choice," she said, looking frustrated. "It's the safe house or my apartment. Right now, I think I'll sleep better in a place where no one would look for me, and where there are armed guards at my door."

"You're not worried about being followed?" Ridge asked, but they were interrupted by Moshe and Sam summoning Alexsana to review the next phase of their excavation plans.

"Thanks to crews working 'round the clock, temporary reinforcements are almost complete," she explained. "The team's moved on to building foundations for the permanent cement piers. You're welcome to go down with Sam. I've got to go," she said ruefully. She gave him a tender look. "I'm really glad you're back." Then, squeezing his hand, she turned from his side.

Ridge watched as she walked away, putting on glasses to review the plans spread on the ground before her. She was the epitome of the intellectual woman he had always admired. And she was in love with him! He felt like the luck-iest — yet the most doomed — of all men. What if someone harmed her? She was on at least one hit list. How many others had she made while he was gone?

The thought made him feel utterly helpless. *Please God*, he prayed silently as he stared at Alexsana. *Please, please keep her safe. It's out of my hands and up to you.*

Looking out past the Haram walls did not make him feel any better. Israeli police had cowed the crowds into dispersing, but the memory of CNN footage was burned into his thoughts. He and Steve had stopped by headquarters in Jerusalem en route to the Temple Mount; memories of film showing enraged faces and a chanting mob still sent chills down his spine.

He glanced from the minaret to the plaza. Below, soldiers patrolled in teams of four, scattering flocks of pigeons in their wake. Even more tension than usual could be felt; the heightened emotions surrounding the Haram were somehow palpable. As he stood, watching, a soldier stopped a Palestinian man, questioned him, then threw him against the wall for a body search. Ridge grimaced.

The smell of frying *falafels* wafted upward, testifying that life went on as usual despite the craziness at the edge of Jerusalem. Ridge's stomach rumbled, reminding him that he had not eaten since breakfast on the plane. It hardly mattered. He could not eat. The city was in turmoil.

And so was his heart.

That evening, the protesters returned in what was becoming a predictable routine. They seemed not to care that both

Palestinian and Israeli soldiers were present to defend the excavation team. Ridge and Steve left the Haram and approached the crowd to film some personal interviews. Against the shouting of the mob, Ridge had to yell to be heard.

"Does anybody speak English? English? English?!"

A young boy waved from behind a wall of Israeli guards. Steve ran over to him and gestured for Ridge to join them.

"Can we ask you a few questions?" Ridge shouted.

"Sure. Very fine," the boy said, grinning.

Ridge frowned. Many young people would say anything just to get on camera, but this youth was the only protester who had responded to their plea. He waved the boy through and, reluctantly, the guards let him pass.

The threesome stepped away from the crowds, seeking a measure of quiet for their interview.

"My name is Ridge McIntyre." He extended his arm and shook the boy's hand. "This is my cameraman, Steve Rains. What is your name?"

The boy spoke rapidly, uttering a name that seemed to Ridge to be unpronounceable. Ridge looked helplessly at Steve, who shrugged.

"Okay. We'll just go with A Concerned Palestinian Youth. Tell me, why are you protesting? The team on the Haram is half Palestinian. So are the guards that are protecting them. For that matter, the project has been approved by Abdallah al Azeh."

"Many of my people think that those traitors were paid many American dollars to do this," the boy said earnestly, surprising both men with his command of the language. "No true believer of Allah would desecrate the Haram or the holy mosque. It is a plot. Our mosque is in danger!"

"Would anything convince you otherwise?"

"Nothing! Even if they are innocent in their work, they still are exposing the Haram to grave danger. The Kahane look for opportunities like this."

"Are you a member of the Hamas?"

"My father will not allow it," the boy admitted. He lifted his chin proudly. "But I may join my brothers there no matter what my father says. Next month I will be sixteen. Old enough to be a man. I can make my own decisions then." He placed his hand on his chest as he spoke, the picture of heroic youth.

"Do your Hamas brothers intend to put a stop to this dig?" Ridge asked tightly.

"I cannot say."

"Why don't you ask me?" came a deep voice behind the boy. Stunned, Ridge watched as Khalil seemed to emerge out of thin air. Upon closer inspection, he noticed a narrow opening farther down the wall where Khalil had entered their quiet alcove.

"Off camera," Khalil directed, looking at Steve. The cameraman continued filming defiantly.

"Off camera," Ridge echoed, and Steve obediently lowered the heavy Betacam.

Ridge noticed a dramatic change in the way the man presented himself. It was evident in his tone, his posture…even his attire. "Khalil," he said. "Dressing for a special occasion?" The man wore khaki slacks and a button-down cotton shirt the color of saffron. With a braided belt and expensive topsiders to complete the ensemble, he looked more like a young American college professor than the head of the militant Hamas.

Khalil smiled, but ignored his comment. He shooed the young boy away, and immediately — eyes wide at hearing his name — the boy obeyed. Khalil turned back to Ridge. "I understand that you are seeing Alexsana."

Ridge tensed and squared his shoulders. "I am."

With his jaw clenched, Khalil circled Ridge, as if surveying the stock of which he was made.

Ridge gave a slight shake of his head to Steve, discouraging any reaction from him.

Khalil stopped, his face inches away from Ridge's. "What makes you think you can protect her?"

Ridge gave him a tense smile. "You might have noticed something about Alexsana Roarke. She's not really one to be squirreled away in some hiding place. The woman's headstrong. And I for one, admire her for it."

"Even if her choices place her in danger?"

Ridge spoke carefully. "I admit, I don't care for that aspect of her work. But I cannot convince her otherwise. I believe you tried to do so yourself and found her equally as impossible to sway. I've decided her safety is out of my hands. I'll do what I can, but the rest is up to God."

Khalil glowered at him. "You can do nothing more with her?"

Ridge shook his head in resignation. "She's on a mission. And no one is going to stop her." He paused, then said evenly, "You might as well know I'm in love with her."

Khalil gave him a penetrating look. "I am not surprised. You know that I loved her once?"

"I guessed as much the first time I met you." Ridge wondered, would Khalil have him killed for loving the same woman? Suddenly, it was hard to imagine that the casually dressed man had the power to order an assassination. Again, Ridge imagined him strolling on an Ivy League campus.

Khalil looked past him and studied the Haram. "I want you to give Alexsana a message. The people who are most dangerous to her are temporarily in hand. I believe I can buy her time to complete the dig, but there are no guarantees. Tension continues to mount within my ranks. If the excavation takes longer than is projected, there will be little I can do.

"But if she can get in and out and prove to the masses that she follows through on her promises — I speak of the fortifications she planned — she will guarantee the safety of her team better than ever before. That is the only reason I do not send her away yet again. Do you understand me?"

"Yes, I —"

"There is no need for you to speak."

Ridge ground his teeth together, willing himself to be patient.

"You and your friend there," Khalil motioned to Steve, "can be useful to Alexsana by airing footage of her progress."

"We were intending —"

"Do it tonight. Tomorrow at the latest. It is imperative. Do you understand?"

Ridge swallowed his pride and glared at Khalil. "I understand."

At that, Khalil turned on his heel and disappeared.

Twenty-Six

May 26

Ridge heeded Khalil's advice. Despite the fact that he and Steve had planned to wait until the following week to air the entire story as a special feature, they talked their superiors into airing a portion of the story on *Headline News*.

By the following morning, the segment had been shown twelve times. The BBC picked up the story and aired it over their radio program. Major networks around the world followed suit. Word was out that the Haram had been excavated and that the foundations were stronger than ever before.

The effect of the press attention was tremendous. The vast majority of the protesters dispersed and failed to reappear for what had become their regular evening demonstration. A few radicals continued to protest, shouting of the Kahane plot and the Muslim traitors who had betrayed them. But despite the continued danger those few represented, those involved breathed a collective sigh of relief. Somehow, several identifiable, angry faces seemed less intimidating than a mob of indecipherable, furious voices.

May 29

Several days after the story first aired, Ridge sat watching Alexsana as she and her team discussed plans for the following day's work. By digging around the clock, workers had made excellent progress. Strata Three had been reached, and the new foundations were complete. Soon they would begin smaller excavation projects, sending teams in either direction down the main pathway, which had been cleared.

She looks exhausted, Ridge surmised grimly. Usually, Alexsana was amazingly well put-together, even in the most difficult of circumstances. Ridge studied her glasses that kept falling off her nose, the victim of a broken stem. Tendrils of hair escaped her thrown-together ponytail, and her customary whites and khakis had faded to creams and browns under a thick coat of excavation dust. There were dark smudges at her temples where she had impatiently wiped dirt away, smearing the dust with tears from her irritated eyes.

Alexsana dismissed the crew and raised her head to look for Ridge. Spotting him, she smiled wanly, looking slightly guilty under his concerned gaze. She walked over, and Ridge pulled her into his arms. Nearby, three huge Israeli guards kept watch. "You're exhausted," Ridge said with compassion.

She melted under his touch, feeling loved, protected, understood. "I am tired," she admitted. "Want to eat with me in my room?"

"I've got a better idea. Grab Huey, Dewey and Louie over there," he nodded at the guards, "and tell them I'm taking you on a date."

"Oh, Ridge. That sounds great. But I'm so —"

Ridge placed his fingers over her lips to hush her. "Trust me. You'll love it. I know you're beat. Trust me," he repeated.

Accompanied by the three bodyguards, Ridge and Alexsana left the Haram after five that evening. Inside the police car that was their transport, Alexsana leaned her head against Ridge's shoulder. As he put his arm around her, she struggled to fight off sleep. "I don't know about this. I'm so tired, Ridge," she began again.

"Sana Roarke," he looked at her tenderly, "trust me."

"Okay," she sighed. "I'll just take a little nap on the way there. Do you think I could grab a shower before dinner? I'm afraid my face will land in the soup bowl if I don't."

"You are a bit grubby," he teased. "But I've got better plans for you. Snooze for a few minutes, love. I promise, you'll feel better in a couple of hours."

"I hope I'm in bed in a couple...." She was asleep against his shoulder before she had completed her sentence.

They arrived at the Intercontinental Hotel fifteen minutes later, and Ridge led Alexsana into the hotel via the service entrance. The Mossad guards melted into the background like trained FBI agents, watching every entrance and keeping contact with one another via earpieces and tiny microphones attached to their clothes.

Ridge escorted Alexsana directly to the spa, where he kissed her, then left her to the care of a kindly, strong Palestinian woman of about sixty. She led Sana into the women's lounge where, delighted by the prospect of some pampering, Alexsana showered, using a heavenly, mint-scented shampoo that made her scalp tingle, a conditioner that coated her hair into a soft sheet of gold, and a body soap smelling of almonds that somehow soothed her aching body.

She toweled off and bundled herself up into a rich, white

terry cloth robe. Next, the awaiting Palestinian woman silently led her into a dimly lit room where soft instrumental music played. The woman motioned toward a massage table, made up with starched white sheets pulled taut, as if she expected a drill sergeant to inspect it.

Gladly, Sana disrobed and lay down upon the table. The woman discreetly covered Alexsana, leaving her back exposed. Sana watched, mesmerized, as the masseuse washed her gnarled hands in a porcelain sink beside the table. Picking up a glass bottle, the woman poured a liberal amount of heavy, spearmint-scented oil into her hands, then began to work on Alexsana's back. Sana was asleep in under a minute.

An hour later, after the massage was complete, Alexsana was awakened and escorted to another room. There, one woman combed out her long hair while another cut, filed, and painted a clear coat of polish onto her fingernails and toenails. After dabbing on some mascara, blush, and a subtle lipstick, Alexsana gazed at herself in the mirror. She looked and felt worlds better than she had several hours before.

A smile grew across her face. *Ridge.* Never had she met a man who understood her needs so completely.

"You look beautiful, my friend," said a familiar voice behind her.

Alexsana's eyes widened as she recognized the new image in the mirror. "Lydia! What are you doing here?" she asked, standing to embrace her friend.

"Sam went home to shower and is meeting me here for dinner. We would join you and Ridge, but I have the distinct feeling that he wants you all to himself. He asked me to deliver these." Lydia held out Alexsana's classic ivory silk jumpsuit and delicate sandals.

"Oh, thank you!" Alexsana said, taking the clothing in her arms. "I couldn't stand the idea of putting on my grubby clothes again. I was considering going to dinner in this robe," she laughed.

"You are welcome. And now, I must go and meet your brother." Lydia's dark eyes danced. "I believe Ridge is pacing, he is so anxious to see you," she said conspiratorially. "That man loves you, Alexsana. More than Khalil ever did. More than any man I have ever seen around you."

"I know," Alexsana said, grinning. "Isn't it *wonderful*?"

Lydia threw her arms around Sana and squeezed her gently. "Yes, it is wonderful," she said, leaving her side. She paused at the door. "Maybe we can convince both men to rendezvous for dessert."

"If I last that long," Alexsana agreed. "I feel invigorated by all of this, but I'm afraid it's bound to wear off."

"I'll come to your table in an hour to see how you are faring. If you wish it, we shall join you."

"If you can convince Sam to share you."

"Yes," Lydia said impishly. "That will be a must."

Alexsana left the spa feeling as if she were floating. The guard Ridge had dubbed "Huey" tailed her while another led the way, but she consciously pushed thoughts about them from her mind. She would not think about the guards, or the ever-present danger. Tonight she only had eyes for Ridge.

Ridge rose from his wicker chair at the top of the marble stairs and came to meet her. Alexsana raised her lips to meet his, then, smiling, wiped away the touch of lipstick that had smeared his mouth. "Thank you," she said tenderly. "No one has done anything so thoughtful for me in my whole life."

Ridge grinned and looked her over. "A bit better than when I brought you here," he pretended to judge with chin in hand.

"I take it you like this outfit," she said, indicating the clothing he had chosen for her.

"You're breathtaking," he said, somehow managing not to sound corny.

A warm sensation flooded through Alexsana as Ridge gazed at her. She felt like she belonged to him, like she had always belonged to him. Keeping her tone light, she pretended to dismiss his compliment. "It's my one claim to a fashion statement that I can make. Glad you think it's okay."

"I think you'll be a suitable dinner companion," he teased, offering his arm. "In fact," he said, leading her to the dining room, "I've never looked forward to a dinner date more."

As dinner progressed, Alexsana's energy increased while Ridge became increasingly quiet. After the waiter had taken their dinner dishes away, Alexana took a moment to study her companion. Ridge had pushed his chair away from the table and was leaning back, his legs sprawled out casually before him. He stared at his palms.

She placed her elbows on the table and folded her hands. "Where are you? You're obviously not here with me any-more," she said gently, without accusation.

He glanced up guiltily. "Oh, I'm here all right. I'm sorry.

It's just that there's something I need to discuss with you. It can't wait any longer."

Alexsana grew nervous at the sound of his tone. Was their relationship ending? Was he sick? Had something happened? She managed to nod. "Okay," she said, urging him on.

Ridge sat up and leaned forward, across the table. He swallowed hard. "I have to tell you something and I'm afraid it will ruin everything, Alexsana. I'm afraid that if I tell you, you'll turn away."

As she saw the sadness and vulnerability in his eyes, her heart skipped a beat. She wanted to hold him, caress his hair, tell him that it would all be okay. "Oh, Ridge," she began, reaching across to take his hand.

"No," he said, pulling away. "I need to be as clear as possible with you, and holding your hand softens it somehow. I don't deserve to have you make this easy for me."

Alexsana frowned and leaned back, stung by his rebuff but madly striving to understand. She prepared herself for the worst. *He's walking away. He doesn't love me after all.* "This seems to be the place that we make frank confessions," she said with a tight smile, trying to lighten the mood.

"It is," he said soberly. He squared his shoulders and sighed. "Alexsana, I —"

"Hey!" Sam's booming voice broke in as he and Lydia neared the table. "Let's skip dessert and hit the dance floor! They have a great…." his voice trailed off as he looked from his sister's face to Ridge's. "I'm sorry. I obviously interrupted something."

Ridge looked down at his hands without speaking.

Alexsana reached out to lay her hand on Lydia's arm. "Can we come join you in a few minutes?" she asked quietly.

"Yes, yes," Lydia said. "Whenever you can."

"We'll be there," Sam said and quickly led Lydia away.

After a moment of awkward silence, Ridge smiled grimly and shook his head. "I'll try again." He raised his eyes to meet hers. "Alexsana, I think you know that I love you. More than any other woman I've ever known. I love everything about you. I want to be with you for a long time. I can't imagine life without you anymore."

Alexsana's heart pounded under the intensity of his gaze. She nodded, wondering where he was going with this train of thought.

"I have a confession to make, and I'm not proud of myself," he said. He paused, then said carefully: "There have been other women."

Alexsana took a deep breath. "Since we met?" she managed to ask.

"No, no," Ridge assured her quickly. "But do you understand? I don't come to you as I believe you're coming to me. You are pure, untouched, and that's a tremendous gift to me. If we were to marry, it would be the greatest gift I could ever be given."

Alexsana nodded in understanding. "You're telling me that you're not a virgin. Did you think that I would be surprised? I pegged you as a womanizer the first day I saw you. I can accept it, as long as I'm the only woman you want to womanize anymore," she told him.

"No," Ridge remained unconvinced. "Don't let me off the hook. I was wrong, Alexsana. I was wrong to be with any woman I didn't feel this incredible love for. And there were many...."

"Stop." She spoke firmly. "I don't want to hear it, Ridge. I don't want to know how many or who they were." She leaned forward. "When you accepted Christ, Ridge, God forgave you. You became a new creation in his eyes. When that happened, you became a new creation in my eyes as well. To me, you *are* pure, untouched."

Ridge smiled timidly, ruefully.

"Truly," she said, willing him to comprehend her words. "If we do marry, we'll share something special, something beautiful. And no, I have not been touched in that way by another man. That will be my gift to you. Your gift to me will be a lifelong, sacred promise that you'll never touch another.

"I've said this before, but I must say it again, Ridge. The most hurtful, hateful thing I could imagine would be to find my husband with another woman. I never want to deal with that. Is that something you could promise me, for the rest of your life?"

Ridge studied her, his gaze unwavering. "Yes. For you, I have no question in my mind that I could do it. But Alexsana," he said, finally taking her hand, "I need to ask you for forgiveness. I'm sorry I didn't wait for you. I didn't know I would feel this way. I didn't know it could be like this."

With her free hand, Alexsana gently caressed his face, feeling the slight trace of beard stubble upon the firm jaw line beneath her fingertips. Ridge's eyes glistened with earnest tears. She remained silent for a moment, thinking before answering him.

"I'm sad that I won't be the only one for you, Ridge," she said at last. "I can't deny that. But I love you, and so I forgive you," she said with compassion. "I forgive you," she repeated softly.

Twenty-Seven

❧

May 31

Alexsana watched as Ridge and Sam came down the excavation ramp, filming interviews with workers along the way. She studied Ridge, remembering their dinner date. His frank confession hadn't really come as a surprise, but the reality of it had been a shock to her system. She had avoided him for a few days, taking time to weigh her feelings.

Ridge reached her side and, after casting a furtive look about, pulled her into his arms for a brief hug and a kiss. She clung to him, not caring who saw them. "I love you, Ridge McIntyre," she said solemnly.

Ridge smiled joyfully. "I love you, too, Alexsana Roarke. It sounds great to hear you say that. Say it again."

"I love you."

His smile grew. "I was beginning to wonder when you started avoiding me after our dinner at the Seven Arches."

"I just needed a little space, a little time, to process it all."

"I understand that," he said soberly, catching her meaning. "And you're okay?"

"Right as rain." She spoke with assurance. "Maybe it's

because I'm in love, but I've never felt anything so clearly in all my life. I think being in love echoes what it's like to have a relationship with Jesus." She released Ridge and smiled impishly up at him, unable to contain her excitement any longer. "Now, come see what we've found. You'll want to bring your cameraman with you."

Ridge smiled back into her eyes with a look of genuine admiration. "What does Dr. Roarke have in store for me now?" he quipped, waving Steve over. They quickly joined Sam and a large crew working below on a column that bordered the main stairway of the Double Gate.

Sam stood in front of the gigantic column, photographing one section over and over, while the crew fairly bristled with excitement.

"This discovery is big, isn't it?" Ridge asked, surveying the workers.

"Yes, it is," Alexsana said. The crowd parted for them like the Red Sea, revealing an inscription in the stone that Ridge could not read.

"Well?" He waited for someone to explain.

"It's Aramaic," Sam said excitedly.

"What does it say?" Ridge asked in exasperation.

"Let me tell him," Alexsana said softly.

"Wait!" Steve said. "Let's get this moment on film." The bright light snapped on and Steve counted down as Alexsana went to stand beside the column.

"In three, two, one...."

"We're here with Dr. Alexsana Roarke under the Temple Mount in Jerusalem where her excavation team has just made an amazing discovery," Ridge automatically introduced into the camera. "After digging for several weeks, workers have made it to Strata Three. We stand at the base of the steps that once led up into the great Jewish Temple that stood during Jesus' lifetime. Dr. Roarke, please tell us what you've discovered."

Lightly, reverently, Alexsana rubbed her hands over the inscription. She read the words first in Aramaic, then translated: "'All praise to the Lord Jesus Christ the Messiah who healed me at...of Peter.' You see, the column has been damaged here, destroying some of the words, but we believe they must have once said 'at the hands of Peter.'"

Ridge smiled, beginning to understand the team's excitement. "How have you come to those conclusions, Dr. Roarke?"

"Acts 3 tells of a lame man who always begged for alms, then was healed by Peter as the disciples entered the temple. Peter said to the man, 'I have no silver and gold, but I give you what I have; in the name of Jesus Christ of Nazareth, walk.' This healing apparently took place upstairs on the Temple Mount, for the Bible says that it happened at 'the gate called Beautiful' and that the people ran to them where they stood in Solomon's portico, both of which are found above us."

Alexsana turned to gaze directly into the camera. She had just read the text again, and it burned in her memory. "The Bible says that the lame man got up and joined Peter and John, 'walking and leaping and praising God.' A man who was handicapped, presumably for most of his life, actually stood, 'walking and leaping and praising God.'"

"It is an amazing discovery indeed, Dr. Roarke," Ridge managed to squeak out, awed. He hoped his voice sounded stronger to the viewer than it did in his own ears. "But tell us, if the man was healed upstairs at the Beautiful Gate, why would the inscription be found down here?"

"This was the central Jewish temple," Alexsana explained. "The Sanhedrin were none too happy to have Christian disciples healing and preaching about Jesus right there in their courtyard. In Acts 4, we learn that Peter and John were arrested and placed before the high priests. They were questioned as to who had given them the power to perform such acts."

Alexsana opened up her pocket Bible and read, "'Peter answered them by saying, "Rulers of the people and elders, if we are being examined today concerning a good deed done to a cripple, by what means this man has been healed, be it known to you all, and to all the people of Israel, that by the name of Jesus Christ of Nazareth, whom you crucified, whom God raised from the dead, by him this man is standing before you well. This is the stone which was rejected by you builders, but which has become the head of the corner. And there is salvation in no one else, for there is no other name under heaven given among men by which we must be saved."'"

Alexsana looked up. "The Sanhedrin didn't know what to say to them. They were two 'uneducated, common, but bold men' who had the living testimony of a healed man standing beside them. They tried to intimidate them into remaining silent, but they failed. Unable to do anything else, the Sanhedrin let the men go, probably hoping that their testimony would be swept under the carpet."

Her face lit up. "We believe that the lame man came here and left a monument to his healing. He was not so bold as to make this inscription on the Temple Mount above us, right under the noses of the Sanhedrin. But, somewhere, he had to make his mark, leave his testimony for all to see. Here, beyond the Double Gate, was the perfect place to do that."

She paused and grinned. "He probably had no idea that the entire world would be looking at it two thousand years later."

"Exactly how significant is this discovery?"

Alexsana's eyes opened wide. "It's very big. Bigger than the stone that mentions Pilate, found in the amphitheater at Caesarea Maritima, or the inscription at Tel Dan that mentions King David. This is almost a complete inscription that directly mentions Jesus Christ of Nazareth. It is an unprecedented find."

"Tell us, Dr. Roarke," Ridge prompted, "how do you know that this inscription is authentic?"

"Because of the paleontography — the shape of the letters — and the fact that the strata it was found under was undisturbed," she said confidently.

"But how do you know it wasn't placed here, say, last week — or even yesterday — by some well-meaning Christian member of your crew?"

Alexsana furrowed her brow at the suggestion, but she quickly realized that this would be the first question on everyone's minds. Ridge was simply giving her the opportunity to cut them off at the pass.

"Well, Ridge, you and your cameraman have been given unlimited access to the dig from the start. You have been an eyewitness to our excavation process, and I believe if you examine your footage from yesterday, you will see this exact column as it stood before the inscription was uncovered. As you know, we've had crews working around the clock. With a crew of over sixty coming and going, it would be impossible to carve these words in such a central location without being seen. The carving itself would take hours. And as you and your cameraman can testify, we just uncovered it this morning."

Ridge smiled at her and motioned for Steve to shut off the camera. Safely removed from the world's view, he picked Alexsana up, swung her around, and gave her a long, tender hug. "Congratulations, my love. This is bigger than I'm sure even you imagined."

"Huge. Gigantic. Incredible," she said, shaking her head and smiling back up into his eyes. "You'll air it tonight?"

"Tonight. Steve and I will tape more interviews with the crew, then head back to the editing room. They'll air it as a feature. Over and over." He beamed.

"Do me a favor?"

"Anything!"

"Try to get the gospel message past editing?" Alexsana begged.

"I'll do my best, Sana," Ridge promised. "I'll get some flak, but I'll argue that the Bible passages are germane to the discovery. I think I can get most of it through."

Alexsana took his hands and squeezed them. "Don't you see? God is going before us. Trust in him, Ridge. He can accomplish miracles, right before your very eyes." She gestured toward the inscription. "How can we not trust him?"

Ridge nodded, and together they stood — side by side — contemplating their God who moved in their world each and every day.

Twenty-Eight

May 31

Ridge whirled Alexsana out onto the dance floor at the Seven Arches hotel. "We're getting to be regulars here," he whispered in her ear.

"I thought the crew deserved the very best," she said. But her mind was not on the crew. All she could think about was the man who held her, his hand feeling warm and wonderful at the small of her back. Just having his face so close to her own gave her an emotional high.

She never wanted to lose this moment. The intensity was so great, it was as though her nervous system was transmitting at a thousand times its normal rate. Ridge leaned back to cradle her cheek and tenderly gaze at her, his touch sending goose bumps across her arms and down her back.

On stage, a woman in a long, sequined gown of royal blue sang Edith Piaf numbers, giving the room a feel more like that of 1940s Paris than of 1990s Jerusalem.

"Thank you, Alexsana," Ridge whispered, his voice just barely audible over the music.

"For what?" she asked, biting her lip at the slight tremble in her voice.

"For loving me. First, for loving me so much that you introduced me to God, and then for allowing me to love you."

She smiled and looked away, embarrassed. "Ridge, you know —" Her voice froze as her eyes locked on a resplendent Khalil, standing in a shadowed corner wearing a formal tux and tails. Noting that she had spotted him, he moved onto the dance floor with the grace of a much bigger, more formidable Fred Astaire.

Khalil came up behind Ridge as he studied Alexsana, trying to figure out what was wrong. Ridge turned and, finding Khalil behind him, scowled.

"May I cut in?" Khalil asked Ridge, staring at Alexsana.

She looked from one man to another, momentarily speechless.

"Just for a moment," Khalil said deferentially to Ridge, then stepped forward before he could protest and whirled her away into the crowd.

"Khalil," Alexsana said, not daring to look up into his dark eyes, "you should not be here. They'll arrest you."

"Nonsense." The man showed no sign of fear. "I move in and out of the city easily. I came to see your boyfriend last week just outside the Haram. He told you?"

"He did. It was a good suggestion you made. Most of the protesters dispersed as soon as the story aired. But you still —"

"I could not keep you locked away, dear Alexsana. Do not try to do the same to me," he said gently, but firmly. "Besides, the Jewish jackals are storming my hideout in the desert at this very moment. I decided it was an excellent time to move to a new location and to see how you are faring."

"Well, as you can see, I am fine," she began. "We are doing well at the dig."

"Yes, I saw the Christian propaganda aired on CNN tonight. I am certain it will be featured in everything I read tomorrow: *The Washington Post, The London Times,* as well as on the BBC.…"

"My, you do manage to keep up, don't you?" she ribbed, relaxing as they continued to talk and dance.

"Yes," he said, ignoring the jibe. "I do my best to be informed. But I am not here merely to congratulate you, my friend."

Alexsana wondered at his use of the word "friend," but forced herself to keep her mind on what he had to tell her. "I'm listening."

Khalil lowered his voice and moved his head closer to her ear. Over his shoulder, she could just make out Ridge at the edge of the crowd, frowning more deeply as they moved closer together. She gave him a small smile that she hoped would encourage him.

"You have found something significant," Khalil began. "Will you now leave all else alone and depart the Haram?"

Alexsana stopped, defensive and indignant at the suggestion, but Khalil swiftly moved her onward, covering her misstep with his own graceful motion.

"Do not stop. You will call attention to us. And I must finish this conversation with you."

"Very well. Get on with it. I have a dance partner," she winced at her own harsh tone, but she could not help herself.

"Understood," Khalil said crisply. "There are still many in the Hamas who want to see this opportunity for the Kahane to end. They speak radically...."

"There's something new and unusual." Alexsana spoke sarcastically, her frustration mounting.

"There is still talk of assassinating you or your crew," Khalil continued calmly. "The new foundations bought you some time. But, Alexsana," he said looking her full in the face, "I am losing my hold on the most radical in the group. They may move again without my approval. If you do not get out now, having proven that you are trustworthy, you might have difficulty going on with your life in the Old City."

"Don't you see, Khalil?" she protested. "There might be other important discoveries down there. We have another week of excavation to do before we completely uncover the steps and the immediate surroundings. When it's clear, we will stop."

"You do not intend to open the gate as it once was, do you?" he asked, fear finally reaching his voice.

"No, of course not. I am aware of the ramifications of such action. The Muslim moderates would not tolerate it, let alone the Hamas. But if we go that far — clear the whole site from just inside the gate to the stairs — we can visualize and model exactly how it would have been in Jesus' time. It is fundamentally important from both archaeological *and* Christian perspectives. I *must* do it, Khalil. I must."

A muscled twitched along Khalil's jaw line. "You have little time. I cannot emphasize that enough. Get out as soon as possible. If you are too stubborn to do otherwise, then I wash my hands of all responsibility."

The song ended and Khalil and Sana stood among the

crowd of people, some moving toward their dinner tables, others back onto the floor. "I will not see you for a while, my friend." Khalil looked over her shoulder at the two soldiers, Alexsana's bodyguards, who stared as if trying to place him.

"Mossad?" Khalil asked.

"Yes," she said without turning. "My own personal secret service agents. Pretty impressive, huh?"

Khalil ignored her joke. "I feel better with them here for your sake. But I'm afraid they would not reciprocate my appreciation. In fact, I think they're about to throw me out or as you Americans say, 'cart me away.' Alexsana, I must go into hiding for a bit, and get to know my new bride."

Alexsana gasped, momentarily wondering if he intended to spirit her off again and force her to marry him.

He laughed softly and bent to kiss her quickly on the cheek. "Do not worry. It is not you." His eyes darted to her guards, who had begun speaking into their tiny walkie-talkies and were making their way toward them. "I will give Sarah your best," he whispered in her ear. "Take care."

Khalil left her standing on the dance floor and stopped to speak with Ridge. The soldiers made their way to Alexsana. "Pardon us, Dr. Roarke," the one Ridge had dubbed "Louie" said in British-accented English. "May we ask with whom you were just dancing?"

"You may. It was Khalil al Aitam."

Both men shot looks at one another, then toward Ridge. But Khalil had disappeared.

Sam and Lydia shared their cab to the Damascus Gate, with the Mossad agents following behind. The guards had wanted

Alexsana to ride with them, but she threatened a scene until they acquiesced. On the way, the four discussed Khalil's appearance at the Seven Arches, speaking without using his name due to the presence of the cab driver. Sam had seen Khalil only briefly as he exited the restaurant by hopping over the low, outdoor balcony. "He stopped at the French doors and looked at me." Sam sounded haunted by the image. "His face was strange. It was like he was saying good-bye."

Lydia took his hand in hers. "Maybe someday, someplace, we can all be together again."

Ridge bit his tongue, but remained silent.

Alexsana squeezed his leg to reassure him and smiled ruefully. "I think that someday is a long way off."

As they reached their destination, Sam leaned forward to pay the driver. Afterward, the foursome walked through Damascus Gate and into the dark shadows of the Old City, ignoring the agents who followed them.

"I think you should consider what he said, Alexsana," Sam said in a low voice, conscious not to use Khalil's name.

"Sam, I —"

"Today was huge. Really big. You know I'm jazzed that I can work on an excavation that means so much to the faith. But he was right, Sana. You should consider quitting while you're ahead. Not only for your sake. You've got a lot to live for these days," he said meaningfully, gesturing toward Ridge. "But also for the sake of the entire team."

Sam's words hit home. "I'll consider it," Alexsana said grimly, irritated that her brother felt he must remind her of her responsibility.

Sam nodded and looked again at Ridge, who squeezed

Alexsana's shoulders in encouragement. They stopped to say good-bye at an alleyway that provided a shortcut to Lydia's house.

"You know I'll be with you to the bitter end, little sister," Sam said.

"I know it. I know you're just speaking for the good of the group. I'll think about it, okay?" She reached out to hug Lydia, then her brother. "It's been some day, huh?"

"One I'll never forget, Sana. See you in the morning," Samuel said, then groaned as he checked his watch, "which is coming *way* too soon."

He reached out to take Lydia by the hand, then the couple briskly walked away.

Alexsana was suddenly aware of her own exhaustion. "Well, you managed to keep me up 'til all hours again, Mr. McIntyre."

"Can't help it if I'm the best boyfriend in town."

"'Boyfriend,' hmm?" she said, smiling and encircling his waist with her arms. "Sounds a bit corny for a woman of my age to have a 'boyfriend.' There's something too teenage about it for me."

"How about 'manfriend'?" he asked, smiling down at her.

"No. That definitely doesn't work." She looked up at him as a nearly full moon came out from behind a cloud bank, illuminating the city and the man before her. Sana's look grew tender, her eyes sparkling in the soft, yellow moonlight. "How about 'fiancé'?"

Ridge pretended to gasp, his eyes widening. "Why, Dr. Roarke, are you proposing?"

"I most certainly am not! I'm simply accepting your proposal."

"Ahh," he said, grinning from ear to ear as he held her. He ignored the waiting guards as he gave her a long, intimate kiss. "Those are beautiful words to this reporter's ears. Shall we make it national?"

"Not yet," she said. "Let's keep it private for now. Don't worry. I won't let anyone scoop you."

CHAPTER

Twenty-Nine

June 14

Despite exhortations from Ridge, Khalil, and Sam to quit while she was ahead, Alexsana pushed forward with the dig, feeling enthralled by every inch of cavern the team unearthed. Nothing equaled the discovery of the column inscription, but over the following two weeks, the grand entryway became easier to visualize with each stone that was removed from the site.

They had cleared the rubble entirely away from both the Double Gate and Triple Gate stairways — seventy meters apart — as well as from the caverns that connected them. Their work was nearly complete. Alexsana stood with Sam just inside the Double Gate, under two pairs of domes that were made of stone and ornately carved with unique floral designs and geometric motifs.

She pointed, her face alight in wonder, and explained the significance of the discovery to Ridge as Steve filmed. "The unique decoration you see above us is a fine example of how Herodian craftsmen adapted Roman decorative styles while conforming to Jewish law, which forbade the representation of human or animal figures.

"Outside, the gate was probably pretty plain — there is no evidence of ornate lintels or a frieze — but that made it all the more spectacular for pilgrims as they entered. This," she gestured upward again, "was a sign of the grandeur that awaited them in the temple above."

Outside the Haram, an entirely new problem gained momentum. As word of the column inscription sped around the world, thousands of Christian pilgrims flooded the city, eager to be among the first to witness such a holy sight. Their presence put both Jew and Muslim on the defensive: suddenly, a new segment of Jerusalem society clamored to lay claim to the Temple Mount.

Within hours, PLO demonstrators had returned, waving Palestinian flags that prior to the peace agreement had been banned. Christians thronged together, singing and shouting demands for entry to Solomon's Stables. Many were ill and believed that one look at the inscription might bring them healing. Jews, worried that Christians might thwart their own agenda for the Temple Mount, also demonstrated, demanding that they be given the Mount back.

Israeli and Palestinian soldiers managed to beat the crowds back and finally even caused them to disperse. But when Alexsana climbed the long ramp at the end of the day, her team was tensely waiting for her in a half-circle. Quietly, Steve filmed the event as if it were a documentary. But Sana did not see him or even Ridge. She was concentrating on her brother. And his face said it all.

"We're quitting?" she asked quietly, fighting to keep accusation from her voice.

"Yes, Sana." Sam spoke with regret, but also with conviction. "It's time. It might even be too late. We need to get out, let things settle down, and allow Eban and al Azeh to figure out how they'll manage this new aspect of the Haram. Our discovery has made things much more complicated."

"Complicated, but wonderful."

"Yes! Yes! You know we're all delighted with the find. But we have weeks of journaling, mapping, cataloguing to do. Let's end the digging. Gain some time to get the protests and anger under control. We'll finish the paperwork and get out."

"But if we —"

Ridge interrupted her with a single gesture. He motioned toward a tiny monitor on some recording equipment beside him. "I think you've been down below so much you've missed the heat of the crowds." He pressed the play button and studied her face as she watched.

Even on a tiny five-inch-square screen, Alexsana could see evidence of the anger and frustration that had arisen once again among the people. Steve had caught shot after shot of close-ups, bringing the message home.

"Twelve were rushed to the hospital today," Sam said quietly. "There will be more tomorrow. And more the next day. If you don't call it quits, al Azeh and Eban will. It would be better if the order came from you."

Alexsana wanted to nod in agreement, but stopped herself. *There is too much to see…if we could just gain a few more feet in either direction.…*

"I'll think about it," she said in dismissal. She looked around defensively. "I will! Give me at least two more days," she said, her tone pleading. "Just two more. We've not even been in the two months we planned on. It's only been six weeks!"

She looked around at the faces of her team members, some pensive, some stricken. Only Jerome seemed to have no visible opinion. She focused on him as she struggled to regain control. "Haidar, tell the digging team that their work is done in two days. Ridge, I trust you can make it public knowledge? That should help alleviate tensions." She did not wait for his response. "Sam, our paperwork will be done within three weeks." She raised her head, daring any of them to defy her authority.

"I hope you know what you're doing, Alexsana," Sam said, shaking his head. "I have a very bad feeling about this."

June 15

Sam paced, feeling extremely edgy from a lack of sleep and his sister's decision to move on. He was further irritated that she still had not arrived. He had given Abu Khadim the go-ahead to start their teams without her, and thought longingly of the bed he had dragged himself from early that morning.

An hour later, Alexsana still had not arrived. When Ridge entered the courtyard on the excavation side of the El Aksa Mosque, Sam hurried over to him. "She's not with you?" he demanded without preamble.

Ridge looked flustered. "No. She's not here yet?"

The two men stared at one another, each fighting growing feelings of fear. Sam looked around and spotted the Mossad chief. He ran toward him with Ridge at his heels.

The man narrowed his eyes as the big, blond man rushed

toward him. Automatically, he reached for his sidearm.

"Call your men!" Sam demanded.

"What?"

"Call them! The men with Dr. Roarke! Call them!" Ridge yelled.

Seeing the genuine fear in the men's eyes, the soldier reached for his cellular phone. Dialing a number from memory, he waited. No one answered.

Ridge closed his eyes and prayed under his breath. "Dear God. Please, God. No. Please be with Alexsana. Please let her be safe."

He opened his eyes, swallowed hard, and leveled his gaze at the soldier. "Call your men outside the house."

The man nodded once, hit an automatic dial button, and waited.

Again, there was no answer.

The safe house had been discovered.

To Ridge, the events that followed flashed past like series of fast-forward and slow-motion video shots. Sam called an immediate stop to the dig and oversaw the crew's exit under heavy guard. Within minutes, Mossad agents stormed the safe house and found the guards dead. Alexsana was gone.

Wanting to be where he could be reached the fastest, Ridge accompanied Steve to CNN's Middle East headquarters. While he waited for Sam to arrive to discuss their next move, Ridge helped his partner edit and file their report, working in a stupor.

A call from a local source interrupted his vigil an hour later: approximately seventy men — heavily armed and apparently backed by the Hamas — had stormed the Temple Mount and seized control from the more moderate Muslims. They blocked any further access to Jews or Christians. Even Muslim worship in the holy mosques was temporarily banned. Jewish faithful dared not approach the Wailing Wall for fear of being shot by snipers high above.

"Ridge, come on!" Steve yelled from across the room. "We're gonna get scooped! Come on!"

Ridge managed to jog over to him, his feet feeling like lead. "I think you had better team up with someone else for this one, Steve. My mind is on Alexsana. Sam's coming any minute. I can't think straight, let alone report accurately."

"Come on!" Steve insisted. "It's after midnight! By the time I get someone out of bed, the story will be *over*. Over, man!"

Years of professional training kicked in, sending a new wave of adrenaline through Ridge's body. The ever-present threat of getting scooped sent his legs into motion when his heart begged him to stay put.

"All right, man!" Steve praised. "Don't worry. They'll know where to find you if word comes in about Alexsana."

Ridge stopped at the receptionist desk and glowered at the young woman in consternation. "Tell Samuel Roarke where I am. And I don't care what it takes: if word about Alexsana Roarke comes in, get me a message right away. Call me, page me, run there yourself if you have to! Got it?"

"Ridge, leave her alone! Come on!" Steve pleaded.

"Got it?" Ridge shouted, ignoring the cameraman.

"Got it," the receptionist managed weakly.

Shehab cursed the bright full moon that rose high above. This was not the ideal night to storm the Haram, but they'd had little choice. He kicked the unconscious woman before him, cloaked in the same black cloth worn by all his men, ignoring her soft moan. She had pushed them to this.

He had not wanted to disobey Khalil, but their leader had proven to have no backbone when it came to the Roarkes. In order to save the Haram, the pride of all faithful Palestinians, Shehab knew he had to act. Fortunately, his work over the last months had provided him with a solid, if small, army of men willing to defect from the Hamas and act for the good of them all.

It had been surprisingly easy to take the woman. Two of his men had been lost in the kidnapping, but none of the Mossad slime were left to tell who had taken her. No one would find her. Shehab allowed himself a tight-lipped smile. Control felt good. This is where Allah had willed him to be. He was certain of it.

The woman moaned again, and Shehab reached down to yank off the hood that covered her head. She winced as he took several thick strands of hair with it.

Raising her head slowly, she sat up and looked at the east side of the El Aksa Mosque. "Why am I here?" she dared to ask.

But Shehab jammed the butt of his rifle into her shoulder, breaking her clavicle and sending her back into blessed unconsciousness.

Thirty

June 16

By morning, every available employee was at CNN headquarters, reporting on events at the Haram. All phone lines were busy. The fax machines spewed forth urgent messages. Computers buzzed and keyboards clicked. People seemed to be climbing all over each other, in places sitting three to a desk.

Ridge and Steve made their way through the throng to file their latest report. From across the melee, Jack shouted and waved them into his office. They closed the door behind them, thankful to be able to shut out the greatest portion of the noise.

"Tell me what you've got in a hundred words or less," Jack demanded.

"We've basically got the beginnings of World War III on our hands over this, Jack," Ridge began, his voice heavy with weariness. *Alexsana. Dear God, please be with her. Alexsana, where are you?*

"Ridge! McIntyre! Stay with me! This is a lousy time for a nap! Tell me *exactly* what's going on!"

Ridge squeezed his eyes shut, then opened them wide, willing himself to concentrate.

"Yesterday, Dr. Alexsana Roarke's team discussed ending active digging and moving forward only on the paperwork. Their thought was that it might help appease the masses outside and bring some measure of calm to Jerusalem. But Alexsana wanted to go on. Just two more days, she said. We aired a clip, telling the world that the end of the excavation was at least near. I had hoped...." His voice trailed off.

Could that clip have sealed her fate? They had shown her disagreeing with the team, urging them on for a while longer. Could her disappearance be his own fault? He turned a grayish green.

His boss swore as Ridge again drifted off into his own thoughts. "McIntyre! *McIntyre!*"

"That's it, Steve," Ridge mumbled. "We made a mistake airing that footage yesterday. We didn't help Alexsana. We set her up. The bad guys heard all about it and decided they could not trust her any longer."

"Hamas?" Steve asked.

"That wouldn't make sense. I saw Khalil not too long ago. I think it might be my old contact Shehab with some renegade, fanatical troops he mustered up."

"More maniacal than normal Hamas?" Jack asked.

"Afraid so, boss," Steve said.

Ridge covered his face with his hands and thought about Sam. His expression of pure panic the night before had unnerved Ridge all the more. His head pounded and his eyes swam before him. He took a deep breath and continued. "We're looking at major consequences," he said. "So far, the prime minister has received threats of repercussions from Syria, Jordan, and Lebanon. If Israeli troops storm the

Haram and take it back, there will certainly be some sort of international response."

"What if they send in Palestinian troops? Wouldn't Chairman Arafat agree to the wisdom of that?"

"We've been trying to reach his office all day. Hopefully, that will be the answer to this chaos."

Shehab directed the soldiers to spread out and guard the entire section of the Haram south of the Dome of the Rock. He could not hope to protect the second, beautiful jewel of a mosque with his limited resources. *Besides*, with the houses that physically bordered the Haram's northwestern side, there were too many opportunities for ambush. He needed to position himself beyond the long, clear sections that could not be taken without a suicidal rush. By waiting at the southern end, his men could pick off anyone who dared to attack. It was at this location that the holy mosque was in the gravest danger.

He dragged Alexsana along the ramp. Although she was conscious once again, she was unable to see as they descended into darkness. She followed her captor helplessly, too weak to protest. Two men carrying lanterns followed. As they reached bottom, another hurried over to a jackhammer.

Shehab dumped Alexsana at the base of the steps. She gave a fleeting thought to the beggar who had once walked there. *Dear God, be with me. Hear me....*

"Dr. Roarke!" Shehab shouted back to the limp woman on the ground. His voice echoed in the cavernous stables. "You made a grave mistake by coming here and desecrating the holy mosque's foundations."

"But I —"

"Silence! You came here to destroy our hold on the Haram, to take it away from us. But you see we are stronger than you. We will not tolerate your abuse of our holy mosque any longer!"

At his signal, two men grabbed Alexsana and chained her to a column in a far corner. As they dragged her into the darkness, she mustered her strength and tried to fight back. But it was no use. She was easily overpowered in her exhausted state. Alexsana bit back a scream as her wounded shoulder was yanked backward and her hands bound together. She sank slowly to the cold stone floor.

From high above, voices cheered Shehab onward. Alexsana closed her eyes against the nightmare unfolding before her eyes. Two soldiers dragged the jackhammer over to the column that bore the inscription. From her perspective, it looked like the light from above shone on it in a heavenly stream. Sunlight, she supposed. Awkwardly, they raised the tip of the jackhammer toward the ancient words.

"NO!" she screamed, seeing their intentions.

"You will see now," Shehab said, "that we hold the only keys to the Haram. You will not use Christian graffiti to gain access. We will not allow it." He nodded toward the men, giving them the go-ahead to destroy the inscription. The noise was deafening, each clang of the jackhammer echoing in Alexsana's horrified ears.

She clenched her eyes shut, praying madly. "Please God. This cannot be happening. No. No. We wanted the world to see those words. To find comfort. To find faith. Where are you? Where are you, God? Put a stop to this! Please, God, stop them!"

Alexsana opened her eyes, realizing that the jackhammer had indeed stopped and her prayer had become audible, ringing through the high caverns of the stables. Dust billowed up in huge clouds that slowly settled around Shehab and his men. Shehab laughed at Alexsana. She ignored him, desperately searching for the inscription with her eyes. But it was gone: blasted to bits by the tip of a single tool.

"Call out to your god all you want, Dr. Roarke. You will die with him here in the stables." He motioned to the others and walked up the long ramp without looking back.

Within an hour the men above had used the heavy excavation equipment to pull out the long ramp and seal the huge hole. Alexsana screamed as a gigantic metal plate was dragged over her only exit, cutting off her cries abruptly.

She was alone in the cold, pitch black of the stables.

And no one outside the Haram knew she was there.

Thirty-One

Within twelve hours of the takeover, the Temple Mount had been cordoned off for an entire square mile. A large portion of the Old City was evacuated as a precaution against the unlikely possibility that Israeli forces would move in with massive air strikes. Around the world, people sat glued to their television sets, aware that the decision that Middle East leaders made to rectify the situation could easily impact lives as far away as the United States.

The president himself flew in to speak with twelve other national leaders, hoping to help moderate the discussion and usher in a peaceful agenda. Other CNN correspondents covered the story in Tel Aviv while Ridge and Steve stayed on top of the progress — or the lack thereof — at the Temple Mount.

There, the troops remained at a standoff, with Palestinian police positioned in front. The renegades on the Haram seemed less likely to take potshots at Palestinians than they were to shoot at Israeli police. Still, the reprieve did not endear Shehab's men to the policemen.

Each policeman knew that the radicals' actions had placed the Palestinians' tenuous hold on self-rule and efforts toward peace at grave risk. Many depended on their new jobs as policemen to support their families and enjoyed a sense of pride of their position, despite the scorn of many.

"Join us, brothers!" a soldier shouted from the Haram. "Leave your false positions! They never intend to give us what we rightfully own! It has come to this! We must fight for what is ours, even the holy El Aksa Mosque! Or they will quietly steal it away as they do our lands!"

Many of the men shifted uncomfortably at the herald's words. These were the questions many asked themselves each day: Was Arafat merely a pawn? Had they become pawns themselves? Most importantly, if it came down to it, could they actually shoot their Palestinian brothers?

Inside the stables, Alexsana drifted in and out of sleep. Her mouth felt like parchment and her lips were cracking. Desperately, she tried to gather enough saliva to swallow, the thought alone a blessed idea, but had little success. She knew she had little time left if she did not get anything to drink.

I am not doing well, Father, she moaned in her mind, unable to speak. *Please do not let me die here.*

Suddenly, twenty feet before her, she saw a small stream of light emerge from the inky darkness. Slowly, it became brighter and brighter. *I'm hallucinating,* she thought mournfully. *Dear God, save me! Surely this is not a good sign! I'm hallucinating!* But the light distracted her from her prayers.

The intensity of the light hurt her eyes, yet drew her like

a magnet draws nails. *I need the light,* she thought hungrily. *It has been hours, perhaps days, since I have seen it…how long?* She searched high above to see if the excavation hole had been reopened, if rescuers were near, but she could not ascertain the source of the light. *It's like a beam from heaven….*

Looking back at the light stream, Alexsana barely saw a figure working at its base. Slowly, the beam dimmed, allowing her vision to clear a little. *Yes, he's working.* All at once the image became clear. A man in rags stood twenty feet away, carving an inscription in the column with a hammer and chisel.

A second figure appeared at her side and offered her a hammered, copper ladle filled with blessed, cool water. The ladle smelled of cold metal as Alexsana took it to her lips. Water, as fresh as if it were directly from a mountain stream, slid over her tongue and down her throat. Before she could raise her head to thank the emissary of light beside her, he was gone.

When she looked to the column, the worker was gone as well. But there on the column, was the Aramaic inscription, just as it once was. Alexsana gazed at it in wonder, even as the beam of light dimmed to a dull glow and she rediscovered her thirst. Alexsana repeated the words over and over, the testimony of the beggar feeding her heart and soul and giving her hope. Then she fell asleep and dreamed of the disciples and the beggar on shadowy steps two thousand years before.

"She's gotta be inside," Sam said, looking up to the tiny, walled off windows that dotted the Haram's walls. "Think about it. There are precious few of those men up there. They could not afford to send any of them elsewhere, so they took her with them. They figure that there are few archaeologists able or willing to lead such a dig...." his voice trailed away.

"So they're just going to hole up in the Haram until she dies?" Ridge paced back and forth in front of Sam, dragging one hand through his hair.

Sam met his gaze. "They want two things: Sana out of the way and to destroy the inscription. It was too unnerving for them when the Christians demanded access. I'll bet it pushed your pal Shehab over the edge. While they're at it, they'd like to gain control of the Haram and to boot out the moderates —"

Sam's exposition was interrupted by rapid gunfire and both men dove for a large stone between them and the Haram.

"What's going on?" Ridge yelled to Steve, who had taken cover ten feet away.

"The guys on the Haram! They're shooting at us!"

Soldiers, half-crouched, ran this way and that. Men screamed as they were hit. Others yelled orders or cried out for help. A Palestinian policeman dove and rolled five feet away, shooting back as soon as he could aim again.

Periodically, Steve took in several deep breaths and stood, shooting footage of the most amazing event to hit Jerusalem since the 1967 war.

"Get down, you idiot!" Ridge yelled.

Steve ducked just as a bullet nicked the stone above him, chipping off a four-inch corner as if it were sand. Steve stared at the corner and then over at Ridge. Their eyes met. "Okay, okay. I'll stay down!" he yelled. "But only if you haul over here and let me get you shooting a report!"

Ridge hesitated, then wondered at his hesitation. A year before he would have moved without thinking, concentrating only on getting the story and prize-winning footage with it. But there was someone who counted on him now. Someone who depended on him to live. And deep inside, he knew that God was urging him not to make foolish choices. His life was precious, and there was greater reason than ever before to preserve it.

He shook his head at Steve. "When it cools off a bit!"

Steve stared back at him, but accepted Ridge's decision without argument. "When you're ready," he mouthed over the gunfire.

The three men watched without further comment as the troops fell into line, their sergeants and captains bringing order to the chaos. As one, they donned their gas masks. Glancing over, Ridge saw that Steve was getting the entire event on film.

A captain yelled out orders as three snipers stood high above, shooting at his men. Soldiers below fell even as tear gas grenades were fired and waves of men stormed the entry ramp to the Haram.

With the attention of the snipers diverted, Ridge rushed over to Steve, who cut back and forth between his partner's report and the action above them. Ridge swallowed hard after completing the speech he had rehearsed in his head, knowing that this news might initiate World War III if the soldiers did not successfully wrest control from the Hamas renegades. "This is Ridge McIntyre for CNN, Jerusalem," he finished wearily.

Steve's camera whipped back to the ramp. He stood without fear, confident that the sharpshooters above had their hands full with the men who were attacking them.

Within minutes, it was over.

Thirty-Two

❧

Ridge pushed through the crowds and when the guards were busy, attempted to pass nonchalantly the checkpoint. Steve and Sam followed right behind him.

"You there! Stop!" a male voice called loudly in Hebrew.

Ridge did not pause to look. He waved his press pass as if it wielded the power to open the White House's front door.

The guard apparently did not appreciate the power of the press and again yelled for them to stop. Ridge, Steve, and Sam froze as they heard several soldiers take off, running, after them. Within seconds, several M-16s were leveled at their heads.

Ridge squared his shoulders. "Where is your captain?" he responded harshly in Hebrew, staring the young soldier down. The man — who was little more than a boy — searched over his own shoulder, looking for a voice of authority to assure him he had done the right thing.

"Where is your captain?" Ridge demanded again. He knew how to say little else in Hebrew, having found that this one lone phrase generally brought about the results he desired. Sam picked up where he left off.

"This is Ridge McIntyre and Steve Rains with CNN, and they have unlimited access to the Solomon's Stables excavation," Sam explained in an appeasing, yet firm manner. "I am Dr. Samuel Roarke. My sister, Dr. Alexsana Roarke, was leader of the Solomon's Stable dig. She is missing. We have reason to believe that she is below."

The soldier studied him for several seconds, weighing his options. "You have identification?" he finally asked.

"I do," Sam said. He looked around at the soldiers, who were still pointing loaded weapons at him. "I'm reaching for my wallet now. Everyone take a deep breath."

He handed his I.D. to the young soldier. Again, the boy looked over his shoulder, but he could see no superior to summon. Speaking quietly, he dispatched one of his fellow soldiers to search for their captain while he studied Sam's papers, apparently unwilling to take on the responsibility of allowing the threesome through.

The other soldier returned within minutes, accompanied by a commander who seemed none too pleased that American journalists were on the Temple Mount. A Palestinian patrol of eight men passed while making rounds of the Haram. It was one of ten groups Ridge had counted since they had arrived. The Israeli and Palestinian police were taking no chances of another overthrow; Ridge was confident that they would maintain control from that point on.

Behind the Israeli commander stood two Palestinian leaders and three men who were obviously CIA. "Oh, brother," Ridge muttered. "Here comes the mighty one and his entourage."

"Ply him with good publicity," Steve said under his breath as they neared. "It might buy us some leeway."

Before the man had a chance to speak, Ridge reached out his hand and flashed a smile. "Hello. Ridge McIntyre, CNN. General, can you tell me about the astounding progress you've made here?"

The American agents interrupted, long accustomed to the schemes used by their country's press. "Sorry, Mr. McIntyre. You and your friends must vacate the premises immediately. This area is secured."

"If I could just get a comment for the camera," Ridge said, motioning to Steve. On cue, Steve turned on the Betacam, blinding the entire group for several seconds.

It was all the lead that Sam needed. Quickly, he slid behind a column of the El Aksa Mosque and, heart pounding, ran toward the far side. The commander noticed the missing man shortly thereafter, and screamed for soldiers to find him.

By the time they located Sam, he had already reached the dig site. He stood at the edge of the hole, dumbfounded, unable to go any farther. A thousand pounds of steel stood between himself and where he was sure his sister lay.

Ridge and Steve ran up behind the soldiers. Ridge fell to his knees, shouting Alexsana's name as he helplessly pulled at the monolith at his feet.

He turned to the commander, all manner of pretense gone. "Alexsana Roarke! Dr. Alexsana Roarke! She's down there! And if she dies while you sit around, it will be on your head!"

The man frowned and studied Ridge for a moment longer. Then he waved for his men to lead the intruders away, exhausted after monitoring the tension-filled hours of upheaval on the Haram.

All three men had to be dragged from the site.

Two hours later, Samuel Roarke Sr. had finally convinced several key officials that his daughter might indeed be trapped beneath the Haram. In conjunction with an investigation geared toward measuring the damage that had been inflicted by the renegade Hamas troops, the authorities allowed a team of government employees to remove the iron ramp from the entrance to the dig site.

Furious at the delay, Ridge spoke to no one. He glared at the soldiers as he passed the checkpoint, certain that they had carelessly endangered Alexsana's life even further. Desperately, he called out in prayer to the Lord, but found no comfort. He was too wrapped up in his own anger to sense God's presence.

This left him feeling cold and empty, and fearful that he had lost the one woman he had loved the most. *Dear God,* he petitioned, *please let her be okay. Is this emptiness I feel a sign that she is dead?* The thought alone made him want to give in to stomach-wrenching sobs. He swallowed hard against the ache in his throat, determined not to cry. Instead, he concentrated on his fury.

To him, the team seemed to take an interminable amount of time to get the steel ramp away from the entry. Ridge paced and desperately searched his soul for the warm comfort he had once found in the Church of All Nations. *I let go of myself,* he remembered. *I believed. I just believed.* In his mind he could hear Alexsana say it as she had that Palm Sunday. *Believe.*

Immediately, a rush of heat flowed through his body and his senses seemed to sharpen tenfold. Ridge looked over at Sam and the elder Roarke, who stood beside him. "He's here," Ridge said firmly. "God is here. He's been watching over Alexsana. She's alive."

The men raised their eyebrows at his statement, but nodded, seeming to find comfort in his words. They never took their eyes off the workmen.

With a deafening scrape, the plate was lifted off by huge cables, turned, and deposited back inside to create a walkway once again. When the machinery was turned off and the dust had settled, the workers stepped forward and lined the dark hole.

A searchlight cut into the darkness below.

For a moment, no one moved. They waited, listening, as their eyes adjusted to the extreme light of the spotlight.

They were greeted by complete, utter silence.

Ridge grabbed a flashlight from a young Palestinian's hand and rushed down the ramp. The way was clear before him, but all about, deep shadows remained. His light caught the heavy dust clouds that still stirred, and he shivered. He did not pause to consider what the frigid temperature had done to Alexsana. His sole purpose was to find her.

Sam was right behind him, followed by Steve, who turned on his Betacam to film the event.

"No camera!" Ridge growled, terrified at what they might find. This was far too private a moment to let the world in on. He wanted Alexsana in his arms, dead or alive, and it was nobody's business outside of the Temple Mount's walls what they found.

The light went off, then Steve turned it on again. "I'm not filming, man. Just using the light."

Ridge turned face forward again and shouted. "Alexsana!"

"Alexsana!" Sam repeated.

There was no response to their cry.

"Alexsana!" Sam called again.

"Over here!" Steve yelled. He swore softly as he hastily set aside his camera and ran toward the woman. "OVER HERE!" he shouted again, fighting to keep the edge of hysteria from his voice. He lifted her hand, deadly cold, as Ridge reached them.

Grimly, Ridge felt for a pulse. "Come on, Sana, come on," he muttered forcefully between clenched teeth. The three men waited silently, not daring to breathe. At long last, Ridge laughed gleefully. "I feel a heartbeat. It's faint, but she's alive!"

Sam whooped and ran to the base of the ramp to call for help. "She's down here! We need an ambulance!"

Ridge found a rock and pounded at a rusty link in the chains that held Alexsana. As the bindings broke, he tenderly lifted her in his arms, emotions flooding his heart.

He carried her to the ramp, looking up into the stream of light as if he were climbing toward the gates of Heaven. "I've got you, love. You're going to be okay, Sana," he mumbled through gritted teeth, as much for himself as for her. "God's seen you through too much to let you die now.

"You'll be okay, sweetheart," Ridge continued gently as he reached the top and was surrounded by people. In a moment that felt surreal, he walked toward a medical chopper, its blades whirring soundlessly.

To Ridge, it felt as though he and Alexsana were alone on the Temple Mount with God himself. From above, a brilliant column of light — which he later learned was more searchlights — followed their path. As the helicopter lifted above him, the "whopping" sound suddenly became audible to him, and Ridge looked across the column of light.

For one short instant, Ridge could have sworn he saw a bearded man in rags.

Behind the beggar stood two men in robes.

Then, in the blink of an eye, the only people visible were soldiers.

Thirty-Three

June 19

Alexsana was released from Jerusalem's Hadassah Hospital three days later after being treated for dehydration, hypothermia, and a broken clavicle. As she walked toward him, Ridge grinned until his cheeks hurt.

"How come you look like a kid who's just run across an abandoned ice cream truck?" Alexsana asked with a smile, reaching up to kiss him lightly.

He gathered her into his arms, mindful of her shoulder, and whispered in her ear. "Because you're better than any ol' ice cream truck. You're the Dreyers of women. The Haagen Dazs of the female gender."

Alexsana laughed and shook her head. "Reaching pretty hard for those analogies, aren't you, my love?"

He smiled back into her eyes. "Perhaps. Are you a free woman now?"

"For the next twenty-four hours, at least. It looks like it will be a while until we get the okay to go back and do the paperwork on our dig."

Ridge nodded, sobering at the mention of their harrowing

night at the Haram. "Come on," he said, motioning toward his rental car. "I want to go for a drive. I need to see the ocean, take a breather from Jerusalem life."

Alexsana looked at him with question in her eyes. "What about work?"

"What about it? You're more important." He took her hand and studied her intently. "Alexsana, you're the most important person in my life. You introduced me to God!" he spread out his arms as wide as possible. "You taught me what love was all about. Work's important. But as I've said before, I'd leave the best job in the world if it meant I couldn't be with you."

Alexsana studied him, thinking. "Let's go for that ride."

Two hours later, they reached a resort town on the coast. Leaving their things in the car, they hurried to catch the last rays of sunset on the beach. Alexsana walked behind Ridge, carefully placing her feet inside his imprints in the sand. She could feel the contours of his toes, heels, and soles in the cold, wet grains. The sensation was oddly intimate. "Ridge," she said.

He stopped and turned, waiting for her to go on.

"I'm so glad you chose me, Ridge." She looked up at him in wonder. "I'm so glad you asked me to marry you."

"You are?"

His voice was hopeful, without ego. To hear it coming from a man like Ridge brought tears to her eyes. "I did a lot of thinking in the hospital," she continued. "About what I want for us. And I was wondering if maybe you and I should synthesize careers somehow. You know, you document archaeological digs or I become a full-time news resource."

Ridge shook his head, not understanding her lead. "But why?"

"Well, Mr. McIntyre, at one point you asked me to marry you," she said as if it were obvious.

"And you asked me back," he said with a smile, waiting for her to go on.

"I'm not going to stay at home while you risk life and limb alone on some assignment in a war zone, or let us work ourselves to pieces while seeing each other only twice a month at some rendezvous point like Paris or Nairobi. As romantic as that might seem at first, it's not what I want for my family."

"Okay." He kept his eyes on hers, listening carefully.

"I do want a family, Ridge. A house. A home. And a husband who will live long enough to see our children grow up. I want to work for God's glory, not my own. My time at the Haram showed me that no matter what I do, no matter what I discover or what I accomplish, it can be destroyed in seconds. But God — our God, Ridge — he's eternal. He saved me. I know he was there."

He nodded, understanding at last. "But you're the one who almost got yourself killed three days ago. I'm not the one who was kidnapped by the head of the Hamas or left for dead at the bottom of the Temple Mount."

Alexsana looked down at her bare feet, then back at up at him. She pulled off her glasses.

"Uh-oh," he said with a laugh. "I'm in for it now."

"What do you mean?"

"You always pull the glasses off when you want to drive home a point."

Alexsana gave him a tiny half-smile. "Yes, well listen to

this one, Ridge. I admit that I made a mistake at the Haram. I put my work ahead of my life. I risked not only *my* life, but the lives of my crew. I thank God every day that I am not responsible for getting any of my people killed. Being trapped in the stables made me think. *Really* think. I even felt like I saw a vision, a tiny glimpse of God. And it over-whelmed me.

"My work is important. Even though the inscription we found under the Haram is gone now, we still have it on film. And this find will go down as one of the greatest in history. But was it worth risking my future with you? What we have together? No. For me, nothing is that important. I've come to that decision, Ridge. Have you?"

He looked back out to sea, his expression unreadable. "I told you I'd leave if I had to, but it's tough. I have to choose: you or my job."

Alexsana fought the hurt that threatened to creep into her voice. "Not your job, Ridge. Your current position. And I'm not forcing you to do anything. This is up to you. I love you, no matter what you decide. I'm simply asking you to consider our future."

"I suppose life with you will be full of tough decisions," he said slowly, carefully.

Alexsana managed a small smile. "Does that mean you'll consider it?"

He looked directly into her eyes and spoke with confi-dence. "Alexsana Roarke, I love you. All the way. Forever. There's no job that's more important. I've said that, and I mean it. You're right. I don't want you to be in harm's way. It's not fair to ask you to feel anything different."

Alexsana smiled broadly and threw her good arm around

Ridge's waist. Bringing his arm around her shoulder, he pulled her tightly against him. They looked out to sea together, watching for a long while as the sky faded to a deep amethyst and a few stars faintly twinkled.

"We'll work it out, somehow," Alexsana said finally.

"Yes, we will," Ridge agreed, pulling her in front of him and kissing her forehead. "I know it." He looked into her eyes and reached for her hand, placing it over his heart. She felt the rhythm of his strong pulse and smiled up into his eyes. "I know it *here*," he whispered earnestly.

"You *believe*," she said through her tears. "In us. In God. In our future."

"I do," he said, his voice returning with a laugh. "How 'bout a jaunt through the stars, Wendy?" he quipped, picking her up in his arms.

"Any time, Peter Pan," she said, her smile broadening. "Any time."

Dear Reader:

Six years ago, I was in Utah when my cousin Bob called, inviting me to visit him and his wife, Pam, in Jerusalem. On fire for Christ, I went. The experience was life-changing. Easter in the Holy City was something I'll never forget, and many of my experiences have wound up in this novel.

I spent nearly a month in Israel and Egypt, and over three days on a whirlwind bus tour of archeological sites with the École Biblique. There I was, hanging out with a bunch of priests and monks and scholars — "me and the boys" — in the middle of Israel! I witnessed a right-wing Israeli group take over a Palestinian block in the Old City that culminated in protests and tear gassing; the Old City at the height of emotion during Easter, Passover, and Ramadan; a Palm Sunday processional from Bethany; an Easter sunrise service from the Mount of Olives. It was in Jerusalem that Bob talked about a man I *had* to meet, one he thought might be able to carry the other half of my own yoke; a man who, two years later, asked me to marry him. (I accepted!)

I cannot express what it means as a Christian to walk where the Savior walked. Biblical text comes alive; the Spirit moves in a palpable way; one stands still long enough to sense that God is present. These are the emotions and passions I hoped to convey in *Chosen*. My goal was to spin an adventurous romance, a hold-on-to-your-hat tale, while still touching upon something vital to us all: salvation. I hope it touched your lives in some way.

Life is indeed rich for me right now. Tim and I constantly laugh and smile at our precious baby girl, Olivia, who will be ten months old at press time. What a joy!

All my best to each of you —

Lisa Tawn Bergren

Write to Lisa Tawn Bergren
c/o Palisades
P.O.Box 1720
Sisters, Oregon 97759

⌁

Look for Lisa Tawn Bergren's next release,
Firestorm, in October 1996!

*She had lost so much one summer
to a blazing inferno — could she now risk loving
a man dedicated to fighting fires?*

Sequel to the best-seller, *Refuge,* available
at your local Christian bookstore.

PALISADES...PURE ROMANCE

∽ PALISADES ∾

Reunion, Karen Ball (July, 1996)

Firestorm, Lisa Tawn Bergren (October, 1996)

Refuge, Lisa Tawn Bergren

Torchlight, Lisa Tawn Bergren

Treasure, Lisa Tawn Bergren

Chosen, Lisa Tawn Bergren

Cherish, Constance Colson

Angel Valley, Peggy Darty

Seascape, Peggy Darty

Wilderness, Peggy Darty (August, 1996)

Love Song, Sharon Gillenwater

Antiques, Sharon Gillenwater

Secrets, Robin Jones Gunn

Whispers, Robin Jones Gunn

Echoes, Robin Jones Gunn (June, 1996)

Coming Home, Barbara Hicks (June, 1996)

Glory, Marilyn Kok

Sierra, Shari MacDonald

Forget-Me-Not, Shari MacDonald

Westward, Amanda MacLean

Stonehaven, Amanda MacLean

Everlasting, Amanda MacLean (May, 1996)

Betrayed, Lorena McCourtney

Escape, Lorena McCourtney (November, 1996)

Voyage, Elaine Schulte (August, 1996)

A Christmas Joy, Darty, Gillenwater, MacLean

Refuge, Lisa Tawn Bergren
ISBN 0-88070-875-1

Part One: A Montana rancher and a San Francisco marketing exec—only one incredible summer and God could bring such diverse lives together. *Part Two:* Lost and alone, Emily Walker needs and wants a new home, a sense of family. Can one man lead her to the greatest Father she could ever want and a life full of love?

Torchlight, Lisa Tawn Bergren
ISBN 0-88070-806-9

When beautiful heiress Julia Rierdon returns to Maine to remodel her family's estate, she finds herself torn between the man she plans to marry and unexpected feelings for a mysterious wanderer who threatens to steal her heart.

Treasure, Lisa Tawn Bergren
ISBN 0-88070-725-9

She arrived on the Caribbean island of Robert's Foe armed with a lifelong dream—to find her ancestor's sunken ship—and yet the only man who can help her stands stubbornly in her way. Can Christina and Mitch find their way to the ship *and* to each other?

Cherish, Constance Colson
ISBN 0-88070-802-6

Recovering from the heartbreak of a failed engagement, Rose Anson seeks refuge at a resort on Singing Pines Island, where she plans to spend a peaceful summer studying and painting the spectacular scenery of international Lake of the Woods. But when a flamboyant Canadian and a big-hearted American compete for her love, the young artist must face her past—and her future. What follows is a search for the source and meaning of true love: a journey that begins in the heart and concludes in the soul.

Angel Valley, Peggy Darty
ISBN 0-88070-778-X

When teacher Laurel Hollingsworth accepts a summer tutoring position for a wealthy socialite family, she faces an enormous challenge in her young student, Anna Lee Wentworth. However, the real challenge is ahead of her: hanging on to her heart when older brother Matthew Wentworth comes to visit. Soon Laurel and Matthew find that they share a faith in God...and powerful feelings for one another. Can Laurel and Matthew find time to explore their relationship while she helps the emotionally troubled Anna Lee and fights to defend her love for the beautiful *Angel Valley*?

Love Song, Sharon Gillenwater
ISBN 0-88070-747-X

When famous country singer Andrea Carson returns to her hometown to recuperate from a life-threatening illness, she seeks nothing more than a respite from the demands of stardom that have sapped her creativity and ability to perform. It's Andi's old high school friend Wade Jamison who helps her to realize that she needs inner healing as well. As Andi's strength grows, so do her feelings for the rancher who has captured her heart. But can their relationship withstand the demands of her career? Or will their romance be as fleeting as a beautiful Love Song?

Antiques, Sharon Gillenwater
ISBN 0-88070-801-8

Deeply wounded by the infidelity of his wife, widower Grant Adams swore off all women—until meeting charming antiques dealer Dawn Carson. Although he is drawn to her, Grant struggles to trust again. Dawn finds herself overwhelmingly attracted to the darkly brooding cowboy, but won't marry a nonbeliever. As Grant learns more about her faith, he is touched by its impact on her life and slowly begins to trust.

Secrets, Robin Jones Gunn
ISBN 0-88070-721-6

Seeking a new life as an English teacher in a peaceful Oregon town, Jessica tries desperately to hide the details of her identity from the community...until she falls in love. Will the past keep Jessica and Kyle apart forever?

Whispers, Robin Jones Gunn
ISBN 0-88070-755-0

Teri Moreno went to Maui eager to rekindle a romance. But when circumstances turn out to be quite different than she expects, she finds herself spending a great deal of time with a handsome, old high school crush who now works at a local resort. But the situation becomes more complicated when Teri meets Gordon, a clumsy, endearing Australian with a wild past, and both men begin to pursue her. Will Teri respond to God's gentle urgings toward true love? The answer lies in her response to the gentle Whispers in her heart.

Glory, Marilyn Kok
ISBN 0-88070-754-2

To Mariel Forrest, the teaching position in Taiwan provided more than a simple escape from grief; it also offered an opportunity to deal with her feelings toward the God she once loved, but ultimately blamed for the deaths of her family. Once there, Mariel dares to ask the timeless question: "If God is good, why do we suffer?" What follows is an inspiring story of love, healing, and renewed confidence in God's goodness.

Sierra, Shari MacDonald
ISBN 0-88070-726-7
When spirited photographer Celia Randall travels to eastern California for a short-term assignment, she quickly is drawn to—and locks horns with—editor Marcus Stratton. Will lingering heartaches destroy Celia's chance at true love? Or can she find hope and healing high in the *Sierra*?

Westward, Amanda MacLean
ISBN 0-88070-751-8
Running from a desperate fate in the South toward an unknown future in the West, plantation-born artist Juliana St. Clair finds herself torn between two men, one an undercover agent with a heart of gold, the other a man with evil intentions and a smooth facade. Witness Juliana's dangerous travels toward faith and love as she follows God's lead in this powerful historical novel.

Stonehaven, Amanda MacLean
ISBN 0-88070-757-7
Picking up in the years following *Westward*, *Stonehaven* follows Callie St. Clair back to the South where she has returned to reclaim her ancestral home. As she works to win back the plantation, the beautiful and dauntless Callie turns it into a station on the Underground Railroad. Covering her actions by playing the role of a Southern belle, Callie risks losing Hawk, the only man she has ever loved. Readers will find themselves quickly drawn into this fast-paced novel of treachery, intrigue, spiritual discovery, and unexpected love.

A Christmas Joy, MacLean, Darty, Gillenwater
ISBN 0-88070-780-1 (same length as other Palisades books)
Snow falls, hearts change, and love prevails! In this compilation, three experienced Palisades authors spin three separate novelettes centering around the Christmas season and message:
By Amanda MacLean: A Christmas pageant coordinator in a remote mountain village of Northern California is reunited with an old friend and discovers the greatest gift of all.
By Peggy Darty: A college ski club reunion brings together model Heather Grant and an old flame. Will they gain a new understanding?
By Sharon Gillenwater: A chance meeting in an airport that neither of them could forget...and a Christmas reunion.

If you enjoyed reading *Chosen*, the following is an excerpt from Lisa Tawn Bergren's novel, *Treasure*.

Prologue

❧

JULY 1627
THE GULF COAST

Above the high-pitched scream of the wind, Captain Esteban Ontario Alvarez heard the wails of his passengers below, but he had too much on his mind to worry about a bunch of over-indulged Castilian merchants. He squinted his eyes against the constant spray of the sea and struggled to maintain hold of the helm with the help of his first mate and a soldier.

The wind was relentless in its drive back toward the coast. Soaked to the skin after battling the storm on deck for four hours, the professional sailors were losing the war. "*Jesu Cristo*," the captain grunted through clenched teeth. "*Salvanos por favor.*" Jesus, please save us.

"*¡Capitan! ¡Capitan!*" Screaming over the wind, Alvarez's cabin boy struggled valiantly to make his way across the deck to his superior. He fell, was swept against the ship's starboard railing, then picked himself up and pushed forward once again. Esteban watched out of the corner of his eye, his heart in his throat, but unable to leave the wheel.

"*¡Capitan!*" The boy pointed frantically, unable to say anything else as terror overwhelmed him.

"*Si! Si! Qué* ...."

But he saw what struck fear in the boy's eyes. *Tierra.* Land. They would break apart on the reef if he didn't slow them down quickly. "*¡La ancla! ¡La ancla!*" he yelled at the boy, wanting with everything in him to release the wheel and run for the anchors himself. Sheer exhaustion threatened to overtake him.

The boy clung, monkey-like, to the torn sails, railing, masts...anything he could grab as he made his way forward to the one thing that might save them. The ship, a giant that weighed over three tons, rocked chaotically. So steep was the incline from starboard to port, the boy feared that they might capsize even if they did manage to slow their rapid advance.

He heaved against a door in the floorboards and scowled at a frightened sailor clinging for his life just below decks. "*¡La ancla!*" the boy screamed. The grimy man nodded, climbed the steep step, and helped the boy release the huge iron hook.

The six hundred pound weight sank quickly, pulling with it yards and yards of chain. Dragging across sand and loose rocks, it struck the ocean floor in under a minute, sinking its teeth into a massive coral reef.

The ship lurched at the force of the anchor's braking power, throwing ten feet every body and loose object aboard. Captain Alvarez and his men gave the wildly spinning wheel room and searched for rope with which to tie it off.

Below decks, *La Canción*'s hasty building schedule was telling. Mahogany ribs, weaker than oak, strained under the burden of heavy seas and a taut anchor chain. Planking popped as boards requiring ten nails each broke free of their scanty two. Waves gnawed at the interior clamp, which held the anchor to the ship. It took only one more watery monster to yank the teeth from their sockets.

"We're moving again!" Alvarez yelled in the Castilian accent of aristocratic Spaniards. "Sound the warning: Abandon ship!"

Seeing that they were moving, his man on the foc's'le deck swiftly threw a second anchor, unaware that the interior clamp was gone, that there was nothing below to keep the anchors from merely sinking beyond the wounded ship. He threw a third. A fourth. Holding the last one, he gazed frantically from the quickly approaching rocks to the chain in his hand, knowing that all was lost.

JULY 1986
THE GULF COAST OF TEXAS

Mitch had rarely scuba-dived with visibility as great as this: eighty feet in any direction. He looked to his friend Hans, provoking a moray eel fifteen feet to his left, then to Chet, meticulously studying the coral reef and its inhabitants five feet to his right. He smiled around the regulator in his mouth. As far as he was concerned, this was heaven.

Catching sight of a lavender and gold striped Spanish grunt fish, Mitch stroked through the water with powerful legs, coasting after the beauty with ease. Over the rise of coral he discovered a huge pile of rocks and moved to investigate. Such exploration had lately become the focus of Mitch's dreams. On each dive, he imagined finding vases, ballast piles, anchors: the beginning clues of valuable and ancient wreck sites. Ever since his introduction to Nautical Archeology 101, he'd had nothing else on his mind, much to his parents' chagrin.

He tried to dismiss the idea of actually finding a wreck on a casual dive off Galveston, but as much as he tried to banish the idea, found himself returning to it again and again. It would only take one wreck to convince his dad. Mom might have to have an emerald necklace that once belonged to Queen Estuvia or a Celtic cross that once hung from a devout monk's neck.

He smiled. *Then.* Then they would not keep hounding him about the cost of a "perfectly good education squandered away on a schoolboy's dreams." *Just one. Come on, God. Think of the ministry potential! Such success could open all kinds of doors!* He laughed at himself, recognizing that one cannot bargain with God. Yet he felt that a life of searching the underwater world was a personal calling, and that the Lord would reward his following.

Mitch fully realized that such action might leave him poor, chasing the siren call of one ship after another for the rest of his life. Yet it was not wealth that enticed him to this life path. It was the anticipated thrill of a find. The spark that lit each successful treasure hunter's eyes when telling of that special dig. *Just one, God.*

The Spanish grunt darted away and Mitch turned his attention to several multi-colored queen angels, their heavenly wings waving to him as they ate from the pile of ballast stones on the ocean floor. *Ballast stones.* Mitch caught his breath and held it. He closed his eyes slowly and then opened them, expecting the pile to disappear.

It did not. He rose fifteen feet, eager to catch the attention of his buddies. Hans spotted his wave first and dragged Chet away from his studies toward Mitch. Seeing his Texas A & M pals en route, Mitch moved back to the pile, carefully examining each rock as Professor Sanders had advised.

Sometimes the kind of rock could help a diver narrow down the ship's port of origin. *If this really is a ship,* he chastised himself silently, willing his excitement back down. He dusted off the rocks, but could not tell what kind they were. Chet, better at such things than he, was already studying the color and texture. Mitch moved on.

Thirty feet away, in the direct line of the current, he found another large, lichen-covered pile. After investigation, Mitch discovered that the pile was made up of hundreds of earthen jars, such as the kind crews once carried, filled with fresh water or delicacies, like olives. Many were intact, even covered with marine life.

Mitch abandoned the vases to see what else might be nearby. As he swam over the next rise, his breathing became labored, and he wondered if what he was seeing could really be true. There, scattered between what was clearly the rotting remains of a ship's timbers, lay thousands of sparkling, gold coins.

His friends soon joined him and the trio excitedly filled the "goody bags" at their waists with as many coins as possible, then swam to their raft thirty feet above. Clinging to the sides, they laughed and shouted while throwing their bounty on board.

"Well, boys," Mitch said, grinning broadly, "I think I finally know what I want to do when I grow up."

AUGUST 1994
OFF THE COAST OF MAINE

Trevor leaned toward Julia and kissed her gently. "I love looking over at you and saying, 'There she is. My *wife.*'"

"I love looking over at *you* and thinking, *my husband*. Husband, husband, husband. It will take a while before that word rolls off my tongue."

"We've got years to get used to it. I didn't expect it to become second nature in the first month."

Julia laid back, soaking in the sun and the sights of Martha's Vineyard. It was the perfect honeymoon destination. Quiet if a couple wanted it to be so, social if they wished it to be otherwise. She and Trevor had been drawn to the solitude and stayed close to the small cottage they had rented for the week.

Trevor looked lovingly at Julia, then gazed down the beach. She followed his line of vision and nudged him indignantly. "Hey, no looking at other women on your honeymoon...or ever."

Trevor smiled but his eyes remained on the attractive woman walking toward them on the beach. "It's just...she looks like someone I should know...."

"Who? A swimsuit model from *Sports Illustrated?*"

"No. You know I never read those."

"Yeah, right."

He kissed her soundly. "I think it was Paul Newman who said, 'Why go out for hamburger when you have steak at home?'"

"I always liked that guy," Julia said, smiling at her new husband.

The figure drew closer.

Trevor looked up again and scrambled to his feet, leaving a bewildered Julia sitting alone. "It *is* her," he mumbled in explanation as he walked toward the other woman. "Christina! Christina!"